LOST CAUSE

(LOST LAKE LOCATORS BOOK 3)

LOST LAKE LOCATORS

SUSAN SLEEMAN

EDGE OF YOUR SEAT BOOKS, INC.

Published by Edge of Your Seat Books, Inc.

Contact the publisher at contact@edgeofyourseatbooks.com

Copyright © 2025 by Susan Sleeman

Cover design by Kelly A. Martin of KAM Design

All rights reserved. Kindle Edition Printed in the United States of America or the country of purchase. Without limiting the rights under copyright reserved above, no part of this book may be reproduced in any form or by any electronic or mechanical means, including information storage and retrieval systems, without permission in writing from the publisher, except by a reviewer, who may quote brief passages in a review.

This book is a work of fiction. Characters, names, places, and incidents in this novel are either products of the imagination or are used fictitiously. Any resemblance to real people, either living or dead, to events, businesses, or locales is entirely coincidental.

NO AI TRAINING: Without in any way limiting the author's [and publisher's] exclusive rights under copyright, any use of this publication to "train" generative artificial intelligence (AI) technologies to generate text is expressly prohibited. The author reserves all rights to license uses of this work for generative AI training and development of machine learning language models.

1

Secrets. They wanted to stay buried. Deep. Hidden, often needing help to rise from the dark.

No matter. Abby Day was just the person to dig them up, starting tonight. She had to. Her friends and fellow teammates were counting on her to get this assignment and keep their company from going under.

She took a firm stance on the nearly deserted ferry as it cut through the turbulent water while powerful engines growled in a low rumble. The double-decker boat navigated through thick fog swirling like a living entity around them. She squinted to see her destination, but mist swallowed the island's rugged outline, hiding the estate.

She shivered and tightened her coat against the damp chill—against whatever awaited her on Ravenhook Island.

The island wasn't just remote—it was ignored by most. If you didn't count the stories and the rumors. They continued to be whispered and shared on a regular basis.

Once home to six lavish houses for wealthy trendsetters, now most properties were in disrepair. Some deserted. A few remained to shelter recluses—long-term occupants like Mr. Lemoine, who'd desperately called the Lost Lake Locator's team to report a mysterious theft on his secluded estate. She couldn't shake his cryptic words.

Another shiver raked over her body.

Stow it. Keep your imagination in check. Think like the former sheriff you are.

Nothing good came from chasing unsettling shadows and jumping to conclusions. Hold back. Wait. Look for evidence. Tangible things. Things she could use in a court of law if it became necessary.

Right. Focus on something else.

Balancing against sudden swells, she zoned in on the lighthouse's rotating beam struggling to light the way to the island. She held on, and the boat soon bumped against a large moss-covered dock with weak lights on tall poles that barely lit the way for the crew scurrying off the boat to secure heavy ropes so she could disembark.

Dressed in a green rain slicker, the burly captain opened the security gate and cast her a concerned look. "Remember, Ms. Day, we leave precisely at nine, and it's the final ferry of the day. This island is the last place you want to be stranded for the night."

"Don't worry." She lifted her shoulders in an attempt to appear fearless. "I'll be back before it's time to leave."

Please make that true!

Her heart kicked into a rapid rhythm.

Chill. You've got this.

She crossed the narrow public road to the mansion's long stairway. Her boots landed on the first step, and she raised her flashlight. Trees twisted with age, and severely overgrown hedges obscured part of the imposing estate, but the mansion's grand front door came into view. Still, everything was cloaked in darkness. Everything.

If Mr. Lemoine was expecting her, wouldn't he have left on a light?

Uneasiness creeping over her, she rested her free hand on her sidearm, pausing to listen. Behind her, distant waves crashed and the idling ferry engine hummed, but otherwise the night remained quiet.

She swung her flashlight through the fog to the 1800s Victorian, revealing thick vines of ivy crawling up the walls. Broken shutters shifted in the breeze.

The most interesting sight? Fragments from a shattered window shimmering beneath the porch.

The likely entry point for the thief? Maybe.

An air of neglect hung heavy in the cool night as she pounded on the thick wooden door. It swung open under her hand, rusted hinges protesting. Cold air spilled out from the darkness. She caught a whiff of damp wood and something older. Something rank.

Abby stood still, pulse ticking in her throat as the door finally settled open wide enough to step through, but just narrow enough to make her wonder if she should.

"Mr. Lemoine?" She poked her head around the door and called out. "It's Abby Day. Are you here?"

Light seeped from under an interior door to the left of the dark, mysterious foyer. She waited for the door to open and Mr. Lemoine to appear, but nothing moved.

Had something terrible happened to him after they'd spoken?

Please don't let this turn into a murder investigation.

She crept into the entry hall. Silence and shadows clung to the dark walls, seeping into corners. Above the grand staircase at the back of the room, light beamed through a cracked windowpane, projecting splintered patterns on the floor.

Creepy was the only fitting word that came to mind, but she had to continue on even if her heart rate shot higher.

She aimed her flashlight to her right and made her way

to the lighted room. Pushing open the door, she found a large library with overflowing bookshelves covering every wall. Peeling paint chipped from the woodwork, and torn, faded wallpaper covered the exposed walls. An odor of old, maybe decaying air clung to the room. But no Victor Lemoine in sight.

Rumor had it he hadn't left Ravenhook Island for decades, having all services brought to him along with supplies and food. She was beginning to believe it.

The large marble fireplace, once opulent, was cold. A ring of soot marked the hearth, the lack of ashes suggesting it had just been cleaned.

She backed into the foyer. "Mr. Lemoine? Mr. Lemoine? It's Abby Day. Where are you?"

No answer.

She was technically trespassing, so did she move ahead or leave?

Call him. She dug her cell out and tapped her most recent call. A landline phone's shrill ring reverberating from cracked plaster walls had her spinning toward a table less than three feet away.

The rotary phone continued to ring. Two. Three. Four times.

She ignored it and eased closer to the sweeping staircase. The sharp trill sounded from above too. His bedroom? The ringing stopped, and her call went to an old-fashioned answering machine.

She pocketed her phone, the urge to leave nearly overwhelming her. But she couldn't. If Victor wasn't answering the phone, it could mean he was hurt and needed help.

She waited, listening to the hall clock ticking down in the musty air. This was pointless. She couldn't just stand there. She crossed a worn Persian runner, muffling the sound of her tactical boots hitting the floor. Her flashlight illuminated portraits of stoic ancestors with pale eyes hanging on the walls. Several frames were missing, leaving hooks and picture outlines on faded brocade wallpaper.

Around the first corner, a stone stairway descended into darkness. Carefully finding her footing, she traversed the stairs and located an antique push-button switch. She held her breath and pressed it down. Light flickered from the underpowered ceiling fixture.

Wow! Oh wow!

A time capsule greeted her of heavy stone walls and iron pots hanging from blackened hooks above a soot-stained hearth. She eased carefully over rough, uneven flagstones to take a better look. A butcher's table stood in the center, covered in knife marks and stains from years of use. She caught the scent of rosemary. Not just the pungent herb. Something older—earthy and metallic permeated the air too. But what?

Footsteps echoed behind her.

She spun.

"What are you doing here?" a male voice challenged from the stairway, hidden in shadows beyond her light beam.

She caught a deep breath. "I'm Abby Day with the Lost Lake Locators. You contacted me and asked me to come right out. I drove down here and took the first ferry to get here as soon as I could."

An older man stepped into the light. Despite his age, his eyes were sharp and unwavering. His hand rested on an ornate cane. His seventy-plus years on this earth had hollowed his cheeks and stooped his frame, but he seemed far from frail. Had to be Victor Lemoine.

"I wasn't sure you would come." He spoke with a raspy, measured voice.

"Is that the reason you didn't answer the door?"

"I apologize. My afternoon rest time ran longer than I expected." His liver-spotted free hand clutched a once-elegant velvet smoking robe. "How did you get in?"

"The door was open."

He frowned. "I was certain I'd locked it."

"I'll check the lock to see if it's been tampered with," she offered, though he'd likely had a senior moment and failed to secure the door. Could be another way the burglar had gotten into his home.

"We can discuss the theft in the library." He pivoted, his posture stiff like a precision soldier.

She trailed him up the stairs and down the hallway. He had a slight limp, his cane thumping on the wooden floor. He didn't bother to turn on a light, something she would expect a man who likely had the poor eyesight of his advanced age might do.

He pushed the front door closed, then turned. "You can inspect the door later. After I provide details on the theft. Then I assume you'll want to check all the entrance points for the house."

"That's fine by me."

From his pocket, he handed her a large ring filled with jingling keys. "You'll need these, along with the blueprint of the house and drawing of the property waiting for you in the library."

She pocketed them and followed him into the lighted room.

Regal looking, he flicked a hand at a nearby loveseat as he settled in a high-backed chair. "Sit."

She hung her soggy jacket on the back of a chair before taking a seat. His deep-set eyes followed and evaluated her. Something about the intense study said he was weighing her very character. She didn't appreciate how he behaved like an aristocrat, and she was beneath him, here to do his bidding and then be discarded. But the team needed him as a client, and she kept her mouth shut.

He tapped a rolled set of documents sitting on the nearby table then poured a full snifter of brandy. He took a long sip and pointed at the table, no offer of something to drink for her. "The blueprint and property layout as I promised."

She swallowed away her irritation and smiled her acknowledgment. "Thank you for calling our team, Mr. Lemoine. You were very cryptic on the phone. So what exactly do you need our help with?"

"Call me Victor." He set the glass down and ran a hand over his head. Wispy and messy silver hair was cinched tight with a tie in the back. "I—"

A long, low creak echoed in the hallway and took his attention. "The front door."

Abby froze. Listened. Heard the rusty hinges. Her heart galloped into high gear, and she shot to her feet. "Probably just the wind. Stay here. I'll check it out."

She rested her hand on her sidearm before starting for the shadowy hallway.

As she'd crossed the bay, a storm had been brewing, but there was no wind in the hallway. No draft. Just the front door inching open into the dim foyer, and she braced herself for whoever would come through.

∼

The Lemoine Mansion hadn't seen many visitors in years, and it showed in the serious disrepair, cobwebs, and dirt surrounding the main entrance. But it welcomed Detective Burke Ulrich with an unlocked door.

Not a good sign after Victor Lemoine's frantic call to 911 about a theft. Not good at all.

He drew his weapon and carefully pressed on the splintered wood. Light spilling into the space to his left illuminated the dark, shadowed foyer and outlined a petite woman facing the door, feet planted, weapon drawn.

"Police!" he shouted as he tried to make out her facial details. "Lower your weapon to the floor."

"You have no worries with me." She dropped her arms, revealing her face.

Say what? Couldn't be!

He knew her—former sheriff Abby Day. The one woman who'd managed to break through the wall he'd built since his fiancée left him at the altar a little over a year ago. What in the world was she doing here?

"I'm Lost Lake Locator, Abby Day. I'm going to holster my gun." Her movements were exaggerated, likely for his benefit.

This county was Burke's jurisdiction, but they'd once worked a murder investigation together when she was a nearby sheriff. The last one she handled before leaving the job to join the new firm of investigators who specialized in finding missing people and things. They'd recently been praised in newspapers and on TV for their good work.

Of all the people!

They hadn't seen eye-to-eye before, and now she was a nosy private investigator. If Lemoine hired her to find his thief, she was bound to be a thorn in his side. Not only as far as the investigation went, but also by raising old feelings he'd worked very hard to banish from his life. Just what he didn't need.

"Detective Burke Ulrich," he said in case she'd forgotten him.

"I remember you, Detective." Her unfavorable memories of their time together came through loud and clear.

He got it. They'd had a love-hate relationship,

disagreeing on most investigative steps, yet finding themselves attracted to each other and fighting it all the way. Could she have left the job because he'd questioned her all the time?

Nah. She didn't seem overly bothered by his behavior. More likely, she left because they'd investigated three young children who'd been abducted on their way home from school and brutally murdered. The horrific details nearly caused him to leave his job. Why wouldn't it do the same to her?

Old news, but her change of careers was important news. Still, now wasn't the time to bring it up—he couldn't allow himself to get lost in memories or his feelings for her. "I assume Mr. Lemoine called your team to investigate the theft."

"I did," an older man said from the doorway, the light behind him accenting his age-diminished build.

"Detective Burke Ulrich." He offered his hand to the gentleman. "You must be Mr. Lemoine."

"Victor." His dry, papery skin rasped against Burke's as he latched on with a surprisingly strong grip. "It's about time law enforcement showed."

Haughty was the word that came to Burke to describe this guy's tone. He could be acting due to stress from the theft. Burke didn't want to make it worse for him by responding with a sharp reply.

"Unavoidable transportation delay," he said. "I would've been here sooner if your call indicated you were in any danger and needed immediate attention."

"It seems your understanding of the matter is quite limited." Mr. Lemoine's upper lip curled ever so slightly. "I'm always in danger."

Burke shot a look at Abby for her reaction. She planted a

hand on her hip, long lashes blinking at him. Apparently she hadn't heard about this either.

He returned his attention to Victor. "Then let's sit down, and you can tell us about it."

Victor didn't speak, but clunked with his cane to his chair in the library and gingerly lowered himself to the worn cushion. Burke waited for Abby to enter the room and drop onto the sofa's plush cushions, slightly uneven from years of wear.

Her black tactical pants and matching polo shirt spoke to her law enforcement training and professionalism, but he saw more than the uniform. So much more. Her chin-length hair hung around her face, and her large brown eyes remained sharp.

Memories of how those luminous eyes often sparked in response to him came back. But more so, they reminded him of everything he respected about her. Resourceful, intuitive, compassionate, quietly courageous. Not to mention grounded in an unshakable faith.

She looked at him, and he jerked his attention away like a teenage boy with a crush.

Seriously? Get control. He remained standing and formulated his line of questioning. "So, Victor, tell us about this theft, and the danger you think you're in."

"Not *think*. I'm in danger. I know I am." He stared at the fireplace, silent and imposing, then whipped his attention back to them. "You must promise to keep the information I'm about to share to yourselves."

Abby met the older man's gaze with the confidence of a seasoned investigator. "If you want us to find your missing item, I'll have to share with my team everything you tell me. We'll keep it strictly between us."

"And you, Detective?" Victor raised a bushy eyebrow. "Can you guarantee this will not leak to the public?"

Burke couldn't offend this guy if he wanted to keep his job, the only thing he had left in his life, but he also wouldn't make a promise that he couldn't keep. "I'm sorry, Victor, but I can't guarantee that. I can assure you that I won't share any information unless absolutely necessary, and absolutely nothing with the public without your knowledge."

Victor sniffed, as if the air smelled foul. "I suppose it's the best I can do. But this has remained a secret since 1887, and I would hate for it to get out now."

"An extremely long time to keep something quiet." Abby ran her gaze over him. "This all started back then?"

"Yes, 1887 in France under the rule of the French Third Republic. Just after the fall of Napoleon III and the monarchy, the Republic saw the Crown Jewels as symbols of tyranny." His brows drew together, forming deep creases across his forehead. "They decided to liquidate almost the entire royal collection, both to make a political statement and to raise funds. The sales included multiple royal crowns—some bejeweled, some stripped. Many were bought by private collectors or dismantled for their gems."

"Interesting story, but what does it have to do with you?" Burke asked.

Victor lifted his pointy chin and aimed it at Burke. "My great-grandfather, Valère Lemoine, was an art historian living in Paris at the time, and he bought the Crown of Napoleon III to bring it back to America. When he returned, he had this house built."

"It's a long way from Paris to the Oregon coast." Burke quickly reviewed information from his Oregon history classes to try to remember what was going on in the state in the late 1800s. "If I remember it right, Oregon was just being developed then. Kind of rowdy and unruly in those days for keeping an expensive item safe."

"Probably not the best place for an art historian to find a job either," Abby added.

Victor wagged a finger at her. "It's not like he ever worked a day in his life. He didn't need to. Not with our family money. He'd gotten an art history degree to please his father, but his heart wasn't in it. He was a real adventurer. After a single trip out here, he wanted to claim land and build before anyone else came along to spoil the nearby beauty."

Again, interesting, but it still didn't explain what was going on. "So what does this crown in the 1800s have to do with your call?"

"Like I said." His tone turned condescending as if he'd expected them to figure everything out by now. "He had this house built, and he included a special hidden display case for the crown. From that point forward, he lived here alone and didn't tell anyone about the family treasure until he was on his deathbed. He then revealed it to my grandfather, who then inherited it. It's been kept a secret and passed down to the firstborn son in every generation, currently my responsibility."

"Oh my goodness!" Abby shot forward on the cushion. "The crown! The crown was stolen."

A swift nod was Victor's only response.

Far more interesting than a simple burglary. "I assume it's quite valuable. Do you have a recent appraisal?"

Victor crossed his arms. "It's politically correct these days to return artifacts to their country of origin. An appraisal would simply draw unwanted attention, and I would likely be forced to return it."

Abby blinked a few times. "But what you're saying applies to stolen items, and the crown wasn't stolen from the French government. Do you have a bill of sale or any proof it was purchased by your great-grandfather?"

Victor nodded. "I not only have a bill of sale, but I also have a certificate of authenticity, both of which are kept in a safety deposit box in the local bank. However, it doesn't matter. It's considered a national treasure of France, and the French government would ignore my legitimate rights and claim it under cultural patrimony laws."

Abby's lips pressed into a line. "Makes sense why you couldn't have it appraised, but you won't be able to determine the value."

"I have conducted internet research for that. As far as the art history world is concerned, its current whereabouts are unknown, and it hasn't been displayed in any museum or private collection. Of course it hasn't."

His laughter came slowly at first, like a creaky door easing open, but then it developed into a gravelly chuckle. "This absence has led to speculation about its fate. They're wondering whether it was lost, destroyed, or remains hidden in a private collection. The crown's disappearance adds to the mystique of the French Crown Jewels, and articles I've read claim it would command up to sixteen million dollars at auction."

Burke let out a low whistle and shook his head. He didn't expect anything like this when the call had come into his office. In fact, he'd thought it was a simple theft and begged his sheriff to assign the investigation to someone else. Didn't happen. Apparently, Victor Lemoine held some political sway, and the sheriff wanted his best investigator on the case.

He'd picked Burke—even after everything. Burke had just gotten off probation after losing it when his fiancée ran off with his partner, Miles Ramsey, leaving Burke at the altar. Burke lost it. Couldn't cope with the betrayal from the two people closest to him. After a fight with Ramsey at the office and the obvious tension between them, Burke got demoted and Ramsey took over. A year later, Burke was back to normal status at work, but one wrong move now, and he could kiss the only thing he'd managed to hold onto goodbye.

Now that Lemoine's story intrigued him, Burke was more motivated to work this case. More than motivated—downright fascinated. "Can you show us the crown's display case?"

Victor gripped the carved arms of his chair and pushed to his feet. "It's just over here."

He hobbled across the room, leaving his ornate cane behind and limping heavily. At the bookshelves, he turned to them. "Take a good look. Can you see the hidden compartment?"

Abby brushed past Burke to the bookshelf and bent close. She was a petite thing, so he stepped up behind her to look over her shoulder, catching a whiff of the same tantalizing citrus scent he remembered from the weeks they'd worked together.

He forced himself to concentrate. "There." Reaching over her shoulder, he stabbed a finger at the third shelf down. "The books are fake. There's something behind them."

"Wow." Abby leaned closer to the shelf. "Your great-grandfather did a good job of camouflaging the display case."

Victor lifted his shoulders and expanded his chest. "Money can buy the very best craftsmanship."

"Show us the case," Burke said.

Victor flicked his fingers as if he wanted Burke and Abby to back up, so they did.

He reached into the space above the fake books. The shelf dropped open until it lay flat, the fake books still connected and hanging underneath. He raised the shelf above it. A light came on, revealing an empty glass-front display case lined with rich purple velvet.

A bare crystal pedestal—the resting place for the crown—cast shimmering sparkles of light glinting over the velvet like little jewels. A crystal pedestal of this size from the 1800s had to be worth good money too. Why hadn't the thief taken the stand too? Perhaps too bulky and too much to carry.

Burke looked at Victor. "Do you have a picture of the crown?"

Victor withdrew a worn photograph from the pocket of his ancient smoking jacket and pressed out a few wrinkles before handing it to Burke. "This is the best one I have."

Abby scooted closer, and they studied the gold-framed crown boasting arches shaped like eagles.

Victor tapped the top of the crown. "This monde or globe-shaped ornament symbolizes the monarch's authority over the world. It's surmounted by the cross signifying divine authority."

He drew another picture from his pocket and handed it to Burke. "This case held the crown when my great-grandfather bought it. It has a mahogany frame with leather dyed deep red. The lining is of the finest velvet, and the royal initials are embossed on the box. It was kept on the shelves below. It's also missing."

Abby shook her head, her eyes wide open. "Now I understand why you didn't want to talk about it on the phone."

"And like I said," he shifted his gaze between them, "you must keep this as quiet as possible."

Burke didn't know how he could enforce Victor's wishes and still properly investigate the theft. Questions had to be asked, often requiring him to give information to get information. But more concerning to him was the sharing of this investigation and information with Abby Day and her team. Not only because she was a former sheriff and would likely want to take over, but he didn't need to have a woman distract him when he was finally on solid footing in the job. And especially not during such a high-profile investigation.

Losing control was the one thing he couldn't afford. Especially if he wanted to keep his job. He would cling to it with everything he was made of, no matter how hard she tried to break through.

2

Abby paced, feeling Burke's eyes following her every move.

Ignoring him seemed impossible—especially when he looked annoyingly good in his sharp black suit and white shirt that was still crisp even at this hour. His midnight hair was longer than she remembered, with a curl falling over his forehead in just the right way. Add in the neatly trimmed beard and those ice-blue eyes that seemed to see straight through people, and he had a perfect mix of danger and control.

Basically, everything she found irresistible in a man—and exactly what she needed to steer clear of if she wanted to stay focused enough to get paid for the missing crown.

She stopped in front of Victor. "When was the last time you saw the crown?"

He shrugged. "Not since last week for sure. Maybe not even then."

"So you don't know when it was stolen?" Burke asked.

"No." Victor's eyes darted from face to face as if searching for something—anything—to ground him. "You must find it before some collector snaps it up or it vanishes for good."

If Abby hadn't felt pressure mount when he mentioned the value of the crown, it had now risen to an uncomfortable level, and she needed to bring her A-game for sure. Assuming Victor was telling the truth, he really did own a crown of such high value, and it actually had been stolen. Whenever a theft of such a valuable item is reported, law enforcement always had to suspect the item's owner of orchestrating the theft for financial gain, as that often was the case.

But she had to tread carefully. Not only did she need to keep him as a client, but as an elderly person, he might have some confusion. "Do you have any thoughts on who might've stolen the crown?"

He shook his head. "I'm the only person who knows about it. I'm getting on in years, and it's about time for my son to take responsibility for it, but I haven't spoken to him yet."

The same reservations Abby was feeling about Victor's potential involvement in the theft flickered across Burke's face, but he quickly masked it. "You've never mentioned having children."

"Didn't I?" He shook his head. "I also have a daughter. After my wife left, I was in charge of raising them, and I readily admit I let my grief take over and I didn't do a good job of it. Thankfully, my father was here for at least a few years to help out. But now, they've both moved away, and I'm not as close to them as I would like to be."

"Back to the safe," Burke said. "If only you knew about it, how could anyone have found out about it?"

Victor pursed his lips. "I suppose I could have been careless, and my estate manager or housekeeper saw me looking at it. I can't think of a time when that could've happened. I only open the shelves when I'm alone in the house. Besides, they've been with me for years, so even if they knew about the crown, I can't imagine either one of them would steal it."

"You never know what people are capable of." Abby's words punched through the silence, hard and direct. She needed Victor to understand that everyone is a suspect in an investigation until ruled out. "I'll need their names and contact information."

He gripped the end of the wooden arms of his ornate chair, his fingers turning white. "I understand you have to question them, but you must be very careful not to mention the crown. Promise me you'll keep it between us for now."

"We can refer to it as a stolen object or artifact for the initial questioning," Burke said. "But I can't promise anything more."

"Still," Abby cast Burke a pointed look, "we'll do our very best."

"We will," he said.

She handed a notebook to Victor. "Please write down their contact information and schedules."

As he started writing, Burke motioned for her to move to the side of the room and turned his intense focus on her. "You'll share the info with me," he said in a low voice.

No "please". No questions. Just a demand. Still, why fight him when he could ask Victor for the same thing? It would only make them both look unprofessional for not being able to cooperate with one another. She wouldn't jeopardize this investigation. Not when Victor was paying the team good money. Their business was still in startup mode and had cash flow problems. They needed every dime to remain solvent.

"Of course I'll share." She eased closer and lowered her voice. "You believe him, right? Believe he owns such a crown?"

"Believe? At this point I'm not sure. He could be using

his dismissive behavior to put us off because he's hiding something. We won't know if he's telling the truth until we're able to obtain the documents and have an expert verify their authenticity."

"And since he's the only one who knows about the crown, we need to watch for any sign he's not being completely honest or lying to us," Abby added and glanced at Victor.

The elderly gentleman didn't look like a liar, but her law enforcement experience told her liars came in all shapes and sizes, and she couldn't let the fact that he was of advanced years keep her from posing hard questions. Like Burke said, Victor's condescending and standoffish behavior could be the very thing he was using to cover up a lie or hide the truth.

"Done." He closed the notebook. "I'll have to look up their addresses, but you can talk to them tomorrow. They'll arrive on the one o'clock ferry and work until six."

"They don't live on site?" Burke asked.

"No. They once did. In fact, Ugo served as my full-time personal valet, but I have few needs now, so I promoted him to estate manager."

"What about your son?" Abby asked. "Where does he live?"

A raw wince stole over his face. "He left for college and never came back here to live. He currently resides in Salem and occasionally visits, but finds the slow pace of life here untenable."

"Sounds like you'd really like him to live here with you. Maybe he will someday." Abby pointed at his hand. "Could you please add his name and contact information too?"

"I need to be the one to tell him about the crown. So promise me you won't tell him without my prior knowledge."

"You have my word," she said and hoped she could keep it.

Victor started writing, his hand moving furiously over the page. He finished, clipped the pen to the cover, and handed them both to her.

She glanced at the information. Vidal Lemoine lived in Salem, Oregon, as Victor had said. The name Vidal was likely French and the V was in keeping with Victor's first initial and his ancestors' names too. Next Victor had listed Sylvia Bass, housekeeper, and Ugo Morell, estate manager. They worked two full days per week and two part-time days.

Abby looked up from the notepad. "And these are the only individuals you think could know about the crown?"

He nodded. "But I honestly don't think my son does. I'm beginning to believe someone randomly broke in and discovered the case."

"But you didn't mention any evidence of a break-in," Burke said.

"I haven't seen any."

Burke arched an eyebrow. "What about the broken basement window?"

"Oh that." He waved a dismissive hand. "Ugo is responsible for the damage. He was trying to repair a shutter a month or so ago and accidentally hit the window with his ladder. I thought it had been fixed by now. I'll have to talk to him about it."

"No offense, Victor," she said as gently as she could, "but why haven't you noticed the window is still broken?"

He looked her up and down, weighing her, and his expression said he found her lacking. "I have no need to leave my house. Everything is brought to me, so I haven't been outside for quite some time."

This could explain the disrepair. Could Ugo be scamming Victor—charging him for repair materials and then never buying them? But wouldn't Sylvia mention the state of the building to Ugo? Or were they in on this together? Questions she would need to ask them.

"Before I leave I need to check the building for any intrusions." She slipped into her jacket and picked up the blueprints. "If you'll please stay here, I'll report back after I've checked all the doors and windows."

Victor gave a solid nod of approval.

She didn't wait for Burke's consent, but charged into the hallway. She put on a pair of disposable gloves from her jacket pocket to keep from contaminating anything.

"Hold up." Burke's voice boomed through the cavernous foyer. "We'll do nothing until we talk about your role in this investigation."

"What's to talk about?" Abby wasn't normally one to seek conflict, but her company came first, and she had to pull out all stops to find this crown. "Victor hired me to investigate, and I'm going to investigate. Starting now by checking the doors and windows for forced entry."

He paused, the time ticking slowly by. "You're a former sheriff and used to being in charge. I get that. But this is now an official crime scene—*my* crime scene—and you're disregarding my authority."

"And you can't limit my access." She raised her hand to indicate the space around them. "I don't see a cordoned off area designated as a crime scene. I see private property of the man who hired me to investigate the theft of his crown."

He stared at her as if he didn't know how to respond.

She squared her shoulders and held up the key ring. "I have keys to every door, and unrestricted access to them—no questions asked."

Burke curled his fingers into fists. "My deputies are locking the place down now. They'll be in any minute to cordon off the library."

Say what? "Deputies? This is the first time you've mentioned them."

"Wasn't sure what I'd be walking into, so I brought backup—just in case."

She eyed him. "Seems like an extreme response for a simple theft."

"Victor's got pull around here, so my sheriff's all over this theft. As soon as he finds out what was taken, I'm betting he'll put me on this case full-time."

"Doesn't surprise me Victor has friends in high places. All the more reason to throw everything you've got at this—wrap it up fast and make your department look good in the press."

He shifted his weight from one foot to the other. "What are you suggesting?"

"That we work together. My team and I will back you all the way—no stepping on toes, no stealing credit if it's due."

He tilted his head and studied her. "Why would you do that?"

"Because, as Victor said, finding this crown is urgent." She intensified her gaze, looking him straight in the eye. "Letting it disappear forever wouldn't end well for either of us."

"You have a point," he said, but with a hesitant tone. "I doubt my sheriff will authorize bringing civilians in on the investigation."

"No problem. We've been in situations like this in the past. The solution—law enforcement swore one or two of us in for the duration of the investigation."

He shoved his hands into his pockets. " Ryder won't likely agree to such a thing."

"But you do think it's worth pursuing?"

"Maybe." His eyes narrowed. "We can't forget the challenges we had working together in the past."

The unpleasant memories of the horrific crime came back, and her stomach cramped. "That investigation involved the murder of three children, and our emotions were on high alert. This is a simple case of theft, and we should be able to work together."

He arched an eyebrow. "And what about this thing between us? This interest in each other?"

She didn't expect him to bring that up or be so straightforward about it, but it was probably a good thing to get it out in the open early on so they wouldn't waste time on it and could focus on the investigation. "We figured out how to work through it before. We can do it again."

He let out a long breath. "I'm not sure I want to put myself through such a struggle again."

"Look." She crossed her arms. "I'm not going anywhere. I've been hired to investigate this theft. Agree or not, but I'll do my best to find the crown. I'll try not to overreach my authority or challenge you, but I'm doing this. With or without your sheriff's blessing. With or without you."

He let silence hang in the air. "I need to think about it."

Okay, good. She had him on the fence—the best she could hope for at this point. He was a man of strong conviction. A trait she admired. But in this case, she had to put aside all emotions and keep pressing ahead. "Since I'm already here, how about we do a quick walk-through together? You can mull everything over as we go."

"I..." He swallowed, his Adam's apple bobbing. "We'll do it your way for now, but I take lead on the walk-through and you don't touch anything."

With all her years running things, she felt certain she knew better than he did how to handle a crime scene and had a strong urge to defend her abilities. But she also knew when to play nice and work together. Tonight, teamwork was what really mattered and what her teammates were counting on her to do. "I can live with that. For now."

The grandfather clock chimed nine, the ring echoing from the ceiling. In the distance, the ferry's whistle blew in long blasts of a foggy, mournful rumble.

Abby flashed a look at her watch to confirm the time. "Oh no."

"What's wrong?"

"I just missed the last boat of the day. I'm stuck here overnight."

"No worries. You can ride back with us."

"Oh right." She resisted, clapping her hand to her forehead. "You obviously weren't on the ferry with me, so you would have a boat."

"We have a search and rescue/interdiction boat. One of the reasons I was late—I had to track down a deputy cleared to pilot it."

The county where she'd served as sheriff was located inland and never needed a boat, but Burke's county bordered the ocean. "Thank you for the ride. I appreciate it."

He studied her. "Quick question about teaming up. If we bring you in, will your whole team try to crash the investigation too?"

She ignored his insinuation. She wasn't crashing anything. Just doing her job. "I took the first call, so I'll lead this investigation and talk to the others about their roles. But since we're hours from the office, I'll probably suggest one other teammate stay here for the duration."

"Here, as on the island? There's no place to stay here."

"I have a good friend in Cold Harbor. She's a Blackwell Tactical team member, and I hope to stay with her on their compound."

"Blackwell Tactical?" He ran a hand over his face. "Don't tell me that team wants to get involved too."

"Okay, I won't tell you." She laughed, but his expression left no doubt he wasn't amused. "They've got serious skills, so if they can help with the investigation, why wouldn't we bring them in?"

"After our discussion, isn't it obvious?" He crossed his arms, his muscular forearms straining the fabric of his suit jacket. "Just more civilians butting in when this is a law enforcement matter."

She raised a brow. "Are you familiar with the team?"

"Everyone in law enforcement around here knows Gage Blackwell and his crew. The guy's built a solid reputation, and their record for high-end training and protection is hard to beat."

"Sounds like you might not mind working with them, then." She would cross her fingers if she believed such a thing actually helped.

"I might respect the team from what I've heard, but I've got the same concerns about them as I do about you and your team." He sized her up with a steady look. "But let's table this for now and get to checking those doors."

She nodded, but this wasn't over. Somehow, she needed to chip away at his resolve and open his mind so she could fulfill her promise to her team. Partnering with him would be a good thing. She'd have access to official reports and information. But if he decided against working together, she would investigate this theft with or without his help. Her friends and her livelihood were counting on her to succeed.

3

Burke put on protective gloves and opened the mansion's front door. He had to ignore Abby as she watched him study the aged brass lock that appeared original to the house. She was buzzing with energy as if she wanted to take over. He couldn't let her. Nor could he let her distract him during the investigation. One false move, and Sheriff Ryder could change his mind about keeping Burke on as a detective.

Ignore her. You have to ignore her.

He tuned her out and intensified his focus. He saw no sign of gouging in the wood or slashes from a sharp object in the lock itself. "Looks like we're clear here."

She moved in closer. Of course she didn't trust his assessment. He couldn't fault her, though. He would've done the same thing.

Keeping the blueprint roll tucked under her arm, she ran a gloved finger over the lock and the strike plate before looking up. "Agreed. But the door was open when I arrived. It likely doesn't latch properly, so someone could've entered without leaving any evidence behind."

"I found it open too," Burke said.

"And that was after I saw Victor shove it closed."

"Means we can't rule this door out as the point of entry, and we need forensics to dust for prints." He thought about who they would get out here, and a heavy, sinking feeling filled his chest. "Our forensic team is tied up with a homicide, and I might have to call in the state."

She rested her hands on her hips and tipped her head. "Can I suggest alternatives?"

"I'm listening."

"My first thought is we bring in a forensic team from the Veritas Center in Portland."

He tried to stop his mouth from falling open, but didn't manage it. "You can't be serious. No way we can afford to pay for a world-renowned forensic team."

"They do work pro bono. I have contacts there and would be glad to ask."

"Putting you in line to receive forensic results first." He scowled. "My sheriff won't go for that, and I won't either."

"They can sign a contract with your agency stipulating your department has exclusive rights to receive the results."

"Okay," he said, but something about it still didn't sit well with him. "What's your second option?"

"Not nearly on the same level as Veritas, but my friend at Blackwell Tactical was a skilled Portland forensic tech before she joined the team. As a bonus, she served as a patrol officer before moving to forensics, making her sensitive to investigative needs. She's built a top-notch lab and would most certainly do it as a favor to me."

Right off the bat, the second option seemed better. He could control one person. Maybe. She was Abby's friend after all, and her loyalty would go to Abby. Could be problematic.

"I'll think about it." He wasn't ready to make a commitment about anything until he had a chance to consider the situation he found himself in. He didn't want to drag his feet on this investigation, but he also didn't want to make a major mistake.

A shadow of concern passed over her face as if she didn't like his answer. Maybe she was worried he would choose a subpar forensic team. Not his plan at all. Part of the decision would come down to who could get to the scene quickest. The rest would depend on his sheriff's preference.

She pulled the blueprints from under her arm and settled them on a round table coated in dust. If it wasn't rude, he'd push her out of the way and take over the plans. He might not be happy she was here, but it wasn't in his nature to be rude to anyone. So he came alongside her while she unrolled them on the table.

The mansion had three entrances in addition to the front door. Four possible places the intruder could've entered to steal the crown, not counting the windows.

"Why don't we work our way down the right side around the perimeter and back?" he asked, instead of demanding. He'd done far too much of that already.

She rerolled the prints. "Follow me. I know the location of the first door."

She took off at a rapid pace through the dingy, dismal foyer, and he stayed on her heels.

"Hold up." He stopped near a wall, the upper half covered in old portraits. "Did you see the dust print from these missing paintings?"

Abby narrowed her eyes. "Victor never mentioned stolen art. Just the crown."

Burke's instincts buzzed—quietly, insistently. He jotted a note on a pad he took from his suit jacket. If the missing paintings had anything to do with the investigation, he would leave no stone unturned.

She continued to focus on the wall. "You don't think he's telling the whole truth."

"No, I don't."

She looked over her shoulder at him. "I think there are more secrets here than he'll ever reveal to us, but are they related to the investigation?"

"Problem is, we have to rely on him to make that determination."

"Yeah. Doesn't bode well for us, does it?" She hurried ahead and rounded a corner, then slowed to make her way down a few stone stairs into what appeared to be the mansion's original kitchen.

Burke took a long look. How could anyone prepare a meal in such a tiny space? Especially service for a large number of guests. If the original owner hosted dinner parties, the crown's identity might've been discovered then. Or maybe he'd been a hermit like Victor.

"The door's straight ahead," she said, tucking the blueprints back under her arm. "I saw it when I arrived and came in looking for Victor. Turns out he was upstairs taking a nap."

"Odd," Burke said. "He's a hermit who knew someone was coming to invade his sanctuary. How could he nap? He surely would've been upset about the theft of the crown at least."

"We might have to accept that Victor is unpredictable."

"Which could make this investigation even more difficult." Burke tried not to sound discouraged, but he liked things more black and white than he was finding tonight.

Stopping in front of a door, she tugged on the handle. "Locked."

She handed him the blueprints. "Hold these for a second, please."

She pulled the key ring from her pocket, the metal clinking in the quiet stone hallway, and fumbled through them until she found one to fit the lock. "The blueprint makes this look like a passageway that doesn't lead to the outside." Pulling the door open, she stared ahead.

Eager to see where it led, he stepped past her to find additional stone stairs leading downward. He returned the blueprints to her and shone his flashlight at the lock. Zero evidence of tampering.

He looked around the space. "No sign of a break-in and no sign of lights, but I do see a few kerosene lamps and matches on the shelf. They'll cover a wider area than our flashlight so I'll light one for each of us."

After stowing his flashlight in his pocket, he fired up the lamps, illuminating the area around him. He handed one to her and took his down the stairway. Six stone stairs in all, the temperature falling with each one until he reached an earthen floor, the dirt packed from many years of traffic. A rank odor clung to the thick stone walls.

With her footsteps trailing him, he held his light out to lead them ten feet down the passageway. The narrow space opened to a wide room with a higher ceiling.

He looked ahead. Blinked. Blinked again.

Couldn't be, could it?

Yeah, he was seeing clearly.

Two eight-by-ten prison-like cells with iron bars, heavy chains, and padlocks filled the room. Each cell held a wooden cot with a straw mattress, a chamber pot, and a small table.

"A dungeon?" Abby's voice bounced off the stone walls. "Why would anyone build a dungeon in their home?"

"At the time this house was built, rural Oregon was pretty lawless," he said as he came to grips with the sight in front of him. "Maybe the homeowner had to take the law into his own hands to protect his property."

"Something to ask Victor about." Frowning, she looked

around, then bolted for the furthest cell and pointed inside. "Look at this. It isn't from the 1800s."

Inside the cell, something red on the cot caught his attention. He moved close enough to pick up an individual paper packet of Tylenol, the top torn and the package empty.

He turned it over. "Expiration date is less than two years from now. If I'm right, the manufacturer sets the dates two years from packaging."

Her face brightened. "So this packet is current and should be processed for prints."

"Maybe our first real lead."

She lifted the mattress. "A penny. There's a penny."

He grabbed the coin and flipped it over with gloved fingers. "Stamped 1992. Another newer item."

"Let's keep going." Her excited tone encouraged him. "See what else we find."

He replaced both items so their forensic tech could photograph them in situ before trying to lift prints. The other cell held nothing of interest, so they continued ahead until they reached the broken window.

He stared at it. "If Victor isn't telling the truth about this window, and it was used to get in, it's suspiciously clean. Too clean. No shattered glass in here, almost as if someone staged it."

"Inside job?" she asked.

"Could be the housekeeper or estate manager, but they really wouldn't have to break a window, would they?"

"Not likely." She started down another narrow passage.

Burke held his light out until they reached a door at the end of the corridor where they extinguished their lanterns and set them on the floor.

"This should lead to the outside." She followed the same procedure as door number one, handing the plans back to him and finding the right key. She tugged the door open, then gave the lock and wood a careful study. "I don't see any proof of forced entry here either."

They exited the building, but he stopped to examine the lock. She was right. No sign anyone forced the door open. She made her way along an overgrown path leading from the building, but his light caught something near her feet.

"Hold up." He crouched to study a set of muddy footprints. "Recent footprints. Not from my deputies. Too small. Narrow stride. Heading away from the house."

Abby bent down. "A woman?"

"Maybe. Or a small man." He stood. "Could've been Victor, too, if he's not as fragile as he lets on. Let's move on. But be careful. Don't disturb the footprints before we get them evaluated."

She looked at him. "Another reason to decide on a forensic team before rain washes these away."

He nodded, but still wasn't prepared to make a decision and led the way down a path that wound upward to the main entrance.

"Keep going," she said. "Around the corner to the next door."

Picking his way through overgrown weeds, he reached the side of the house. He directed his light at the wall, running it back and forth, spotting the outline of a door swallowed by a thick coat of ivy. Completely inaccessible. "No one's opened this door in many, many years."

"It's not even on the blueprints. Let's move on, and we can come back if we need to."

She led the way this time. They checked every window they passed, but all were locked and intact. Around the corner, at the back of the house, they reached a paved veranda with glass French doors. She opened them with a key on her ring.

A small office greeted them, but Burke couldn't see much in the darkness. He lifted his flashlight, when a crystal lamp switched on. Dusty like nobody'd touched it in years, it threw light across a heavy-looking desk and matching chair. All of it sat on some thick rug that probably cost more than his truck tires.

Abby stood near the edge of the room, nowhere near the lamp.

"Did you turn the lamp on?" he asked.

She shook her head.

He traced the cord. "It's on a timer to go on and off several times a day."

"Could be a security measure." She crossed the room to the fireplace.

"Looks like it." He found and hit the light switch.

An old chandelier flickered to life, dust clinging to every edge. The place looked like something straight out of an old French postcard, worn but trying to hang on to look fancy.

Abby crouched on the tiled hearth. "The grate's still hot. Lots of fluffy ashes, and the wood's barely charred. This was a quick burn. Paper, maybe?"

"Maybe, but it would be hard to tell if someone burned something from this room. We need Victor to look through his things." Burke circled the room, and the floor near the mantle creaked under his feet. He bent to study the wood. "A loose floorboard."

He pulled out a pocketknife and pried the wood free, revealing a hollow space, perfect for storing secrets.

She stood over him. "It's empty."

"Maybe someone took something out of here and burned it in the fireplace." He looked up at her. "Documents? Letters?"

She glanced around the room. "Victor might've decided to get rid of something incriminating before we arrived."

"Could be." Burke pivoted to take in the firebox and agreed with her assessment of the ashes. "Couple this with him being the only one who knows about the crown, and no sign of forced entry makes his involvement more likely. Let's grab him to check out the room."

He didn't want to confront the older guy. If he was indeed connected to someone high up in the county, and if Burke started lobbing accusations at him and was wrong, Burke could lose his job. But no matter the pressure his boss might put on him, he would do the right thing.

From the far end of the hall, a door closed with a sharp click.

"We're not alone," Abby whispered.

"Could just be Victor," Burke said, but still reached for his gun.

"Or not. It sounded solid. Like the front door, and he said he never goes outside." She drew her sidearm. "Besides, I didn't hear his cane hitting the floor."

"We won't know until we check it out." He rushed toward the door, leaving the blueprints behind.

Abby followed and they moved in sync, years of law enforcement training converging instinctively. They found the foyer empty, the front door still closed. No wind. No creaking floors.

And no noise from Victor when they entered the library. Except for the soft snores escaping through his open mouth. Eyes closed, he reclined back in his chair, a plaid blanket over his knees. A nearly empty snifter of brandy sat on the table beside him.

"Obviously Victor didn't make the noise," Abby said.

"But we both heard someone slipping out of a room or from the mansion."

"The question is, who?"

"Let me check with my team outside to see if they

spotted anyone." Burke removed a small radio clipped to his belt, but before he could say anything it crackled in his hand.

A voice cut through the static. "Unit one, we've got movement near the greenhouse. Lights on inside. It'll take us a few minutes to get over there to check it out. You're closer and might want to investigate."

"Ten-four, unit two." Burke warned Deputy Ewing about the potential suspect who they believed exited the house.

"Will keep an eye out as we head toward the greenhouse," Ewing responded.

"We're on our way." Burke shot a look at Abby. "Greenhouse? Where is it?"

"Don't know, but the blueprints are in the office." She holstered her weapon and raced to the office, halting by the desk. She ran her finger over the top page, then tapped the faded paper. "East side of the property. There's a warning note here. It says locked and condemned. Too dangerous to enter."

Burke met her gaze. "You might as well leave a red flag telling us to check it out."

She gave him an excited nod. "Fastest way to get there is through the French doors."

They exited through the veranda, their flashlights sweeping across the overgrown garden paths. In the distance, the greenhouse took shape in the shadows, large and imposing against the backdrop of night. The moon broke through the clouds, and the light silvered against the glass walls.

Inside, a light flickered, then went out.

Burke whipped out his sidearm. Abby too. After a quick glance, they eased down the path, picking their way through greenery that had already been disturbed.

They reached the door.

"Wait here." He held up his hand and inched forward. Surprisingly, she stayed behind. He pulled on the handle of an aged wooden door with glass panels. The hinges rasped open.

Inside, the air was thick with heat and rotting vegetation. Overgrown vines curled across the dirt floor. A broken bench lay beneath a tangle of weeds, faded blossoms gray with dust.

And in the center of the floor?

A single shoe print similar in size to the prints located outside the dungeon exit. Had the person started here and gone to the mansion or vice versa? Seemed likely.

Next to it lay a piece of torn velvet, deep purple, embroidered with a decorative pattern using antique gold thread.

A noise sounded behind him. He spun to find Abby standing at the doorway.

Of course she didn't stay put, but he wouldn't take time now to argue about it. He held up the scrap of velvet. "Could be part of the crown's case."

She showed no interest in the velvet, but stared over his shoulder.

He swiveled, seeing nothing unusual. "What is it? What do you see?"

"Look at the overturned planter."

He squinted and made out an item barely poking out beneath the rim.

Abby picked her way through weeds to drop to the ground. She pried the pot free and tipped it over, then pawed through the weeds and soil like a frantic dog. Suddenly, she stopped and glanced back, her face alive with excitement.

He crept closer. Closer. Until he caught a faint hint of her sweet perfume.

She snatched an item up and held it to a shaft of moonlight, illuminating a small brass locket.

She examined the necklace front and back. "What could this possibly be doing here?"

"Look inside," he said, catching her excitement. "A picture might help explain it."

She wiped the dirt from her hand on her knee and dangled the chain over her palm, then maneuvered the locket between her fingers.

Neither of them spoke, the suspense keeping them both waiting.

He lifted the bright beam of his flashlight to the locket, the light revealing cracks and a burnished finish that could only come with age. She pinched the edges, and the top flipped open.

One side of the frame held a faded, water-stained image of a woman. The other, a picture of a much younger Victor.

Burke shifted his light to better illuminate the locket. "See the frayed paper edges behind her picture? There's something back there. Can you take it out?"

She picked at it with a fingernail, releasing the photo. She turned it over and gasped.

"It's a name etched in script." He bent closer to make out the name. "Estelle Lemoine. Likely some relation to Victor, right?"

"His wife." Abby's voice trembled. "I saw her picture in a story and it looked just like this one."

Not the reaction he expected. "Why is that upsetting you?"

"I read in an article that she vanished forty years ago. No hint of where she's been."

Burke stood slowly, the implication settling in. Sure, the locket could simply have been dropped here years ago and accidentally buried, but couple that with her disappearance, and it would be too coincidental. He didn't believe in coincidences. If a woman lost such a sentimental piece of jewelry, surely she would go looking for it.

No, it looked more like someone had come to dig it up tonight, but they'd been interrupted.

Abby's expression mirrored his thoughts.

"This just became more than a theft," he said, but wished he didn't have to. "We could be dealing with Estelle's murder, and Victor might know something about that too."

4

Burke could barely keep up with Abby as she plunged through the overgrown yard, up the narrow driveway, and through the mansion's front door. But he did his best and entered the library moments after she skidded to a stop just inside the door.

She looked down at the sleeping homeowner. "Mr. Lemoine? Wake up. We have news to share."

The older gentleman stirred and grumbled but dropped back to sleep. His chest rose and fell, his lips flapping as he breathed.

"Victor! Victor!" She stepped closer as if she wanted to shake him awake, but her hands remained curled at her sides. "If he wasn't breathing, I'd think he was dead."

At the small, circular table near Victor's chair, Burke pointed at the near-empty brandy snifter. When he last saw the glass, it had held a healthy measure of liquor. "He's probably sleeping it off."

"I could see where one of those would make him drowsy, but knock him out like this?"

"Older folks can't handle alcohol like younger ones. If

he's not a regular drinker, this amount might've left him out cold."

Abby's shoulders sagged as if the air had gone out of her. "I'll leave him a note and tell him I'll be back first thing in the morning."

"Remember, this is my crime scene. Until I say otherwise, I haven't decided if you have a role in this investigation."

Abby straightened. "Unless you cordon off the whole property with crime scene tape, I have every right to enter the building. With or without your permission."

He liked her feisty personality, but not when directed at him, and he couldn't let her interfere with the investigation. "After finding the locket in the greenhouse, not only will my deputies cordon off the mansion, but I'll instruct them to include the entire property in the perimeter."

She cocked her head. "And here I thought since we were getting along so well you'd gotten over this whole jurisdiction thing."

"As I told you, I need time to think about it."

"If you knew me, you'd know I don't plan to one-up you or take over your investigation. I only want to cooperate and be of assistance while also being included in the findings. I'm just not the kind of person you seem to think I am."

She didn't have to tell him that. Not when he'd experienced her integrity firsthand. Even as a sheriff in an agency other than his, she was always ready and willing to lend a hand. Always positive with her staff, lifting and building them up. Not taking credit when goals were achieved, but giving them their due.

Still, he couldn't do what she wanted. Not yet. "I'm not worried about you one-upping me, but I won't jump into making a decision without giving it careful consideration."

The frustration in her expression melted. "And how long will it take for you to decide?"

"I'll have an answer to you by morning."

She gave a sharp nod. "There's nothing else we can do until Victor wakes up. Figure he's out for the night. We should take off so you can start thinking about our potential partnership."

"Go ahead and wait for me at the boat while I give my deputies instructions."

"Will do, after I write Victor a note." She lifted her chin as if she thought he might argue. "I assume I can tell him at least one deputy will be assigned to protect the scene and him."

"I'll have a couple of deputies on site overnight, but with an active murder investigation going on in my department, I'm not sure how many resources we can spare."

"See, this is a perfect opportunity for our team to help. We're trained in proper procedures and have the ability to help you maintain scene integrity."

"Duly noted." She made a good point, several in fact, but he still wouldn't decide anything without thinking it through. He'd been a detective for years and was used to making snap decisions on the job.

But in his personal life? Not so much. Being raised in a religiously strict household, where his parents equated his every fault and mistake to sin and punished him for it, had left him afraid to make a mistake. He'd never totally outgrown that way of thinking. And since his fiancé and partner betrayed him, decision making had become even more difficult. Especially when he had so much weighing on making the right decision.

He swallowed. "Go ahead and write the note, then meet me outside."

"I saw paper and a pen in the office." She exited the room.

Good. Alone at last. Able to think clearly. Something he struggled to do when she was near. Before he left, he would take a quick look to see if he'd let his distraction stop him from seeing something important.

He went straight for the hidden compartment and checked the other shelves to make sure nothing else was hidden here. Everything seemed to be in order, but hopefully a good forensics tech would catch anything he missed. Another decision he had to make. He liked the idea of using one of the people Abby recommended. In either event, he would get quality work done. Given their solid rep, the Veritas Center would've screened and trained all of their staff, and Gage Blackwell's reputation said he wouldn't hire anyone who wasn't at the top of their game.

Question was, would Ryder go for either one of these options or would he insist on using state forensic techs? Only one way to find out. Talk to him. Burke would do that as soon as he reached the mainland again.

He finished searching the perimeter and stopped by Victor's chair. "Victor? Are you awake, Victor?"

The man didn't stir. If anything, he snored louder.

Shaking his head, Burke went outside and made his way to Deputy Ewing, who was standing near the doorway. Burke gave a quick rundown of everything they'd found, making sure not to say the word crown.

"I'm heading back to home base," he said. "You and your partner stay here. Lock down the perimeter—entire property."

Deputy Ewing raised an eyebrow. "The whole thing?"

"That's right. We'll need daylight and additional personnel to process this scene properly. First thing in the morning, I'll schedule reinforcements to relieve you. Until then, once the perimeter's secured, plant yourself at the base of the stairs. No one gets through unless you clear it with me personally. Understood?"

"Yes, sir," Ewing replied.

"That also goes for Abby Day. No one gets in. Including her or anyone on her team. Don't ask. Don't second-guess. They're not authorized. End of story."

Abby gasped from behind him. He cringed. She'd heard his orders.

After their earlier conflict, he hated to upset her more, but the truth was, he had a job to do, and nothing would pull him from it. Not her, not anyone. Respect for her or not, he would keep moving forward. Still, those warm brown eyes had a way of throwing him off balance, making him want to forget the hard lesson he'd already learned about trusting women.

No. He couldn't forget their duplicitous behavior. Wouldn't forget such a thing. Not ever.

~

Abby couldn't believe the silent treatment she was getting from Burke. Not a word. Not a single word uttered since they took seats near each other in the boat for their ride back to civilization. Nor did he apologize for so forcefully instructing his deputy to keep her and her team off Victor's property.

She should just accept the silence, but the only way she wouldn't stew about it all night was if she hashed it out with him. "After the way you so strongly instructed your deputy to keep us away from the crime scene, I thought it might be a good idea to talk a little more about working together."

He swiveled his seat to face her. "I didn't mean anything personal by it."

"It sure feels like it—you thinking the worst of me all the time and not giving me the benefit of the doubt."

He didn't answer for a long moment, but stared over her shoulder. "I'm sorry about that."

"I appreciate you recognizing it and apologizing, but the big question is, how can we avoid it in the future?"

"You don't need to do anything." He leaned forward, his arms on his knees. "Look, the guy you've met so far isn't the man I want to be, and I sure don't *want* to act like this. But there's something about you that gets under my skin. I'm not saying it's your fault. It's all on me. I'm still attracted to you, but I don't have room in my life for such a distraction, and it makes me mad that I can't get control of it."

He needed to be in control. No secret to her. She'd seen the same trait in him before, but it was more exaggerated now. He was a man who was assertive about the way he felt and the way he wanted things, and quick to react when it didn't go his way.

A personality she avoided at all costs. Reminded her too much of her family of pushy defense attorneys—both her parents and three siblings. All who looked down on her for her career choice, never missing a moment to jab her about it. For her own mental health, she'd had to walk away.

The consequences of her decision broke her heart. Unfortunately, her mother died unexpectedly a little over a year ago, and Abby hadn't had a chance to reconcile with her before then. But Burke appeared to be different from her family. He recognized his behavior, at least when it came to this issue, and seemed to want to change. Big questions were, could he recognize it in other situations and actually change?

Only time would tell, and he wasn't the only one to blame for their current situation.

"I have a part in this, too," she admitted, but had no

plans to tell him about how he reminded her of her family. "I'm also still attracted to you and finding it hard to ignore. If I'm conveying my interest and making things worse for you, I'm sorry. I have zero time for a relationship. We're too busy getting our business up and running and barely making ends meet. I need to put all of my attention on this investigation and locate the crown for the generous payment Victor is offering us."

She expected him to ask how much money Victor was shelling out for their services, but when he didn't, she continued, "So what say we do our best not to put ourselves in a position where we have to work extra hard on the way we react to each other?"

"Deal." He held out his hand.

She clasped it, but at the warmth of his touch, she wanted to ignore the pact they'd just made.

So when the boat bumped up against the dock and Burke jumped out to tie it off, she caught up and quickly made her way to the side of the boat.

He held out his hand to help her disembark. Touching him now might undo their whole conversation, so she ignored his hand and climbed onto a bench seat, then onto the slippery dock. She nearly face-planted, but righted herself at the last moment.

Burke was probably laughing under his breath, but she refused to check. She felt like some sulky teenager and couldn't shake it, no matter how dumb it seemed. The kicker? Acting like this wasn't her at all. She was usually easy-going and went with the flow. But something about him set her on edge, and she didn't like who she became around him.

She took a deep breath and let it out, forcing away her irritation and focusing on being more positive.

"Thanks for the ride." She took out her business card

and handed it to him. "I'll be up all night working on background for this investigation. If you have any questions or comments or just want to discuss something, give me a call."

He glanced at the card, then dropped it into his jacket pocket. "I don't think I'll be needing to call you, but I'll let you know by morning where I stand on working together."

His professional tone when she had so many emotions flowing through her, irked her, but she forced out a smile. "And the forensics?"

"It's up to my sheriff. I'm leaning toward going with one of the people you suggested instead of the state. But it depends on who's available first. It'd be ideal to get someone on scene first thing in the morning."

He didn't want much, did he?

"I'll give both of them a call to see who's available, but if you want someone first thing, you'll need to let me know your decision as soon as possible."

"Sheriff Ryder's on duty, and I'm headed back to the office to talk to him now."

"Then I look forward to your call." Thinking she'd done everything she could to plead her case and move this investigation forward, she strolled away as if everything was okay with her. She could feel his eyes tracking her as she negotiated the slippery dock and climbed the stairs to the walkway leading to the parking lot. The wind, fishy-smelling from nearby fishing boats, battered her body until she reached the nearly deserted and poorly lit parking lot. Once in her vehicle, she made quick work of exiting onto the beach road.

After her drive that took a little longer than usual—thanks to the fog and winding country roads—she pulled into Blackwell Tactical's fenced driveway. A high-powered and motion-activated security light clicked on and cut through the fog, illuminating a heavy-duty metal gate.

She'd been to the compound countless times to visit Sam and her family, but every time the military base-like compound on a remote stretch of Cold Harbor backcountry made her hesitate. But Gage was a private man with high-end gear and a serious arsenal—just the type of equipment and weapons thieves would love to get their hands on, and he had to keep the weapons out of the wrong hands.

She pushed the call button, alerting whoever was on duty of her arrival, and smiled at the camera.

"Ab-by-yeee!" Sam's excited voice came over the squawk box. "You're so late. I wasn't sure you were going to make it."

"Sorry. The mystery theft was more involved than I imagined. I'll tell you all about it once I see you."

"Okay, now you've got me curious, so get down here and spill already."

The gate buzzed, then swung open, revealing a long driveway opening into a clearing ringed by tall pines. Gage's log house sat beneath a towering maple, its shadow stretching across the building. The grounds were neat and practical and looked like an ordinary homestead. Most people couldn't imagine that a training facility existed on the property.

Abby knew better. Knew the blacktop drive to her right led to another clearing beyond the thick woods.

She turned onto the blacktop and caught sight of the familiar staff cabins—each one designed by the original five team members. Sam's cabin was a traditional log home with a porch and a modern addition she and her husband, Griff, had built after their second child arrived. Other original team members moved on, buying houses off-site for their growing families. But Sam and Griff lived here for free, helping them save money to start a business.

She'd no more than parked in front of Sam's cabin when

the door flew open. Sam darted out, her shoulder-length blond hair flying behind her.

Abby felt a rush of love for her friend as she climbed out.

Sam, nearly a foot taller than Abby, enveloped her in a strong hug. "I've missed you, my friend. I don't know why we don't get together more often."

Abby squeezed hard, then pushed free. "Because I've been working day and night trying to get our business off the ground."

"Sounds like it's going well." Sam curled her hand in the crook of Abby's arm. "Let's get inside, and you can tell me what this mystery is all about."

Abby was instantly at home in the casual space Sam had painted a cool gray. She added warm orange accents with pillows, throws, and the easy chair Griff currently sprawled on. They'd installed bookshelves around the room, but brightly colored toys for babies and preschool children overpowered most of the available space.

Griff looked up from his computer tablet, eyes a stunning sapphire blue locking on Abby, and assessing her. "Day! Long time no see. How's life?"

"Life. What's that?" She laughed. "The business is taking so much time I don't have much of a life outside of it."

"Sounds like the way we live." He ran a hand over dishwater-blond hair cut spiky short. "Always taking on as many side jobs as we can to build our savings account while working full-time and raising two little kids."

"You can see how much we need a bigger house." Sam dropped onto the couch and patted the seat next to her. "Enough small talk. Park it here and start dishing. What's the deal with the mystery?"

Sitting, Abby described the theft of the pricey crown, she made sure to call an artifact. "It's worth up to sixteen million dollars, so we have a sense of urgency to find it before it's fenced and we never see it again."

"Wow!" Sam shook her head. "You weren't kidding that this guy downplayed the mystery. I'll bet you're glad you took the call and caught the investigation."

Did her friend's tone hold jealousy? Maybe she missed official police work. Might bode well for Sam wanting to handle forensics for them. "Yes and no. I have to partner with Detective Burke Ulrich."

"I heard he was agreeable. Well, agreeable as far as detectives go." She laughed.

"Agreeable, hah! He's pushy, methodical, and extremely skeptical."

"Hmm." Sam cocked her head. "Sounds like someone else I know."

Abby blinked at her. "Who? Me?"

"Yes, you, and I'd add slow to trust, but it's interesting how you've learned so much about him in just one evening." Thinking, Sam tapped a finger on her knee. "Oh, wait! Don't tell me he was the detective you had a problem with on your last investigation."

Abby really didn't want to go there. "Okay, I won't tell you."

"Oh my goodness!" Sam grabbed Abby's hands. "So now you have to work with the detective who gave you a run for your money. The only guy I've seen you interested in."

"No. Not going there." Abby refused to discuss her love life tonight, especially not with Griff listening. "I'm going to be rude and ignore you so I can check in with my team."

"But it's after ten."

"Like I said, we work all hours, and they need to know about the artifact."

Sam shook her head. "And I thought we were bad with our hours."

"Speaking of that, I might have an opportunity for you to handle the forensics for this investigation if you'd be interested. Burke and Sheriff Ryder are deciding who to use, but Burke wants someone to start tomorrow morning."

"*If* I'd be interested?" Sam's eyes lit up. "Are you kidding me? A mystery like this? I wouldn't miss it."

"Umm, honey," Griff said, "you might not be on assignment for Gage tomorrow, but I have to work, and the kids' daycare is closed."

She buried her face in her hands. "Right. Right."

"That's okay," Abby said. "I'm also going to call Sierra at Veritas."

"No, don't." She grabbed Abby's hand. "I'm sure if Hannah's free, she'll watch the kids."

Not only was Gage a great guy and boss, but his wife was super supportive of the team and their families too.

"Well, don't call her this late. It isn't a done deal. I'm waiting for Detective Ulrich to call. For all I know, they could decide to use the state lab."

"He sure won't get anyone from there first thing in the morning. I can tell you that for a fact."

"Agreed," Abby said. "It's unlikely someone from Veritas could arrive so quickly either. They'd have to do the work pro bono, and the partners always meet to decide such cases."

"I'll still call Hannah first thing in the morning, so you know if I'm available. I'd do it pro bono, but I'd rather be paid the same amount they would pay the state. It'll help our saving goals."

"Sounds reasonable to me." Abby stood. "Were you able to get a cabin for me with such late notice?"

"One of our trainee cabins is available for the rest of the week." A flicker of irritation crossed Sam's face as she got up.

"I don't like it though. I wish we had enough room for you to stay with us."

"You did until you started popping out kids." Abby laughed but was envious of their little family. "I know you'd let me stay with you if you could."

Griff pushed out of his chair. "Think of it this way. You're escaping the terror of two preschoolers, so I would say the cabin is a win for you."

Sam swatted him. "Says the guy who thinks he wants four children."

"Actually, I want enough for a baseball team, but I'll settle for the four." He laughed.

She glared at him, but it was in jest. "If we're going to get this business off the ground, we can't afford even two of them, much less a whole team."

Abby admired their dedication to their goal. No doubt they would succeed once they met their savings goal and could get started.

Sam picked up a plastic rifle keychain from the island. "I'll walk you to your cabin."

"You don't have to."

"It's bad enough I don't have room for you here, but I won't shove you out the door to find your cabin." She quickly crossed to the door.

"Just roll with it," Griff said. "It's the easiest thing to do when she's all fired up about something."

"I heard that," she called back at them, a hint of amusement in her voice.

"See you tomorrow," Abby said to Griff, then hurried to catch up with Sam, who was already standing by her car door.

The moment Abby unlocked the door, Sam whipped it open to grab Abby's tote bag and computer case, then turned toward the traditional, one-bedroom log cabins built to house trainees.

"This is it. Number three." Sam pushed the door open and released a pleasant orange smell. "I did a quick cleanup before you got here. Gage pays for a cleaning crew, but still, you never know. Some of our trainees aren't exactly neat freaks."

"You really don't have to worry about me," Abby said. "If you saw the inn where my team lives, you wouldn't be apologizing."

"Hmm." Sam set Abby's bags inside the door and flipped on a light switch. "If only someone invited me to visit the inn, I might know what you mean."

"I'm sorry, I really am. We've just been so slammed. We haven't had any friends over."

She waved her hand. "I'm just messing with you. With our crazy busy life, it's likely I would have to say no."

Abby looked around. She expected a stark, no-frills place. After all, it was basically an Airbnb for buzz cuts and way too much testosterone with the occasional female thrown in the mix, but it was even more bare bones than expected. Thick logs made up the walls, and the floors were rough-hewn wood. The back wall held a tiny kitchenette and a small pine dining table with four chairs. The living area consisted of a dark brown sofa and matching chair, a coffee table, and an end table with a lamp.

"Sorry it's not fancier," Sam said.

"It's perfect. I really appreciate you letting me crash here. Tell Gage thanks, too, okay?"

She nodded. "I stocked the fridge and cabinet with snacks and drinks. Nothing for a full meal, but I figured you wouldn't be hanging around much during the day. Please swing by for breakfast in the morning."

"Breakfast sounds good. Depends on my schedule."

"We usually eat around seven," Sam said. "Come if you can. No big deal if you can't. Call your team, but text me with the decision on forensics. No matter the time."

Abby gave her friend a quick hug. "Seriously, it's so good to see you. We'll catch up properly once I get a grip on everything."

"No worries. I totally get it."

Sam left, and the moment the lock latched, Abby got out her laptop and made a video call from the dining table to the team's conference room. She sat in the rigid chair and tapped her foot as she waited for someone to answer.

The screen suddenly came alive. Gabe Irving's image shifted as if he were positioning the laptop so the camera caught his full face. Soon, his wide jaw covered with a dark, close-cut beard, and his narrowed eyes came into focus. "Yo, Abby. We all wondered if you'd check in."

"Is everybody with you?"

"Nope." He leaned back in his chair and clasped his hands behind his head, muscular arms bulging under his shirt sleeves. "I wouldn't be here either, but I have a ton of paperwork Nolan's been nagging me to get done. I'm pulling an all-nighter to get him off my back." Gabe could be classified as a bad boy who leaned toward the wrong side of the line most of the time. He detested sitting still for something as boring as paperwork.

She disliked it too. Especially after her stint as a sheriff, where the county created more paperwork than she'd ever dreamed possible. But Nolan, who founded the business, liked things tied up nice and neat. They were all partners in the business, but he basically ran things, and they tried to cooperate.

Gabe yawned. "Everyone else's crashed in their rooms."

Really? She'd texted to say she'd be late and had an exciting update. "Well, I'm disappointed," she said, trying not to whine. "I promised I'd give an update about the investigation. Any chance you can call a team meeting?"

"Maybe." He arched a dark eyebrow. "Give me the CliffsNotes version of your day before I take my life into my hands and wake them up."

She didn't like going through him as the gatekeeper, but she valued his usual devil's advocate perspective, and he would tell her whether the team needed to know about the theft of the crown right now. She gave him a quick rundown on the crown and locket.

"Wow!" He snapped his chair forward. "Yeah. Yeah. They'll want to hear about this tonight."

"I figured as much."

"Let me pull everyone together, and we'll call you right back." The screen went dark.

She'd wanted to tell Sam about the crown, but couldn't unless she took part in the investigation. So it felt good to tell Gabe, and it would feel even better to get her whole team's viewpoint. Hopefully they could shed light on tonight's mysterious happenings and help her formulate a plan to find this most prized missing artifact in time.

5

In his cubicle, Burke stared at Victor Lemoine's DMV record on his monitor. The man didn't have a criminal record, not even a speeding ticket. No surprises there. He'd received his Oregon driver's license forty-one years ago, had listed the Lemoine Mansion as his home address, and had regularly renewed it when due.

A 2012 all-electric Nissan Leaf was the only vehicle registered in his name. Burke had expected a larger car for a man with such opulent taste, but it made practical sense to have a small, all-electric vehicle on the island. None of this information helped, especially since Victor was a self-professed hermit.

Burke opened his notes on his phone and typed, *Ask Victor when he last left the island.*

He entered Estelle Lemoine's name into the county database, hoping her record provided a lead. Her picture confirmed the photo in the locket. Her driver's license had been issued on the same day as Victor's, but she failed to renew it when it came due, which would fit with her disappearance. He made another note to ask Victor about the official date of her disappearance. He also noted that she was ten years younger than Victor, though he didn't know if that was of any significance.

Shifting to his department's investigation database, he entered her name. The search returned a missing person investigation but zero details. Many of the department's old paper files hadn't been digitized, and hers were probably buried in basement storage at the Sheriff's Department's old location. The only way to get them was to file a request, requiring Ryder's approval.

Burke leaned back and stretched his arms overhead. When he first arrived at his office tonight, he checked to make sure Ryder was in, but didn't stop to talk. Burke wanted to wait until he knew for himself what he'd like to do about the forensics and partnering with Abby and her team.

The preliminary information they'd gathered indicated this could be a much larger investigation than expected. His department didn't have the staff necessary to assign additional people to this case, and he wasn't about to fail in finding the crown. If he could contain Abby's pushy behavior, partnering with the LLL team would be a good idea.

And the forensics? No one had been hurt or killed, or at least they didn't have proof of a murder yet. Just a simple theft, so the state lab wouldn't prioritize their case. Could mean a serious delay in processing, resulting in an equally serious delay in his investigation. Also risking the crown's disappearance. Poof. Vanished. Gone. Just like Estelle.

Decision made, he sat forward.

He would propose using one of the forensics teams Abby suggested, and he would form a partnership with her. Ryder would have to decide if their partnership included deputizing her or not.

He pushed away from his desk, sending the wheeled chair bumping into the cubicle wall and bouncing back at him. Before talking to Ryder, he needed to slow his roll and take hold of the jitters he hadn't been able to shake since seeing Abby. His boss was an intimidating guy and extremely perceptive. No way Burke wanted him questioning his ability to do the job, especially because of a woman.

He strode down the hall, took a deep breath, and poked his head into the office.

Ryder sat behind an old metal desk, stretching nearly the width of the small space. At roughly six feet tall, he had military-cut, sandy-blond hair and a hint of his summer tan on his face.

He looked up. "I hoped you'd stop in so we can give a positive report to Commissioner Blankenship in the morning. We gonna close this burglary fast?"

"About that," Burke said, dreading telling him it was going to take longer. "It's not as straightforward as we thought."

Ryder gestured at a chair in front of his desk. "Sit and bring me up to speed."

Burke lowered himself into the padded chair and updated his boss on the situation.

Ryder ran a hand over his stubbled jaw. "No one had any idea about this?"

"The way Lemoine wants to keep it, if possible." Burke explained Victor's reasons.

"We can do our best, but you know we can't promise it won't get out."

"I know," Burke said. "We can refer to the crown as a 'missing artifact' when talking to others."

"That works."

"The wife's disappearance could be related to the theft," Burke said. "I'll need your permission to request her missing persons file from storage.

"It'll take time to retrieve it, but bring me the form, and I'll fast-track the request. Hopefully, I'll have someone available to send out there first thing in the morning, and I'll pressure them into getting it to me by end of day." Ryder steepled his fingers. "You need to get this thing closed fast if you want the powers that be not to question removing your probationary status and keeping Ramsey permanently at detective."

Burke couldn't screw this up. If they demoted him again, he couldn't possibly survive having to work under Ramsey on a permanent basis. He would definitely have to leave his job and start over at another agency. Might mean going back to patrol and working his way up. Not something Burke wanted to do for sure.

"What resources do you need to get this investigation going?" Ryder asked.

He told his boss about Abby and her team, plus Blackwell Tactical.

Ryder picked up and toyed with a pen. "I've run into Day a few times. She's got a good rep. Was a solid sheriff. Don't know her team, but I'm willing to give them a try."

"*Willing*, as in deputizing them? Or do you want me to simply coordinate with them?"

Ryder grimaced. "Nothing simple about that. Not with all of them being former law enforcement officers. They're trained to take charge. We deputize the ones we need. Hopefully only one or two. They're less likely to go rogue if they have to report to you."

As much as Burke didn't want Abby reporting to him on a regular basis, Ryder made a solid point. "I'll get with Day to discover necessary personnel and get back to you tomorrow."

"Sounds like a plan."

"One more thing," Burke said. "Forensics. What are the

odds one of our techs could get on this first thing in the morning?"

Ryder snorted. "Fat chance. Wexler homicide trumps everything. No way I'll pull a tech off that and reassign them to your investigation."

"As I expected." He shared Abby's suggestions for forensic staff. "I figured if they both did the work pro bono, we'd use the first one available."

Ryder snapped his chair forward. "You can't go wrong with either one. If Gage Blackwell hired someone, that person has top-notch skills, but the Veritas Center will have far more resources. I'll leave it up to you to decide. In either event, all results come to you first."

Burke took this as a sign their conversation had ended and stood. "I'll let you know what I decide."

"I'd like a preliminary report on my desk by eight. Make it detailed but vague on the crown in case the commissioner asks to see the investigation details in writing."

"Roger that."

"And Ulrich," Ryder locked his eyes on Burke, "I'm glad to have you back where you belong, but don't let me down on this investigation or you just might find yourself in the hot seat again."

Burke nodded, but couldn't find the right words to say, so he took off. Back in his cubicle, he developed a to-do list. First, he would fill out the request for the old files. The next item he didn't much like. Calling Abby Day. No biggie, right? There were often tasks he didn't like in his job.

"Yeah... right," he mumbled, feeling that familiar edge of caution. "Like talking to her would be anything like talking to any other ex-sheriff."

Abby's phone rang. Expecting her team's video call, she opened her laptop and looked at the screen. Whoa! Not a video call and not her team, but ID for the county sheriff's office appeared. Had to be Burke. Should she talk to him when she hadn't spoken to her team yet? She had to. She'd promised to let Sam know as soon as possible if she was needed in the morning.

Her friendship with Sam trumped her unease in taking the call.

"Abby Day," she answered, trying to keep her voice light when she was exhausted.

"It's Burke Ulrich," Burke said, sounding as fatigued as she felt. "I've made a decision on the forensics. I'd like you to contact both parties to see who might be available first thing in the morning."

"I've already left a message for Sierra at Veritas, and I'm waiting to hear back from her, and I've spoken to Samantha Griffin at Blackwell. She's available, but not pro bono. She'll work for whatever wage you'd pay a state tech. And that's a real bargain."

He let silence answer for him.

She wouldn't give in easily on offering Sam's services pro bono, so sat back to wait him out.

He finally cleared his throat. "If Veritas isn't available first thing, I'll check with the sheriff to see if we can offer Ms. Griffin any payment."

"Perfect."

"I've also spoken to the sheriff about you and your team. He's agreed to deputize you and any of your teammates who you feel are vital to this investigation."

"Deputize... oh, uh, I didn't expect him to agree to that."

"Sheriff Ryder wants this case closed quickly and believes it's the best way to accomplish it."

So she'd be reporting to Burke as her supervisor. Could

she report to him? She wouldn't answer now and would give it some thought. "I haven't met with my team yet."

"No worries. We can meet at Victor's estate at eight a.m. sharp, and you can let me know your decision then." He disconnected before she could agree or add anything else.

Probably a good thing. The more they limited their conversations, the less likely they'd get into an area that would be uncomfortable for both of them.

Her phone chimed with the team's video call, and she quickly answered it on her laptop. Nolan Orr, Hayden Kraus, Jude French, Reece Waters, and of course, Gabe were present. Simply seeing her teammates—friends she'd known since college—helped ease her stress, but she wouldn't waste time this late at night with greetings. She brought everyone up to speed on the crown theft and finding the locket.

"Whoa!" Reece said.

"I told you it was big time." A gleam of eagerness shone in Gabe's eyes. "And before anyone else says anything, if Abby needs backup onsite, I'm calling dibs."

"Not so fast!" Jude shot forward. The former FBI agent ran a hand over his near-black hair trimmed with military precision—just like the beard, it clearly got VIP treatment. "I'd like in on the action."

"You snooze, you lose." Gabe blew on his fingernails and rubbed them across his chest. "I'm the man for the job. End of discussion."

Jude grumbled, but the team had an unwritten rule of calling dibs, and if it made sense for the investigation, whoever called it first got the assignment. She waited a moment, glancing at the others, but no one objected.

After finding the locket and the possibilities it raised, the investigation could very well turn out to be something big. She needed the full team's support, but specifically someone with her at the mansion for backup. But was Gabe the right person?

As a former Oregon state trooper, he certainly was qualified to do the job, but was it a good idea to bring in someone guaranteed to butt heads with Burke? Gabe pushed the boundaries all the time, and he didn't have an extreme amount of tact and could often be sarcastic.

Problem was, people outside the team didn't know that a lot of his behavior stemmed from his childhood, and he often used sarcasm as a defense mechanism when he was uncomfortable. They also didn't know he was the type to step up for anyone in need. All they saw was the sarcasm and his forthright behavior.

If she chose him, she could help tone him down. Or maybe the opposite was true. Maybe she needed someone like Gabe who could unquestionably hold his own against a strong detective. And she respected Gabe's investigative skills and his motivation.

She looked into the camera. "Before volunteering, you might want to know whoever works this investigation will be deputized and report to Detective Burke Ulrich."

Gabe pinched the bridge of his nose. "So we'll have to do this by the book."

"As much as possible, but the investigation and our client come first. I'm sure we'll be standing our ground more often than Burke would hope."

Gabe rubbed his hands together in front of the camera. "Then I'm your man."

"True, but I hope you'll tone down the sarcasm."

"I can do that. Or at least I can try." He grinned.

"You'll need to stay in a cabin on the Blackwell compound for the duration," she said, hoping there was another one available so she didn't have to bunk with Gabe.

"No worries. I can rough it with the best." He flashed a smile. "Do you want me to leave right now?"

She shook her head. "I'm meeting Burke at the mansion at eight a.m. I'd like you there. When you figure out your departure time, you need to factor in the ferry ride to the island. You have to be on the six a.m. departure to make it on time."

He groaned. "Early mornings aren't my thing, but I'll make it by six. I'll grab a few hours of sleep then head out around two-thirty."

"I can pack snacks and send them along with him." Reece shifted to eye Gabe, keeping the flawless posture she'd learned as a runway model in college. "The box will be sealed, and it better arrive the same way."

Gabe's stunned expression was so fake it bordered on theatrical. "But it's a three-hour drive. How ever will I survive that long without food?"

"Don't worry. I'll make a care package just for you." Reece always mothered them with homemade goodies and cooked nearly all of their meals.

"That's more like it." Gabe grinned.

Abby smiled. "Once we're in the thick of things, we'll both appreciate having your home-baked goodies."

"What about clothing and toiletries, Abby?" Reece asked. "I know you didn't plan to stay overnight, so I can pack a bag for you."

Abby had hoped she would volunteer for this task. "I'd very much appreciate your help."

"So," Reece said. "Are we going for business wear, business casual, or just plain casual?"

She couldn't get rid of the sight of Burke's tailored suit and crisp shirt even at the time of night they'd met.

Fine. Admit it. He's good-looking. Even thinking about him sent her heart somersaulting.

Not good. Not in front of the team. She cleared her throat. "Ulrich wore a suit, looking like he'd stepped out of a detective fashion catalog."

"Is there something going on there?" Reece wiggled her eyebrows. "Do tell!"

"Nothing to tell," Abby said firmly, hoping to put an end to her teammate's suspicions. "I should dress the part, but maybe throw in some business casual. Never know when I might need to get my hands dirty. And something chill, in case there's actually any downtime."

"I'd contribute to the conversation, but all my shirts are the same so..." Jude laughed.

The others nodded too, and just like that, the warmth she felt for her friends pushed aside the worries crowding her head. They'd had her back since college, through every high and low, and she knew without a doubt she'd do anything for them—no questions asked.

Nolan cleared his throat. "I think we can all agree this is settled, and if you want to discuss it further, you can do it without the rest of the team. The biggest thing you both need to remember is how important it is to keep Victor happy as a client and find the crown. Our future here depends on it."

Abby didn't need to be reminded of the importance of their mission. Based on Gabe's frown, he didn't either. Not only did they need the money for the team, but these guys were her family, and she didn't want to let them down.

"What other resources will you need?" Nolan asked.

Abby shifted her focus to Hayden. "Can you do a deep dive on Victor Lemoine and his wife, Estelle? The only thing I know is that he inherited the estate from his father, and he and his wife settled in Oregon over forty years ago. She went missing a couple years after they relocated and has never been found."

"Missing woman?" Hayden's typically serious expression lifted, revealing a spark of interest. "Now that's more like it. Sounds more exciting than the usual routine background checks you dump on—I mean *give*—me to do. I'll get right on it."

"Thanks." She ignored his attempted humor so she didn't get distracted and focused on Nolan. "It's safe to assume the crown's headed for the black market. Might be an open market, or the thief already has a buyer. I can't imagine buyers around here have pockets deep enough to afford it, so it's not likely a local deal. But a local expert could know where it's going or a collector who would buy it."

"Wouldn't an expert for a pricey artifact be rare around these parts too?" Reece asked.

Nolan sat forward. "Last weekend, Mina dragged me to an antique shop. The owner's sharp and aware of what's going on in the antiques market. I could go back and ask if he knows of an expert—fence—in the area. Mina could come with me. She speaks their language."

Excitement about this potential lead lifted Abby's tired shoulders. "I like the idea of you talking to him, but don't take Mina."

Nolan raised an eyebrow. "Why's that?"

"She might just be your girlfriend to you, but she's also the local sheriff. He might've recognized her or she could've talked about her job. If she goes back with you to discuss fencing stolen goods, he could very well clam up."

"You have a point. With reelection around the corner, he could've seen her campaign posters or billboards. I can go there alone first thing tomorrow and report back to you."

"Thanks," Abby said. "But I need you to hold off for now. With Burke's permission, I'd like to overnight the locket to you so you can show it to the shop owner. Get an idea of its age and where it could've been made or purchased. That kind of thing."

Nolan nodded. "Just let me know when to expect it, and I'll take it straight to the shop."

"Will do and thank you." She jotted Hayden's and Nolan's assignments on her notepad.

"All right, boss lady," Jude said, a hint of his usual humor in his voice. "Should I start with something productive or just sit here looking handsome and confused?"

Gabe rolled his eyes. "I get confused, but handsome? Nah. Not that."

A soft smile tugged at Abby's lips as she watched her team—her people—and felt a comforting warmth inside. "I hope to take Lemoine to his bank tomorrow morning to retrieve the crown's certificate and bill of sale from his safety deposit box. *If* I can get a guy who hasn't left home in decades to go outside and leave the island."

"So what do you want me to do?" A sharp glint burned in Jude's eyes. "Come along and drag him out if he doesn't want to leave?"

She stifled a groan. "We won't force him from his house. I need you to find an expert who can review and validate the documents once I have them."

"You think Lemoine is lying to you about the validity of the crown?" Nolan asked.

A good question. One she hadn't answered one way or the other yet. "The guy is quite condescending, but he's also elderly. He might not be thinking straight or he's covering something up. Authenticating the documents from his safety deposit box will confirm his story."

"Could he be trying to scam his insurance company?" Reece asked, not surprising. As a former FBI agent she would be familiar with insurance scams.

"Not likely." Abby shared Victor's reasons for keeping

the crown quiet, then looked each teammate in the eye. "You're not to mention the crown to anyone. If you have to discuss it at all, just call it a valuable artifact."

"Whoever validates the certificate will know," Jude said.

"We have no choice but to provide the details to some people. We'll have to count on their discretion and limit the number of people we tell. I'll get Victor's permission to share it with the expert and if you have to share it in the future, be sure you talk to me first." She stifled a yawn. "That's all I have for now. I'm sure my morning meeting with Victor and Detective Ulrich will bring up additional action items."

"Keep us updated," Nolan said. "And if you need us there, just let us know."

"I don't think that's likely," she said, instantly regretting it.

They couldn't predict when one of their investigations took a completely different turn, pitting them against a life-threatening emergency.

6

Burke eased his friend's boat through choppy waves to the Ravenhook Island dock and checked his watch—precisely six-ten a.m. On the other side of the long pier, the ferry's mooring lines strained as the large vessel bobbed in the water.

He secured the last knot for the boat, then satisfied it wasn't going anywhere, he scanned the mansion's stairs.

What? Why in the world was Abby here so early when they were meeting at eight?

Not only here on the island, but she'd slipped under the crime scene tape deep in conversation with two people he didn't recognize. She wore a razor-sharp business suit and combed her windblown hair back with her fingers.

An aqua blue cooler sat at her feet, and in front of them, a pair of hand trucks held stacks of large plastic storage bins. A tall blonde stood behind one stack, her hair catching the breeze as if she were filming a shampoo commercial. The guy next to Abby looked like he'd been dragged off a football field—broad shoulders, cargo pants, and a T-shirt that read: *Off Duty. Try Not to Ruin It.* Judging by his scowl, he meant every word.

Had she arrived early in hopes of one-upping him? Sure, she claimed not to be that kind of person, but was she really? He'd stupidly hoped she wasn't. Trusted in her words. Trusted her as a former law enforcement officer.

Surprise. He'd fallen victim to another woman's distrustful actions.

But the biggest surprise? The ache in his gut over being attracted to a woman who wasn't who he thought she was. Just like Tiffany, though the stakes were much lower here. But what if Abby hadn't shown her true colors yet, and he'd ended up getting involved with her?

Foolish. Just foolish thoughts. Keep your mind on the job.

He grabbed his clipboard from the boat and set off at a rapid pace, but the soles of his slick dress shoes slipped. He slowed to keep his feet out of the standing water and to avoid face-planting on the wet dock. He should've dressed casually today, but he always wore suits to work. Some might say he was rigid. At worst, he believed he was predictable.

Once on solid ground, he stormed ahead, trying to release his anger at her with every step, but it grew instead.

Abby looked his way, then leaned in and whispered something to the brawny guy next to her. Eyes the color of cold ice gave Burke the once-over—head to toe—sizing him up. He clearly wasn't impressed.

Burke stopped in front of Deputy Ewing, whose shift had been extended due to a lack of resources, and now recorded the names of all crime scene visitors. "I gave you strict orders last night. No one was allowed on scene without my permission."

Even more color drained from his already pasty face. "They said they were working with you." His words seemed to barely make it past a closing throat.

At the young guy's strangled reply, Burke almost felt bad

about taking him to task, especially when he'd worked most of the night and had to be tired. But Ewing had a promising future. *If* he learned to follow directions at all times. If he didn't, it could cost him his life or the lives of others. At crime scenes, if he didn't keep out potential contamination, the case could get thrown out of court and a murderer set free.

"I *am* working with them." Burke kept his gaze pinned to the young man. "But I particularly mentioned Day and her team weren't allowed on site."

"Yes, sir." Ewing ringed his finger around his collar. "I won't make the same mistake again."

"See that you don't. We don't want dangerous criminals escaping prosecution because we didn't properly manage a crime scene."

Ewing bobbed his head and lifted up the fluttering yellow tape, probably hoping Burke was done reading him the riot act and would leave him alone.

But Burke wanted to drive this important lesson home. "The housekeeper, Sylvia Bass, and the estate manager, Ugo Morell, will be arriving this afternoon. I want to be notified the moment they get here, and you are *not* to let them inside the perimeter. And be sure to check with me before allowing access to anyone else who shows up while you're on duty."

"Yes, sir." Ewing lifted the scene barrier higher.

Burke dipped under the tape and turned his focus to Abby and her team. He didn't want to call another person out, but he had to set standards at the beginning of their work relationship.

Preparing himself for an argument, he took the stairs two at a time to the landing at the base of the crumbling stairs. "After you pulled this little stunt, I have half a mind to cancel our partnership."

"Hey now." The chiseled guy at her side raised his hands and stepped forward. "I need you to back off."

"It's okay, Gabe." Abby grabbed his forearm. "Detective Ulrich might sound like a real tough guy, but he's harmless." She shifted her attention to Burke, her mouth turning down at the corners. "What stunt are you talking about?"

He didn't know if she was playing dumb or if she really was clueless. "Arriving here before the time we arranged to meet. Crossing the crime scene barrier when you knew I didn't want you to. Probably hoping to question Lemoine without me and keep the information to yourself."

Her nostrils flared. "Before you jump to conclusions, how about looking at the ferry schedule? We had two choices. Six or nine a.m. You're a smart guy. Do the math. Which one would you take not to be late for an eight o'clock appointment?"

His anger deflated. He'd let his temper get the best of him, jump to conclusions, and made a fool of himself in front of people he hadn't even met. But he wouldn't retreat.

"Right. Sorry." He ducked his head to show the sincerity of his apology. "So, are we good to move forward?"

She gave a sharp nod, but he could tell she didn't agree. She turned to Gabe. "Let me officially introduce you to Gabe Irving. I guess you can figure out he's on our team, but you might not know he's a former Oregon state trooper."

Burke offered his hand in a gesture of goodwill. "Hopefully we can move past this too."

Gabe shook hands as if he was trying to dislodge Burke's arm from his shoulder. "Just know I have my eyes on you."

The warning didn't surprise him. "Understood."

"And behind the storage bins is Samantha Griffin." Abby spun. "She's the fabulous forensic expert I told you about."

He was glad Sheriff Ryder had decided to pay her for her

services. "Thank you for coming at such short notice, Samantha."

"Sam." The tall, slender woman with friendly greenish-blue eyes smiled. "Everyone calls me Sam."

He nodded toward the bins. "Let me help you get these up the steps."

"I got it." She quickly tipped back the hand truck. "And before you're impressed with my brute strength, you should know the bins are empty for evidence storage." She chuckled.

Burke laughed with her. "All the same, I'd feel better about helping."

"Hey, no worries." Gabe pushed back from the other cart. "I've got nothing to prove, so feel free. Take my stack. And before you start up the steps, these aren't empty."

Well played! The guy left Burke with no choice but to go over to the other stack. Not if he didn't want to have another altercation. He wasn't certain about having Gabe around. Could be problematic. Was he here because Abby wanted to include him in the investigation? If he was on the LLL team, he certainly had to possess redeeming qualities.

"After you all." Burke motioned for them to go ahead and grabbed the hand truck, the metal cold beneath his fingers.

Abby picked up the cooler, and they all started up the stairway. While the others went ahead, Burke took his time, getting a better look at the surrounding area. Daylight removed some of the intimidation from last night. In fact, the sun sparkling through the trees brought a sense of peace. Not so, once he caught sight of the building itself.

The shutters appeared as if mere threads kept them attached, and a good percentage of the dark blue, almost black paint had chipped away from the siding. Several tiles were missing from the slate roof, and their once dark-gray color had faded into a lighter pewter. The massive wooden front door, though impressive in size and intricate carvings, was weather-worn and needed a good refinishing. The broken basement window stood wide open to the elements.

Victor was neglecting his property, and the place would fall into ruin if he didn't act. If the man couldn't convince himself to go outside, he could at least have his estate manager take pictures to share with him. Or maybe he'd done that, and he just didn't care. Burke couldn't understand his behavior. Not at all. If he ever owned property, no matter how busy he was in life, he'd respect God's blessing and do his best to care for it.

By the time he reached the top landing, Abby was approaching the door.

He settled the containers on the heavy stone walkway, making sure not to drop the clipboard he'd braced on the top bin. "Hold up, Abby. Can I have a word first?"

She fixed appraising eyes on him, but turned and joined him on the landing. "What is it?"

"First, I wanted to apologize again for the way I handled things when I arrived." He made sure his sincerity sounded in his tone. "There was no excuse for my behavior. I won't let it happen again. Okay?"

"Okay," she said, but her skeptical gaze told him he still had a lot to prove.

The sight of her might leave him out of control, but he would do everything within his power not to behave so childishly again. After all, he didn't want to feel this way. Not when he didn't have the time or inclination to get involved with anyone.

So shut it down, man, and don't throw a tantrum again.

"One thing, before the day gets going," she said. "I'd like your permission to overnight the locket to Nolan so he can take it to an antique dealer to authenticate. He won't mention Estelle or Victor, and he won't show him the pictures inside."

Good. Great even. She was focused on the case instead of their conflict and running things past him before acting. "Sounds like a good plan."

"Then after Sam adds the locket to her inventory, I'll have her overnight it today." She cocked her head. "Was there something else you wanted to talk to me about?"

"Yeah, Gabe. Do you want him to be involved in the investigation on a daily basis?"

"Is there a problem?"

"No, no problem. It's just that I want to deputize you before we talk to Victor, and if Gabe will be working with us, he'll need to be sworn in too, but I only brought credentials for you." He took from his pocket a shiny brass shield he'd picked up for her. "Next time I go back to the office, I'll grab one for him."

She took the badge, an eyebrow raising. "So you want to do the swearing in right here?"

"I know it's unconventional, but yes. It would be good if you were officially sworn in before this interview."

"Makes sense." She turned to the door. "We need you over here, Gabe."

He jogged down to them and once he planted his tactical boots on the steps, Abby explained the situation. "When I mentioned being sworn in, you didn't raise an objection, so I assume you're good with it."

"Good? Not sure that's the word, but I'm okay with it."

"Okay, then," Burke said. "You'll both have full powers of the job, but I hope you won't take advantage of that."

"Man," Gabe said. "And here I was ready to declare my room at the inn an official crime scene so I didn't have to clean up the mess." He cracked a smile.

Abby rolled her eyes. "Your room is a disaster and looks

like many crime scenes I've responded to, but the joke was pretty lame."

Burke agreed with her, but he held out his hand for a fist bump. "Bonus points for creativity though."

Gabe flashed him a surprised look, just the thing Burke was going for. Keep the other guy guessing, but also try to change the narrative after their less-than-stellar introduction.

Burke glanced at the top sheet on his clipboard. "I'll make this quick. Raise your right hands, and I'll read the oath of office. You repeat back to me. Then you'll sign the official form, and we'll be done."

"And at that point we report to you." Gabe's piercing look cut through Burke.

"Yes," he said, and moved right into reading the oath of office. Both of them took the oath and signed their names to their forms.

"That covers it." Burke took the clipboard back. "Except don't make me regret asking the sheriff to agree to this. Not that I think you'll do anything to cause that to happen, but in the heat of an investigation, bad decisions can be made."

He handed the shield to Abby and explained to Gabe why he didn't have one for him.

"Don't worry," Gabe said. "I'll wait to cry about it in the car later." He ended with a playful grin.

Abby smiled back at him. "As you can see, Gabe is always good for some humor."

The exact opposite of Burke. As much as he didn't want to compare himself to this guy, Abby's smiles directed at Gabe made him rethink his seriousness. Did this guy have a thing for her, the reason behind his treatment of Burke? He didn't get such a vibe from either of them, and after years as a detective, he didn't often misread interpersonal cues.

"Okay, let's get this interview done." Abby proceeded

straight to the door and pounded on the aged wood with the side of her fist. The solid thumps echoed over the quiet island, competing only with the ferry engine's rumble as it pulled away from the dock.

Victor finally opened the door wearing the same dressing gown. His hair was tangled, and dark bags hung under his drooping eyes.

He looked like they'd woken him, and they would have to do some fancy talking to get him to let them in this early. But Burke was up for the challenge. They had to get inside to collect forensic evidence. Every room in this house could hold secrets, each one a potential key to unraveling the mystery.

Or if Estelle had indeed been murdered, they could even find a clue to locate her killer.

7

Abby entered the dining room and took a good look at the massive space. A dust-covered crystal chandelier hung over an equally dusty table with sixteen ornately carved chairs. She could easily imagine the room sparkling clean, the table set with fine china and silver, and formally dressed men and women arriving for dinner in the 1800s.

Gabe stood at the end of the table, watching the doorway.

"Anything of interest?" she asked him as Burke stepped in behind her.

"If you consider silverware that looks like it requires a user manual, then yes—very interesting." His eyes twinkled with humor. "But as far as the theft goes, doesn't look like it's a room we should waste any time on."

Burke pointed at the large antique sideboard. "Did you check all the drawers?"

Abby expected a negative reaction from Gabe over having his work questioned, but he simply nodded.

"Then let's have a seat and hope Victor doesn't take long to get ready." Burke pulled out a chair for Abby.

The guy had old-school manners. Both in this gesture

and offering to take Sam's cart up the stairs. She liked his kindness. Would appreciate it, even. *If* she knew the reason. Was it a sign of respect, or was it patronizing—thinking women didn't have the same abilities as a man? Even worse, did it indicate he was brought up with a privileged lifestyle that he adopted for himself? A lifestyle like her snooty family lived. They looked down on people who hadn't been raised in the same social standing. True, he was a detective, and her family would no more approve of his job than hers, so she was probably overreacting.

Gabe plopped down on the chair next to her. She'd avoided placing her arms on the dusty table, but Gabe didn't care. He propped his elbows on top and put his chin in his hands. "I wonder how long this dude'll take to get ready."

Victor had spent the night in his chair in the library, and he hadn't had a chance to change clothes. Still, he'd been kind enough to let them in and took Sam to the library to begin processing the forensics and take his fingerprints to eliminate his from others she might locate in the house.

"We have to remember his age," Abby said. "He's in his seventies and won't move as fast as we do."

"Don't worry," Gabe said. "I got the hint earlier. Dial it down a notch and be more respectful."

She laughed. "See. Now that's why I brought you along."

Expression still serious, Burke dropped onto a chair across the table and held up his phone. "I made a list of questions for Victor last night, starting with the simple things we learned and building to Estelle. If it's okay with you, I'd like to take lead here."

"Sounds like a good plan," Abby said, amazed he'd asked instead of ordered. "It's fine with me as long as you don't mind my input along the way."

"Two heads are better than one." He swiped his screen with a long index finger.

He seemed to want to get along. She did too, so she would make sure to keep things light and friendly between them. "Thank you for your consideration."

Gabe looked between them. "I don't know what's going on with you guys, but your conversation is bordering on sappy sweet."

Abby probably shouldn't venture out of the professional realm, but she couldn't resist giving Burke a playful grin.

He took a sharp breath and laughed. "Maybe it was a *bit* over the top."

Gabe crossed his arms. "You grilled us on our early arrival, Ulrich, but you never said why you showed up at the crack of dawn."

Burke stared at his phone as if he wasn't going to answer, but then cleared his throat. "Our department boat is booked for a training today, and I had to borrow one. My friend couldn't be late for work to hand it over to me, so we had to meet early. I figured, why hang on the mainland when I could get started here."

Gabe scratched the back of his neck. "You always dress like a banker?"

"Gabe!" Abby shook her head. "Filters, man. Not all thoughts are meant to be spoken."

He shrugged, his gaze still on Burke. "Well, do you?"

Abby groaned.

"I like to dress professionally at work." Burke lowered his phone and returned Gabe's stare. "If it offends you, so be it."

Abby waited for a fireworks show between the two of them, but Victor came to the door. Perfect timing.

His hair was slicked back against his head, bringing to mind a freshly waxed car. He wore a shabby blue sweater she suspected was pricey cashmere, but several holes ruined the appearance of luxury. He'd paired it with formal black wool trousers patched at the knee.

Burke nodded at the chair at the head of the table. "Have a seat."

Gaze wary, Victor took a seat and clasped his hands together on the tabletop. "This seems so formal."

"Formal is an interview at the station." Burke smiled but it looked forced.

Abby took out her notepad and pen and set them on the table. "It always helps to get the victim's viewpoint on the crime committed against them."

Victor's shoulders relaxed a notch. "Then go ahead. I'll do what I have to do to locate the artifact."

"You can stop calling it an artifact in this room," Burke said. "We all know it's a crown."

"But I thought—" Victor shot an irritated look at Gabe, then back at Abby. "I thought you weren't going to share this information with others."

"Remember, I said I would share with my team, and Gabe's a team member."

"Fine. But I better not find out you've told other people. Like that forensic tech out there. She doesn't need to know what's missing."

"Actually, she does. Having as much information as possible allows her to do her very best. Except for my team, I haven't told anyone else, and everyone knows to keep it quiet."

"Ditto for me," Burke said. "The sheriff's in the know, but he'll be discreet."

Abby told him about the dealer Nolan had located. "I'd like your permission to share a picture of the crown with this dealer."

"No. No! Absolutely not! He's just the kind of person who would spread the information like wildfire."

"But I—"

"I said no. Now leave it alone." That patronizing expression she was getting tired of seeing was back as he folded his arms.

Pushing further right now would be a mistake. She could lose him as a client, and she couldn't let that happen. "Last night we discovered the fireplace grate in your office was warm to the touch. A fire had burned there shortly before we arrived in the room."

His eyes narrowed. "I didn't build a fire in there yesterday. In fact, I haven't lit one since Sylvia cleaned it last. Tuesday is her regular cleaning day."

Based on the state of the place, Abby had no idea what the woman cleaned, but she wasn't about to ask and further irritate him.

"There's no question someone set a fire in there." Burke's tone had grown a bit more forceful. "And the ash residue seems to be from paper, not wood."

Victor lifted his chin. "What exactly are you saying?"

Burke sat forward. "Perhaps you remembered documents you didn't want anyone to see and decided to burn them while we were checking the door locks."

"Preposterous!" Victor slammed his hands on the arms of his chair. "I don't have anything to hide. As you said, I'm the victim. Why would I hide something?"

"Let me speak candidly," Burke said. "We both get the feeling you aren't telling us everything you know about the missing crown."

He glanced between her and Burke, then lifted his chin. "I don't know why you would think that. Like I said, I have nothing to hide."

"Then why didn't you tell us about the hidden compartment in the floor in front of your fireplace?" Burke asked.

Victor's eyes widened. "Compartment? What are you talking about?"

His sincere expression led Abby to believe him, but she continued to watch him for any deception. "A hidden hole in the floor by the fireplace. If you didn't know about it, who could've installed it?"

He shrugged. "Any of my relatives who owned the house before me. Their families."

"What about your housekeeper or estate manager?" Gabe asked.

Victor tapped his chin with a gnarled finger. "I suppose it could've been possible when I used to leave home, but since I've been a homebody? No. No. The noise would've alerted me. Besides, what reason might they have to install such a thing?"

"A question we'll ask when we interview them." Burke glanced at his phone for a long moment, then looked at Victor again. "One of the doors we were checking took us down to your basement. The one with prison cells."

Victor's lips pursed. "I was as shocked by them as you are, but they were installed when the house was built. Rumor has it my great-grandfather kept indentured servants down there, but I've never found anything to confirm such a rumor. Regardless, I know they weren't used by my grandfather or father, and of course I don't use them. I haven't gone down there since the day I moved in and my father took me on a tour."

Burke arched an eyebrow. "Then why did we find a 1992 penny and a Tylenol packet there?"

Victor tilted his head. "Now that's a most interesting question. Like I said, I've only been down there once, and that was back in the eighties."

"What year did you move here?" Gabe asked.

"Late March of '85. Just when the cherry trees out front

were in full blossom." He stared ahead as if he could see them, and his expression softened. "What a sight that was. Estelle especially loved them."

"How would Estelle feel about the terrible state of the property and grounds now?" Burke asked.

Victor balled his fists. "I think you're exaggerating. Sure, there's some deferred maintenance, but it's not as horrific as you declare."

Gabe snorted. "When's the last time you went outside and took a look around?"

Victor blinked at him. "It's been some time."

"How long?" Gabe asked. "It looks like repairs haven't been made or landscaping trimmed in decades."

Victor sniffed the air. "What does any of this have to do with the stolen crown?"

"Perhaps nothing." Burke shifted his weight slightly, his posture open rather than defensive. "But in the early stages of an investigation, we look at every detail."

Victor sighed. "Okay, well, in that case, '92 was the last time I successfully stepped outside to go to the mainland. I might not have succeeded then, but I had to sign papers at the bank."

"And you haven't tried to leave since then?" Abby asked.

"I tried to go to the 2000 New Year's celebration in Surfside Harbor. But as soon as I reached the ferry, I knew I had to turn around and hurry back up here."

Wow. He hadn't tried to leave the property in over twenty years, preferring to be shut up in this place. Abby couldn't imagine it. "Anything special about that party to make you want to leave the mansion?"

Victor shrugged. "It was a once-in-a-lifetime event, but an uneasy feeling stopped me. I tried going outside a few times after that and couldn't get over the threshold."

"Have you ever considered working with a counselor to

solve the issue?" she asked as gently as she could, so he would answer and she would know how difficult it was going to be to get him to go to the bank.

"Why should I? It hasn't been an issue for me. Without Estelle, there's nowhere I really want to go. I have enough money to have anything I want brought to me." He held up his hands. "I know. I know. You can't understand it, but when Estelle went missing, I lost interest in everything. She's the love of my life. Not knowing what happened to her has devastated me. Broke me."

"I'm so sorry, Victor." Abby maintained soft eye contact, letting her silence communicate support. "I can't imagine how difficult this is for you. When did she disappear?"

Victor didn't hesitate but rattled off a date forty years earlier. "It was just a normal day. She took our small skiff into town to get groceries just like she did every week, but she never came back. Leaving our family without a wife and mother."

"I can tell you miss her a lot," Abby said sincerely as she thought not only about his loneliness, but also about his children without a mother.

"Every minute of every day." His eyes turned glassy with tears. "She's the most special woman. Kind, compassionate. Friendly to all and not a lick of prejudice in her. Oh, and she's funny. Such a good sense of humor. And beautiful, of course. The best wife a man could ever hope for. But she's gone now, and dwelling on it doesn't change that fact."

"What do you think happened to her?" Gabe asked.

Victor shook his head. "I honestly don't know. Our marriage was strong. Sure, at first, she really didn't want to leave Paris to live here, but she made the best of it and soon came to love it here."

Burke leaned in slightly, displaying thoughtfulness not confrontation. "Could she have gone back to Paris?"

"I don't think so. I hired a private investigator to look for her there. He didn't find any trace of her, including flights or ship passages with her name on the manifests. So if she did somehow get back there, she's not living under her real name."

"Not to be insensitive," Gabe said, "but do you think she's still alive?"

Victor looked down at the table and fitted his fingers together. He held his pose until his fingers turned white. "I can't—won't—give up hope. I need to believe she is."

Burke opened his mouth. A knock sounded on the doorframe, shifting everyone's attention to Sam, who stood there.

She poked her head into the room. "Sorry to interrupt, but can I talk to you for a minute, Abby?"

Sam wouldn't interrupt this questioning unless it was important, so Abby rushed to the door. "What is it?"

Sam leaned close and whispered, "I found something you and Burke need to see right away."

Abby stared at her friend. "Can it wait? We're just getting to the important questions."

She glanced over Abby's shoulder, her concerned focus directed at Victor. "I think you'll want this information before you finish your questions. And I recommend you and Burke leave Gabe here to keep an eye on Victor."

Of anything Sam had said, this comment raised Abby's concern the most. "Let me get Burke."

"I'll meet you in the library." Sam backed away.

Abby went to Burke and leaned close. "Sam needs to see us in the library. Now."

"What is it?" Victor asked, sitting up higher in his chair. "What's wrong?"

Abby ignored the questions and looked at Gabe. "I need you to stay here with Victor."

Gabe gave a subtle nod.

"But I…" Victor let his voice fall off as if he didn't know what to say. Or maybe he was too afraid to find out the answer to any of his questions.

"Be right back." Abby hurried through the door, her mind unable to let go of the fact that Sam wouldn't have asked Gabe to watch Victor if she didn't suspect the old man of being involved in this theft. So what on earth had she located in the library to give her such a negative impression?

8

Burke had no idea someone as petite as Abby could walk so fast, but he had to race through the foyer to catch up with her. He came alongside her. "Did Sam tell you what she found?"

She shook her head. "She's being cryptic. Very unlike her."

His gut tightened. "Then it must be something big and not likely something good."

"We'll soon find out." She swung through the library doorway.

The heavy curtains were open, flooding the space with sunlight, and revealing the room's true neglected and shabby state, but at least this room had recently been dusted.

Sam stood in the corner, holding the edge of a closed curtain in a gloved hand. She pointed at an open bin containing her supplies. "You'll want to glove up for this. Put on shoe coverings too."

After a considerable amount of foot traffic had already gone through this room, Burke didn't see the point, but he followed directions.

Abby reached the bin before him and handed him a pair of blue booties and large disposable gloves. "Why all the secrecy, Sam?"

"I didn't want to mention my discovery in front of your homeowner. I think he's lying to you, or at least withholding information and possible evidence."

Interest piqued, Burke hurried to slip on the protective coverings. Abby had been right about Sam's experience and professionalism. Many green forensics techs would've raced into the dining room and announced their findings without regard to the impact on the investigation.

Burke followed Abby to Sam's location, their paper booties whispering over the wood floor.

With a great flourish, Sam drew back the curtain.

Burke had no idea what he should expect, but a blank wall wasn't even in the realm of his consideration. He stared, taking it in, and thinking he must be missing something. "A wall? You brought us in here to see a wall?"

"Well, the curtain is definitely not hiding a window," Abby said.

"Then why would they put it here?" Burke eased closer to look for anything that made sense to call them down here.

"I had the same question." Sam turned to the wall. "And then I found this by accident." Pressing on a spot where the edge of the open curtain would fall, the wall parted and swung in.

"A door!" Abby's eyes flashed up to Sam. "A hidden door. How very mysterious."

"And very appropriate for a place like this." Sam's eyes were flooded with excitement. "And it leads to a long corridor. What it holds, I don't know. I didn't go in. Figured you'd want to be the first ones in there, but I did shine my flashlight inside long enough to discover I was looking at more than a closet, so I came to get you."

Abby looked over her shoulder at him. "I can't imagine Victor doesn't know this hidden doorway is here."

Burke agreed. "Which of course makes me suspicious of what we might find."

Abby swiveled toward Sam. "Great work. Really great. It must've been hard to wait for us and not go in there."

"You have no idea!" Sam laughed, cutting the tension.

"Do you have flashlights we can borrow?" Burke asked Sam.

She jerked a thumb over her shoulder. "In the same tote as the gloves."

He retrieved two small but powerful LED lights and handed one to Abby.

Sam faced them both. "I don't have to caution you about not moving anything before I take photographs, but I'm going to so you don't let the excitement get to you."

"Thanks for the reminder," he said. "We'll let you know when we need you, Sam."

"Then have at it." Sam pulled the curtain further back to allow them easy access.

Burke pointed at the opening. "After you, Abby."

She aimed the beam from her flashlight ahead, revealing a long hallway he couldn't see the end of. Pointing his light at dingy gray plaster walls, he found an antique brass push-button switch and pressed it. A single bulb overhead cast a weak yellow light, barely illuminating the area, but bright enough to reveal a gallery of old portraits lining one of the upper walls.

He squinted for a better look at the first ones. "These pictures resemble the ones in the hallway."

Abby turned her light on the other end. "Likely ancestors."

"Sounds like a good possibility, but why hide them here? Why not display more of them in the open?"

"And for that matter, what happened to the missing paintings in the hallway? Are they important to our investigation? Is any of this important to our investigation?"

"Good questions." He ran his beam down the wall, studying the mixture of old sepia portraits. Stern-looking men and women dressed in 1800s and early 1900s formal attire stared back at him.

Abby paused her light on a woman in the middle. "Something's off about her."

The young woman in the picture wore a white dress, the neckline cut down far lower than the more prim and proper dresses in the other photographs. The square neck was trimmed in lace, and a large black fabric flower was fastened to one side.

"Do you mean the clothing style?"

"No. Part of the portrait looks like it's in 3-D." Abby wiggled the flashlight beam over the woman's bust. "See how it appears raised right here?"

He leaned closer to get an angle from the side. "You're right. Seems like there's something behind it and stretching the canvas."

"Quick." Her excited tone bounced off the walls. "Grab Sam to snap some photos of the portrait so we can take it down."

Burke bolted out of the passageway. "Bring your camera, Sam. Now!"

He didn't wait for her to agree, but rushed back to Abby.

She was still studying the woman. "What do you think's behind there?"

"People hide safes behind pictures all the time," he said. "If the dial and lever aren't recessed, they could cause a lump."

"That makes perfect sense." The thrill of the hunt gleamed in her eyes. "If you're right, I hope it holds something to help solve this mystery."

Carrying a flashlight of her own and a small bin, Sam came down the hallway. "What do you need me to photograph?"

Burke jerked a thumb at the picture and explained their reasoning. "Do whatever you need to do so we can get this thing down quickly."

Sam ran a critical eye over the painting and looked up at the light. "Step back. I need the right perspective and to record the picture size compared to the surrounding ones."

As they backed away, she mounted a flexible ruler on the wall next to the portrait for scale, then lifted her camera, that was hanging around her neck, up to snap photos of everything from various angles. When Burke first met her, she seemed relaxed and carefree, but her concentration now would rival his when on the job.

"Done." She eased away from the wall and scanned the hallway as she stepped away.

Burke carefully lifted the picture down. An ancient-looking safe protruded out of the wall in the same shape as the misshapen canvas. The safe's rusted metal had originally been black, but most of the paint had chipped away, revealing the raw steel underneath. A circular handle along with a round combination wheel were mounted in the middle, and heavy hinges secured the door.

Burke glanced at Abby. "A safe, just like I thought."

She inched closer to it. "Clearly an antique. Must've been here for some time."

"Do you think Victor knows about it and has the combination? If he did, when we mentioned the hidden compartment, why not tell us about the hallway and the safe too?"

Abby's eyes tightened. "I'll add one more question. What could possibly be inside there?"

"And, more importantly, is it related to the theft of the crown?" Burke asked. "We need to question Victor about it and get him to open it."

"I'll just get this stuff packed up." Sam tapped her small bin.

Burke turned his light down the hall. "Let's see where this hallway goes, then we'll talk to Victor."

"Sounds like a plan," Abby said, but didn't move for some reason.

"Hopefully, he hasn't purposely been withholding this information." Burke looked down the hallway, eager to see what else they might find. "If we discover this *is* related to the crown and he hasn't been open about it, we can't rule him out for stealing his own crown. In fact, even without an obvious motive, I'd move him to the top of my suspect list."

⁓

Abby took one last look at the safe. She wanted to give Victor the benefit of the doubt. Believe he didn't withhold this information on purpose, but she couldn't help but think he knew about it. Burke could be right. By Victor not mentioning it, he could be involved in the crown's theft. Sure, they couldn't see a motive right now, but that didn't mean he didn't have one. Between the hidden passageway and the safe he'd kept secret, what else wasn't he telling them? The very question she would ask him as soon as they finished checking out this hallway.

Burke waved her ahead. "After you."

She took a few steps but slowed to let him come closer. "Not that I'm complaining, but what's up with all of the 'after yous', pulling out chairs, and offering to help Sam with her cart and bins? Or do you seriously still do things the old-school way?"

He looked at her. "You don't need to worry—I'm not working some hidden angle here. I know I haven't exactly shown it, but I was raised in a strict Christian home. I was taught to respect women, to step up and help when I can."

She stopped and faced him. "Because we're the weaker sex?"

"No way. The Bible says men should respect women the same way they'd respect their own mother or sister. I don't agree with everything my parents drilled into me, but this is one thing I've carried into adulthood." He held her gaze. "It's not about thinking women need a man to intervene—it's about giving the respect God expects me to show."

Was he being real, or just trying to play her? His voice and that dead-serious look didn't leave much room for doubt. Maybe he actually was one of the good guys—the kind any woman should be glad to have around. So why was every part of her itching to tune him out?

"Hold up," Sam called out from behind them. She was squatting, studying a spot on the floor. "There's something else here. It's some sort of oil, but it'll take detailed analysis to tell you the kind."

Burke crouched next to her. "Do you have the tools to analyze a sample or is it beyond your scope?"

Sam stiffened. "I may not have a world-class lab like the Veritas Center, but thanks to Gage, my lab is very well appointed. So yes, I'll take a sample of the oil today and let you know what I discover."

"Sorry, I didn't mean anything negative by that," he said.

Sam continued to study the spot but didn't speak.

"I told you Sam was good at her job," Abby said, proud of Sam for standing up for herself. "Not only processing unusual evidence but locating it in the first place. She noticed this spot when we both walked right over it, and it could turn out to be important."

"Or not." Sam stood, her irritation gone. "You never know until you know." She laughed and headed toward the library.

"I like her," Burke said. "I put my foot in my mouth, and she's already over it."

"I should've warned you it's a hotspot for her. Her lab is small and not well known in the law enforcement field, so she often gets questioned by skeptical officers."

"From what I can see so far, she seems quite capable. Plus, for a science nerd, she's quite personable." He chuckled.

Abby grinned along with him. "Now that's something she doesn't mind hearing."

"Anything else I should be wary of?"

"If you were to question her skills just because she's a woman, she wouldn't be so easy-going."

"I know men in our line of work still do that, but I never would."

Abby wanted to get going so they could get back to Victor, but she couldn't leave this alone. "So you're okay with women in law enforcement? Not afraid that a woman doesn't have the strength and ability to have your back?"

"I'm good with it," he said. "Would I question her to see if she's well-trained before we partner together? Sure, but I'd do the same thing with a guy. If I found them lacking, I'd make sure they got the necessary training before I'd trust them in the field."

Oh yes, trust. This seemed like a hot button for him too. She couldn't miss the signs. Not with her own lack of trust every time she contemplated getting involved with a guy.

"Let's get going." Step by step, she visually examined

every inch of the original pine floor, but didn't locate anything else she wouldn't expect from a floor that seemed original to this house.

At the end of the corridor, the passageway turned to the left and ended at a worn stairway. Abby started up the steep steps. With no handrails, she had to run her hand along the wall to steady herself. The plaster was cool under her fingers, and a chill came from beneath the closed door at the top of the stairway. She turned the antique glass knob, and the door opened.

She aimed her flashlight ahead and stepped into a large bedroom with an ornate four-poster bed, matching dresser, wardrobe, and another tall cabinet. Victor's dressing gown lay on the mattress.

"This must be Victor's room," she said.

"So the hallway is just a shortcut from the library to the owner's bedroom suite."

The letdown over not locating another lead hit harder than she'd admit. "I was hoping we'd find an answer to some of our questions."

"Someone could've used the passageway to move around the house last night to light that fire without us knowing about it."

"I'll ask Sam to process the knob for fingerprints." Abby glanced around the room again. "I don't feel right about searching his personal possessions. Not without his knowledge."

"Then let's head to the dining room to bring him back to the hallway to open the safe and ask why he didn't tell us about the secret passageway or safe."

Abby carefully made her way back down the steep stairs and along the hallway into the library.

Behind her, Burke took a picture of the secret doorway. "To show Victor when we talk to him. In case he denies it, the picture will save us time." Burke pulled off his blue booties but kept his gloves on.

She searched the room for Sam and found her swirling black powder over a window lock with her fluffy brush.

Sam glanced at her. "Anything else I can do to help right now?"

"Yes," Abby said. "Assuming Victor has the combination to the safe, we'll bring him back here to open it. Can you dust for fingerprints right now? Then the picture frame, and the doorway at the end of the hall, up the stairs."

Sam gave a solid nod. "I'll start right away."

"Perfect." Abby ripped off her shoe coverings but, like Burke, left her gloves on since they would be returning.

She hurried out of the room, Burke following her. In the dining room, he brushed past her and made a beeline to Victor. He stopped across the table from the older man and peered at him.

Victor raised troubled eyes to Burke. "What? What is it? What's wrong?"

"Looks like you withheld something else from us." Burke's tone was measured and deliberate, but less intimidating than she might expect from him when talking to a potential suspect.

"I have no idea what you might be talking about." Victor seriously looked baffled.

Abby felt bad about having to question the older guy. It was hard enough for a younger person to handle an investigation, but someone of Victor's advanced years might take more offense at the questions they were asked. Not only didn't she want to offend him as he was essentially her employer, but she didn't want to see him suffer either.

Burke opened his phone and held it for Victor to see, but didn't speak.

"Oh that." Victor let out a long breath. "It's just a

shortcut to my bedroom. I rarely use it and didn't even think of it as related to the theft."

Burke's shoulders relaxed as if he believed Victor. "I need you to remember your house is a crime scene. Everything about it is important to us because you never know what could be related to the theft. With that in mind, is there anything else you'd like to tell us about?"

Abby appreciated the way Burke took the time to gently explain the situation and not come right out and accuse him of withholding other information.

Victor drummed his fingers on the table, then shook his head. "Nothing comes to mind."

Burke's eyes darkened as if he wanted to go off on Victor, but he simply stood up and put the phone in his pocket. "We just talked about the hallway, and it has a hidden wall safe."

Victor's fingers stilled. "Oh, right, the safe. I don't ever use it, so I forgot about it. My father died a few years after I moved here. Shortly before then, he gave me the combination and said it was a secret. He made me swear not to give it to anyone else. It was empty, then, and I've never opened it. Why bother when I'm the only one with the combination, and I didn't put anything in there?"

He sounded convincing to Abby, but there was no way to prove he was telling the truth.

Burke shifted his stance. "If it's empty, then you won't mind opening it for us."

"Mind? No." His eyes narrowed as he stood. "I wish you'd just believe it's empty, but I'll come with you to prove it."

He thumped past Burke, spearing him with an indignant stare as he went.

"Guess I'll wait here," Gabe said. "Unless you need me at the safe."

"We're good," Abby said. "Quick question before I go. When you were alone with Victor just now, did you get any sense as to his honesty or innocence in the theft?"

Gabe rubbed his chin. "He seemed to be on the up and up. He's still broken up about his wife disappearing. Finding out what happened to her is the only thing he wants before he dies."

"So you don't think he had anything to do with her disappearance?"

"Nah. Like I said, he was on the level."

"Thanks." Abby rushed out of the room, feeling like a yo-yo going up and down the hall.

In the large foyer, she jogged past Burke to come alongside Victor, whose shoulders were thrust back and his cane pounding the floor as he limped along—an anger-filled walk if she'd ever seen one.

When she reached him, she slowed. "You seem upset with Detective Ulrich. He's just doing his job. In our line of work, we need facts behind the information we learn, and the facts so far say you might be involved in the theft."

He ground his teeth. "Believe me, I understand that more than most people might. When Estelle went missing, the sheriff thought I had something to do with her disappearance, and I was under far more intense scrutiny then."

He paused and pounded his cane on the floor in a single thump, the sound reverberating up to the high plaster ceiling with thick cracks running through it. "I should be able to let this roll off my back, but when you act like you don't believe me, I had visions of those past interrogations."

"I can see how that could happen, and I'm sorry it did, but try to see it from our point of view. We continue to find things in your home that make us call into question your involvement, and seem even more suspicious because you didn't tell us about them."

His shoulders sagged. "I guess I can understand that. When you're done with me today, I'll take some time to think about what else might be odd around this place."

"Thank you, Victor. We'd very much appreciate that." She moved ahead, leading him into the library and handing him booties and gloves. "The hallway hasn't been processed, so please don't touch anything until we tell you to."

Leaning heavily on his cane, he put on the booties. She and Burke both slid on a fresh pair, finishing before Victor.

When he completed the task, he hooked the cane over his arm to slip on gloves. One corner of his mouth twitched, anticipation written all over his face. "Let's get the safe open so I can show you it's empty."

"Follow me." Burke took off for the hallway and stopped just past the safe. He pointed at it. "Open it. Touch nothing else."

Victor attempted to spin the dial to the right, but it was sluggish.

"Use more force," Burke said.

Victor grunted and turned it to three different numbers.

"Done," he said, and pulled the handle down but didn't open the door.

Had he been lying to them? Did he know there was something inside? Otherwise, why not open it to prove his innocence?

"Stand back," Burke said, sounding impatient. "I'll do it."

Keeping his eyes on the safe, Victor moved far enough back to allow Burke access.

He jerked the door open, then looked over his shoulder at Victor. "Empty, huh?"

"Yes, why?" Victor blinked innocently.

How could he look innocent when Burke had clearly located something inside?

Burke slipped his hand into the safe and pulled out a

stack of worn leather-bound books. "What do you call these?"

Victor's mouth fell open, his eyes fixed on Burke's hand. "Those look like Estelle's missing journals." He reached out to take them.

Burke moved his hand. "Your wife's journals were missing?"

"She wrote in one every day, but after she disappeared we couldn't find them." He frowned. "I never read them, of course, but Detective Orman, he's the guy who bungled the investigation, thought I destroyed them. I always assumed she took them with her."

Burke took a half-step back, eyes fixed and unblinking. "I don't understand how you can possibly be confused about their location. You're the only one with the combination to the safe. Means you had put them in here."

"But-but-but I..." Victor shook his head. "I didn't do it. Maybe Estelle or the person who kidnapped her—if someone did—somehow figured out the combination."

Abby wanted to believe him, give him the benefit of the doubt, but it seemed improbable that anyone else could have the combination. "How would they figure it out?"

"I don't know. I just don't know." The pain in Victor's eyes was almost tangible, calling into question his guilt of putting the journals in the safe. "He said he'd never shared the combination with anyone and implored me to keep every bit of history and secrets regarding the mansion or our family to myself. Maybe he wasn't telling the truth."

"So there are more secrets beyond the crown," Abby said.

"Maybe secrets isn't the right word. Like every family, we have stories in our history we don't want shared in public. That's all. No big secrets related to the crown."

Abby didn't like that they couldn't rule out this elderly

gentleman of his potential involvement in the theft. If it were up to her as an individual, she'd be inclined to believe him. But as a law enforcement officer, she wasn't sure he could be trusted, and she couldn't give him the benefit of the doubt. They would now have to keep their eyes on him for duplicitous behavior and other secrets he might be hiding.

9

Burke settled the journals in the safe for Sam to process. The only thing he could believe from Victor's story was that the safe combination was a secret and only Victor knew it. Everything else the guy claimed—like not putting the journals in the safe—was out of the question until they had facts to prove otherwise.

He met Victor's troubled gaze. "Head back to the dining room, and we'll be right in to finish our questioning."

Victor's eyes creased into slits. "It feels like you're looking for a way to accuse me of some crime. Maybe I shouldn't answer your questions."

Abby gave him a placating smile. "We're just trying to get to the truth. Nothing more. Nothing less. If you answer truthfully and don't withhold other secrets like the safe, you'll be fine."

He curled his fingers into his hair, looking like he wanted to pull it out. "I told you. I didn't hide the safe from you. I just didn't think of it. You both seem like reasonable people. Why can't you give me the benefit of the doubt?"

Burke shoved his hands in his pockets. "Not something we do in an investigation. We have to go by verifiable facts."

"I can understand that. Doesn't mean I like it. I'll await your further questioning in the dining room." He stomped down the hall, moving faster than Burke had seen him go.

Trailing Victor, Abby glanced at Burke, frustration clouding her eyes. "I don't have a clue if Estelle's journals can help us find the crown. But if you couple it with her necklace in the greenhouse, someone trying to dig it up last night could mean the journals are related to the theft."

"Seems possible to me," Burke said. "But it could be as simple as Estelle knowing the safe combination and that Victor would never open it, so she stored them there for privacy."

Abby peered over her shoulder at the end of the hallway. "Hopefully any fingerprints Sam lifts from the safe will prove that."

Burke nodded and looked around the library. Victor had already exited, and Sam was dusting another window lock.

She looked up, brush stilled in midair. "Victor didn't look happy when he raced through here."

"He's not." Burke told her about the journals. "I left them in the safe for you to process and take into evidence. They need to be secured at all times. I don't want Victor anywhere near them."

With a toss of her head, Sam flipped her ponytail over her shoulder. "That could be a challenge. I don't have a vehicle to lock them in like I usually do. Maybe Victor has a room where we can secure them."

Abby shook her head. "We could never be confident he doesn't have a key."

"Then, the only way to secure them is to watch them all the time," Burke said.

"We'll get Gabe to do it," Abby said.

"Perfect solution." Burke met Sam's eyes. "Be sure to let us know if you find anything else out of the ordinary."

"Will do."

He moved into the foyer with Abby. The strong, musty scent the house oozed seemed to get stronger. "Now that we have the journals, I'd like to hold back some of our questions for Victor until after we've had a chance to read them. We'll keep the locket, velvet scrap, and the person in the greenhouse to ourselves."

Abby cast him an appraising look. "You think the journals might give us reason to suspect him of harming her?"

"The more time we spend with him, the more I think anything's possible."

"Which means you also think he could've participated in the crown's theft." She fell silent for a moment, their footfalls echoing off the high ceiling. "I'm leaning that way, too, but I don't have a clue what his motive is."

"He could be trying to frame someone to get them out of his life."

"It's conceivable, but it's a bit far-fetched, don't you think?"

"Perhaps, but we need to keep all avenues open."

"Maybe he told his son about it," she said. "And he's threatening to give it back to France. Victor doesn't want that to happen, but he can't take it with him, so he's selling it."

"Then why call us?"

"So his son believes it was stolen."

"Could be."

She stopped outside the closed dining room door. "I'll go along with you wanting to withhold information and questions for now."

Glad she saw his reasoning, he gave an affirmative nod. "I'll take lead again, if you don't mind." He waited for her look of agreement.

She frowned instead. "I'm fine with that, but I have a recommendation."

The last thing he wanted at the moment was to be told how to do his job, but he'd promised to keep an open mind with her. "Go ahead."

"Dial it down a notch. Be less aggressive. Try to empathize with him."

Her comment didn't surprise him, but... "You were pretty hard-nosed as a sheriff. Seems like you've changed. Why?"

She rested her hands on her hips and stared up at him. "It's not like I made a conscious decision to change. I was under a lot of pressure as a sheriff to succeed. That hasn't changed. I still have intense pressure. How could I not when lives often depend on us? But it's different. I don't have a whole county watching and judging me. Just myself and my peers. So I've relaxed. Let go of the need to please others and feel more free to be myself."

He understood, but who was the real Abby? Was she this softer, more compassionate version or was it all an act? He didn't know, and he didn't like the uncomfortable feeling that left behind. But it wasn't the time to get into it. Now was the time to get some answers.

He opened the door for her, then followed her into the room. Looking bored, Gabe remained seated in the chair at the end of the long table. Victor sat to his immediate right, his face tight and angry. Directly across from him, Abby settled on one of the chairs and offered Victor a pleasant smile as if she was trying to soften him up.

Burke would follow her suggestion and take the kinder, gentler approach. He dropped onto the chair next to her. "When we checked the basement door locks, we found a set of footprints on the path outside. They're small, like a woman's or a small man, and lead away from the house. Who might've used this exit?"

Victor's eyes narrowed. "No one, as far as I know. Who would even want to go down there?"

"Who has keys to that door?" Abby asked.

"You know I do, but also Ugo and Sylvia. As far as the footprints go, if it was one of them, that's more likely Sylvia's size. But I can't imagine why they would want to exit that way."

Burke could. "Perhaps they wanted to remove something from the house and didn't want you to know about it."

"I highly doubt it, but let's say they did. Why bother when they could take things out the front door every time I go upstairs to nap? Which I do every afternoon for several hours. I have to trust them to be honest, and I do."

So if they knew about the crown, they could easily have stolen it. Burke needed more details about them. "They've worked here a long time. How and when did they start?"

"Ugo began working for our family in France, then came to Oregon with me. Sylvia was recommended to us shortly after we moved here, and she started then. And as I've said, they've been loyal servants for so long and haven't given me a moment's hesitation. I trust them implicitly."

Burke could never be so trusting. Sure, the servants were like family to Victor and had never done anything to betray his trust. Burke and Tiffany had been together five years before their engagement, and there had never even been a hint that she would betray him. Then out of the blue she falls in love with his partner. Seriously? His own partner. In his opinion, if a person could betray someone they were in love with, much worse could happen between employer and employee. Even ones who'd been together for so long.

"We plan to interview them when they arrive this afternoon," Abby said. "We can ask about it then."

"Good." Victor lifted his chin, an action he was coming to associate with him. "I know they'll put your mind at ease, and I'm sure they'll help you realize I'm not the monster you're trying to portray me as."

Burke didn't really think Victor was a monster, but he still hadn't ruled him out as a suspect. "We also located oil spilled on the floor in your secret hallway. Any idea what type of oil it could be?"

"No idea. Not something *I* put there." He'd said he didn't use the hallway before, so that wasn't a surprise.

"I also wanted to ask about the missing paintings in the foyer," Burke said. "The discolored wallpaper says they'd hung there for a long time."

"They belonged to my great-grandfather. He commissioned an artist in the late 1800s to paint them. He had them made for his own enjoyment, but then the artist became famous. Now they're valuable, but nothing like a Monet."

"What happened to them?"

Victor rested his cane on the chair and planted his hands on the arms. "Again, I don't know what this has to do with the missing crown."

"If you sold the paintings because you needed money, maybe you still do and are running some sort of scam involving the crown."

Victor gritted his teeth. "I don't need the money. If you don't believe me, Ugo can show you my latest bank statements when he gets here."

Burke would definitely review those statements. "If you didn't sell the paintings, then what happened to them?"

"Estelle brought her personal maid with her from France," Victor said. "Dominique had been with her since childhood, but she couldn't adapt to the Oregon lifestyle. Less than a year here, she gave in to her homesickness and went back to France. Estelle wanted to recognize her many years of service, and Dominique really enjoyed those paintings, so we agreed to give them to her."

Another logical explanation and one they should be able to prove or disprove. "Can you provide her contact information so we can confirm your story?"

Victor leaned his head back and stared at the ceiling. "We have her family's address, but she's not there. When Estelle went missing, I thought Dominique might know where she was, so I had the private investigator put her under surveillance. He watched her house in France for several weeks and didn't see either of them. Before he left the country, he checked with her family and friends. Not one of them had seen Estelle or knew where Dominique had moved to."

Most suspicious that both women were missing. "And you believe them?"

Victor shook his head. "But wherever she'd gone, they weren't talking, and the PI said he doubted anyone would get the truth from them. If you'd like, I can have Ugo hunt down the last information I had for her."

"We'd appreciate that," Abby said. "Did Estelle hire someone to replace Dominique?"

"No. Life is much more casual in Oregon than it was in France, and Estelle didn't feel like she required someone to help with her personal needs." Victor let out a long sigh. "I'm getting tired of all these questions. Are you about finished?"

Abby lifted a finger. "I have one more thing. We need to get the crown certificate and bill of sale from your safety deposit box. To do this, the bank will require an in-person visit, and we hope to escort you there."

Victor shot forward in his chair. "You know I don't ever leave this place and can't go with you."

"You can't because you have agoraphobia, or you just prefer to stay here?" Burke asked.

"Not agoraphobia." Victor placed his hands on the table,

but they were trembling. "I fell into a deep depression after Estelle went missing and couldn't face the world. Thankfully, a wonderful counselor came here, and I found my way out of it. But our past social life rang hollow to me, and I didn't see any point in resuming it. By then, I'd developed a network of delivery people and other professionals who would come to me. So why leave?"

"You've never needed a medical test?" Burke asked.

"I've never had any serious medical issues, and for the basics, so many things are portable these days."

Burke could see losing interest in society, but he would still have gone outside. Not important to their real issue here. "Would it be helpful if we made the trip in a private boat and not on the ferry? It would be much faster."

"I guess." He carefully intertwined his fingers as he stared at them. "When would you want me to go?"

"If Burke is willing to take us in his boat," Abby said. "Ideally as soon as we finish this conversation."

Victor pulled back as if someone had slapped him. "I... I will do my best, but you must promise if I demand to return to the house you will bring me back."

"I promise, "Abby said and gave Burke a pointed look.

"Yeah, sure, we can do that," Burke said, but he wouldn't promise anything—couldn't promise Victor anything. Not until they ruled him out as a suspect in the theft of a multi-million-dollar crown.

∼

Abby wouldn't let any time pass before going to the bank. She didn't want to give Victor a chance to chicken out, but she needed to have a quick talk with Gabe before they departed.

She smiled at Victor. "Go ahead with Burke. I'll meet you at the door."

"Okay... I..." His words fell off, and he came to his feet, but he couldn't have been more hesitant.

"You can do this," Burke said enthusiastically.

Victor didn't catch the excitement. A deep scowl drew down his face as he trudged out of the room, putting his weight fully on his cane and exaggerating his limp.

Abby turned to Gabe. "I have another exciting job for you."

He arched an eyebrow. "Already sounds like grunt work, but lay it on me."

She told him about Estelle's journals. "Someone has to guard them to keep them away from Victor and his associates."

"So babysit journals? All this tactical brilliance up here" —he tapped his forehead—"and you want me to babysit journals?"

Just the reaction she'd expected from him. "It might not seem like it, but it's an important job."

"Something you tell rookies when you hand them cleaning supplies after a drunk has hurled in your backseat." He laughed. "But fine—I'll do it on one condition."

She cocked her head. "Which is?"

"You keep me looped in on everything else going on. No blackouts."

"Not a very big ask. I was going to do that anyway." She grinned. "This is just like *Survivor*. We're stuck on an island, and you're my ally. I need you."

"Difference is, backstabbing is encouraged on *Survivor*. Contestants often turn on their allies. You know I don't operate that way."

"Right back at you." She shared a fist bump with him.

"Sam has the journals. Just keep them in your sight at all times."

"Don't worry so much. Sitting around doing nothing is my specialty." He relaxed back in his chair and cupped his hands behind his head.

She laughed, though it wasn't true. Gabe was one of the most active members of their team. "It would help if you read the journals while you're waiting. See if Estelle knew anything about the crown back in the day."

"Bonus. Reading a woman's internal thoughts she didn't mean to share with anyone." His sarcastic response trailed her out of the room, but she could count on him to do the job. In every event, but especially now when the stakes were so high for keeping their business alive.

The front door stood wide open, a cool breeze blowing in. She'd hoped Burke would have coaxed Victor outside, but he was frozen in the doorway, one hand glued to the frame. Outside, Burke rubbed a hand over his face as if he'd lost all patience.

"Everything okay?" she asked.

"Victor says he can't leave." Burke's words came out in a sharp cadence.

His irritation didn't surprise her, but she wouldn't let Victor remain unmoving. It was either time to push the issue or scrap the idea of going into town.

She pressed past him and reached for his free hand. "Come on. It'll be okay. We're both with you, and we'll support you all the way."

At her gentle tug, he crossed the threshold. He took a good look around, his eyes widened, and his mouth formed an O of surprise. His steps faltered.

"You're doing great. Keep going." She didn't let him stop, but tugged him along with her as she backed toward the steps. She took comfort in the sound of his cane thumping with every shift of his feet and marking their progress.

Burke followed closely behind. Perhaps too closely, as if he intended to trap Victor between them. She only hoped he didn't reach out and touch him, or the squeamish old man could bolt and run back inside.

At the steps, she let go of his hand and started to turn.

He slowly pivoted to look around. A deer caught in the headlights look took over his expression, but finally, he shook his head. "You're right. This place really is in disrepair. And the landscape. What have I done?"

Abby feared she was losing him. The overgrown weeds, leaves needing raking, and moss consuming every shady spot presented such a big problem that he'd finally recognized the state of his property. Recognized, but didn't have the wherewithal to do anything about it, overwhelming him.

She gave him her best wattage smile. "Don't worry about this now. There's nothing wrong that can't be fixed. Let's focus on getting down to the boat where you can sit and enjoy the beautiful fall weather."

The corners of his mouth actually tipped up in the hint of a smile. "It *is* a beautiful day. The sunshine on my face and the cool breeze blowing fresh air feels wonderful. It's been so long." His voice broke, the last words strangled from his throat.

She took his hand again and used her most cheerful voice. "Ready to go?"

Without waiting for him to respond, she started down the steps, signaling for Burke to fall into place behind them. Thankfully, he'd remained silent and let her do her thing. Victor followed her, pausing to ensure his cane found purchase on each worn rock. His timid movement continued at first, but then he picked up speed until they reached the bottom.

"Just listen to those waves lapping against the shore." Bewildered, he shook his head. "Why have I been so afraid to come out here? Makes no sense."

Abby didn't want to get into such a discussion now. She was certain if she got him onto the boat, they would make it to the mainland. How he would react when he had to encounter other people, sounds, traffic of a bigger town, she didn't know, but they would face that problem when and if it arose.

"Our boat is ready for us." She pulled him forward. "Be careful on the dock. It can be slippery."

Burke continued at their rear, and the three of them reached his borrowed boat. He slipped past them and boarded.

"Our friend is a little unsteady on his feet," Abby said as pleasantly as she could muster to make Victor relax. "Could you help him into the boat?"

"Sure thing." Burke jumped into action and soon had Victor settled in the middle seat, his cane resting beside him and a lifejacket over his shoulders.

He tapped the bench seat next to him. "Sit by me, please."

"Of course." She took a lifejacket from Burke, cushioned it around her neck and sat in the empty place at Victor's side.

Burke quickly untied the boat and revved the motor to get them away from the dock. Victor gasped, and Abby held her breath, waiting for him to insist they return to dry land. But he remained silent, clutching her hand as he looked around.

She had to give the man credit. He was overcoming his unease. Maybe it was the glorious skies—the clearest of blue with fluffy white clouds floating past—and the smooth water. As they motored toward the mainland, a cool breeze danced across the boat, and an occasional spray of water misted her face. The only other thing to make this perfect was if the bay was empty. Several colorful speedboats, two large sightseeing or charter fishing boats, and a pontoon boat dotted the water.

She had no idea if Burke was an experienced boater and could maneuver easily around these vessels, but she doubted his friend would've given him the boat if he didn't have solid skills. He did look odd sitting behind the wheel in his tailored suit, white button-down shirt, and dress shoes. Seemed like something in his past had caused him to dress so formally. Was it a uniform he was hiding behind? She had to admit to being utterly intrigued by the mystery he presented, not to mention how fine he looked in a tailored suit.

She jerked her gaze back to the harbor before he caught her watching him. Anchored vessels bobbed like obstacles in bumper cars, and Burke brought the boat through the traffic without any harm.

The motor revved on one of the larger fishing boats. The bigger boat shot into action, the bow pointed straight toward them. Odd. All the other boats were either anchored or heading to or from the island. This boat was running parallel to the mainland, most likely headed to a preferred fishing area.

The large engine gunned, and the front of the boat rose from the water.

What were they up to? She sat up and glanced at Burke. He cupped his hand over his eyes and swiveled in the other boat's direction, then pushed the throttle forward.

The engine roared. The boat kicked ahead. She grabbed on to the seat.

"What's going on?" Victor cried out, his gaze shooting in all directions.

She didn't answer. How could she? This poor man was terrified just to be on the water. She wasn't about to tell him the larger vessel's pilot seemed ready and willing to ram into them. At the very least, capsizing their boat—most likely ending their lives.

10

Burke swallowed to control his panic. The large vessel was whipping through the water, on course to ram them. Could their little boat move fast enough to move them out of harm's way?

Doubtful, but he had to try.

He pushed the throttle to the max, the engine groaning under the effort. Their boat jumped ahead and cut through the water. Good. He chanced a quick look at the other boat. It shot toward them like a torpedo. Burke's boat was like a dead duck in a carnival shooting gallery. The craft with the higher horsepower would win this game. He, Victor, and Abby were helpless, easy targets.

Depending on him alone. What did he do?

He didn't know. He only knew the basics of piloting a boat. That's it. Nothing more. Certainly, no evasion or defensive handling skills like he possessed for driving a motor vehicle.

Think, man, think.

If he could somehow bring their boat alongside the big craft it couldn't ram them. He had to judge the timing perfectly and wait until the last second, then hook a sharp turn. Such a large vessel wasn't as maneuverable as his friend's boat and shouldn't be able to react quickly enough to stop them.

If he succeeded, he could maneuver around the back of the big boat, completely out of immediate danger. He could then become the aggressor, charging after it to obtain identifying information.

"Hold on," he yelled over the motor before he lost his nerve.

He hadn't offered a prayer since Tiffany left him at the altar, but now, he couldn't help himself.

Please help me to do this. Please keep the others safe.

He eased up on the throttle a bit, kept his eyes on the advancing boat. Counted.

One one thousand. Two one thousand. Three one thousand.

Now!

He jerked the wheel and hit the throttle. The boat rose in the front and nimbly responded. Turning sharply in the nick of time. He'd completed his maneuver, fully coming alongside the bigger boat before it T-boned their vessel.

Thank You. Thank You.

He pressed the throttle harder, circling around the other boat's wake until he faced its stern.

Now they were the pursuer. Burke kept the throttle pressed forward and didn't let up. Chasing the larger boat. Staying back to safely ride the water churned up by the bigger boat.

The boat veered off to the left, and Burke stayed on his tail. They soon neared the beach. Good. He'd have to slow down, and Burke could find out who was piloting the vessel. He waited. A minute. Two.

No slowing. The boat continued to race ahead at high speed.

Closer, closer to the shoreline! He didn't let up, even as they were seconds from crashing.

The large vessel barreled onto the shore, coming to a sudden stop and beaching the boat.

What in the...?

Burke jerked back on the throttle before the propellers hit ground and bent them. He slowly came to a stop. Half tempted to leap into the water and swim to shore, he opted instead to call dispatch and order a patrol unit to the area, keeping his focus on the beached vessel.

Someone in a black ski mask bolted over the side of the boat, hitting the sand hard. A guy, judging by how he ran. About five-foot-ten. Fit, except for the start of a beer belly. He lost his balance on the sand and lay there as if stunned. A trio of beachgoers raced toward him. One man knelt beside him and held him down.

Good. Keep him there until the patrol vehicle arrived.

The boat captain freed his shoulders and shoved to his feet. He quick-stepped up the beach toward a thick stand of grass and trees growing on a long sand dune. He scrambled up. Fell back a few feet, the sand cascading down with his body. He got up. Clambered to the top and disappeared into the shadowy darkness of the trees.

"He's getting away." Abby jumped to her feet. "I'm going after him."

Burke grabbed her wrist. "By the time you swim to shore, he'll be long gone, and you'll have risked your life in the cold water for nothing."

She glared at him and jerked her wrist free.

"You know, I'm right," Burke said, planning to tackle her if necessary. "It might be a nice day, but the water is still extremely cold. Without a wetsuit, you wouldn't make it."

She shifted her gaze to the water. Her chest rose and fell under angry breaths, but she dropped down onto the seat, all of the fight going out of her. "You're right, but I don't have to like it."

"What was that all about?" Victor cried out, his tone bordering on hysteria. "Why did that boat try to run into us?"

Burke's number one question. Number two was who was piloting the boat. Answer question two, and he'd probably have the answer to number one as well. "It might have something to do with the crown. Maybe someone's been watching us. Someone who's targeting you, Victor."

Victor shuddered.

"Hey." She took his hands in hers. "Breathe. Just breathe, and once you calm down, we can talk about it."

She gained his full attention and took a few exaggerated deep breaths, letting them out, until he was breathing along with her.

Burke and Abby might've always butted heads, but he'd heard wonderful things about her as a sheriff. Now, the more time he spent with her, the more he could see she was indeed a very special person. She not only had law enforcement skills, but she could connect with people in a way Burke had never been able to do. She deserved his respect.

She glanced up at him. "While Victor catches his breath, I'll call Sam. Get her on the next ferry over here to process the boat for fingerprints."

He nodded his agreement as his phone rang. "Detective Ulrich."

"Deputy Mullen here," the woman said, her tone calm but alert. "I was dispatched to handle your call. Can you bring me up to speed?"

Burke told her about the boat and described the man who'd taken off. "Forget about the boat for now. Get on the radio—have dispatch alert all units in the area to search for our suspect. We're going after him with full force."

"Copy that." The call went silent.

He looked at Abby. "I'll get to the dock, and we'll proceed from there."

At the dock, he and Abby helped Victor out of the boat. The older gentleman shivered and struggled to walk. He'd left his cane in the boat, and his steps were erratic, like a drunken sailor, and he appeared as if he might collapse. They should probably go back for his cane, but if they did anything except move forward, Victor might insist on leaving.

"Let's get you on solid ground." Abby put her arm around his back and under his elbow, gently leading him down the long pier.

As Burke followed the couple, the pier's sway felt more pronounced. The breeze flowing over his face turned sharper, and the sunshine on his back seemed more intense. All reminding him how lucky he was to be alive.

God had spared him. Them. With only seconds left. Just enough time to show Burke how blessed he was to be alive. To simply be breathing.

Right, nothing simple about that. Something incredibly, extraordinarily wonderful. Each day was a blessing. Had he been squandering his days since Tiffany betrayed him, living in his disappointment and distrust?

Something he needed to give strong consideration, and to God's role in his life too. But not now. Now he had an attempted murderer to find and bring to justice. That had to take priority over everything. And to do that, he had to find the crown.

"Hold up at the deputy," Burke called after them. "We need to get Victor out of the open air."

A wide-eyed female deputy with blond, almost white hair pulled back in a bun waited for them at the end of the dock. She'd parked her patrol vehicle as close to the dock as possible, the lights twirling and drawing attention they really didn't need.

"Thanks for manning the dock." Burke flashed his credentials. "That your cruiser?"

"It is." Her suspicious scrutiny was typical for a uniform officer in such a high-pressure situation.

"I'm commandeering it to house Mr. Lemoine until I can secure additional backup to safely transport him."

The deputy—Mullen, by her name tag—scowled at him. "No matter your rank, you're not leaving the scene with my cruiser."

"No." He would never leave an officer without means of transport. "Just need to sit in it for now."

She fished her keys from her pocket and handed them to him. "Then have at it."

He took the keys. "Any news to report?"

She settled a hand on her sidearm and shook her head. "We haven't located the suspect yet, but the sheriff made it a top priority, and all available resources are continuing to search."

Right. The sheriff. Shocking that Ryder hadn't called Burke yet. Maybe the sheriff was giving him space to take care of things. Regardless, Burke had to report as soon as Victor was secure. "Set up a perimeter around the beached boat. No one, and I mean no one, including you, boards the vessel. I'm holding you personally responsible for this."

"I've got it." She lifted her chin. "You can count on me."

He hoped she was right. "Call me if you locate the suspect or find any leads."

"Roger that," she said.

Burke turned to Abby. "Let's move. Straight ahead to the patrol vehicle."

As they walked toward the cruiser, Abby kept hold of Victor's arm. Burke remained close to them, his hand on his sidearm while surveying the area. He really didn't think they were in danger, but when a law enforcement officer relaxed from such thoughts, people got hurt.

He unlocked the vehicle and opened the back door. Victor slid into the middle, and Abby got in next to him, then closed the door. Burke sat behind the wheel and swiveled to face the others.

Abby took the trembling man's hands in hers. "We'll stay here until we have backup, and then we can go to the bank."

"The bank?" Victor gaped at her. "I want to go home. Please take me home."

"You feel like that now, but you've gone through so much to get this far. Don't you want to finish your job?"

"I do, of course I do. But I don't think I can."

Burke tried to make sure he didn't come across as demanding. "Don't make a decision now. Take a minute. Let the adrenaline recede and calm down. Then if you still want to go home, we'll take you there right away."

Victor bit his lip. "Sounds reasonable, but can you arrange safer transportation than that bathtub toy we came here in to get me home?"

If only Burke had an alternative to offer. "The guy who tried to ram us is long gone, and his boat is beached, so you'll be safe in whatever boat we use. I'll station deputies at the dock where they can check identification for each person wanting to launch a boat. They'll have orders to detain anyone who acts the least bit suspicious."

"That's comforting." Victor's shoulders sagged, and his eyelids drooped.

Ah, yes, his adrenaline was abating, and fatigue would soon threaten to take him down. Best to get him moving before the physical release following such a rush fully hit him, and he asked to go back to the island again. "So what do you say? Should we head to the bank? It's just down the street, and after a quick visit, we'll have you on your way home."

"I... I..."

"I'll arrange for a deputy to search the bank building for any threat, and additional officers to escort you."

He suddenly firmed his shoulders. "Yes, yes, I'll do it. But hurry before I lose my courage."

"The added protection will be perfect," Abby said, but gave Burke a look that suggested he move fast.

He turned to the dash and called Ryder.

"I'll be with you and help you through this," she said softly in the backseat. "I'd also like to pray for you. Would it be okay?"

"I don't believe all that mumbo-jumbo, but it couldn't hurt."

Couldn't hurt indeed. In fact, when someone with strong faith like Abby prayed, it not only couldn't hurt, it could help immensely. Burke needed to observe her and take a lesson from her on faith in action.

In that very moment, he believed prayer and trusting in God was his way forward in life. If only he could let go of his distrust in everything—in everyone—and rediscover enough trust and faith to resume a regular prayer life. Then not only would he once again have his confidence back in his life, but maybe he could move forward in a relationship with Abby too.

11

Burke dropped the accordion folder containing the crown's official certificate and bill of sale on the dining room table. They'd successfully retrieved it from the bank, then got Victor home without incident. He actually seemed calm on the boat ride. That changed the moment they'd reached the island and he charged up the stairs and into the house. Inside the door, he issued a warning not to be disturbed until he emerged from his nap. Period. End of subject. He didn't wait for disagreements, but moved equally as fast up to his bedroom. And honestly, Burke was thankful for a break from the older gentleman, whose moods were as mercurial as a thermometer.

He turned his attention to Abby. She stood across the table, unloading the cooler she'd carried in that morning. When he first spotted it, he'd thought it contained forensic supplies. Not so. She'd thoughtfully brought lunch for the team, including him. He couldn't be more thankful. His adrenaline had abated, and he was starving.

"Okay." She looked around the room where Gabe and Sam had joined them. "I've got roast beef, ham, and turkey sandwiches, potato salad, chips, fruit, and cookies for dessert. Before you're impressed and think I somehow made all of this for you last night, Reece took care of food prep for us. So have at it, and please thank her the next time you see her."

"If Reece made it, I'll double my number of sandwiches for sure." Gabe stepped up to the food, grabbed a plate in one hand, and a wrapped sandwich in the other.

"Reece and I know you, Gabe. Two sandwiches are your requirement." Abby wrinkled her nose at him, then looked at Burke and Sam. "Feel free to have two as well."

"You don't need to tell me twice." Chuckling, Burke circled the end of the table.

"No way I can eat two and have a cookie," Sam said. "And I definitely won't miss out on one of Reece's chocolate chunk cookies."

Burke loaded his plate and had just settled in place when his phone rang, the call from Officer Mullen.

"You're not going to like this," she said, and her urgent tone led him to believe her. "The beached boat was reported stolen yesterday."

Burke ripped open a roast beef sandwich. "So the boat registration won't likely tell us anything."

"Sounds doubtful, but I'd still be glad to check into it."

"Much appreciated. Thank you." He ended the call and shared the information with the team. "I'll let you know when I get the registration details."

Abby frowned. "But as you said, it's likely a dead end unless the fingerprints prove the thief was related to the owner."

Burke turned to Sam. "Do you know when you'll be able to process the boat's forensics?"

Sam set down her unwrapped sandwich. "I called in my assistant to help. She's arriving this afternoon. I'll give her instructions for the work here, then head back to the mainland to handle the boat. Depending on what I find, I should have it done today."

"Perfect," Burke said. "Thank you for being so flexible."

"She always is." Gabe's expression resembled a parent's look when their child had done well. He nodded at the file in front of Burke. "Those the documents from the bank?"

Burke nodded. "The crown appears to be the real deal, but I want to have the document authenticated for age."

"I'm already ahead of you." Dipping into the potato salad, Abby looked up. "Our team met last night and tasked Jude with finding an expert who can authenticate it. After our interviews with Sylvia and Ugo, I'll give Jude a call."

Burke was impressed with her initiative. He'd been bone tired when she left him last night, but she still managed to hold a team meeting. "Did you decide on anything else? I don't want to replicate the work."

She brought her plate to sit next to him. "Hayden's our computer guy. He's searching for background information on Victor and Estelle. Nolan will visit the nearest antique shop to find out who in the area might have the right connections to fence a high-priced antique like the crown. He'll also ask about the locket."

"He knows to be discreet and not mention the crown, right?" Burke popped open his bag of chips, being careful not to explode the chips all over the room.

"You can count on Nolan to be discreet."

"I might be questionable," Gabe said. "Not Nolan. He's a professional through and through." He laughed and shoved more of the sandwich into his mouth.

Abby reacted to his comment with a groan. "Reece is trying to find someone to date the torn velvet we found in the greenhouse."

"Good," Burke said. "This is all very helpful."

"Why don't I schedule an update video call with the entire team for three o'clock?" Abby asked. "We can find out if they've learned anything new."

"Sounds great." Burke met her gaze. "I really appreciate this, Abby. You have resources our department doesn't have."

She beamed with pride. "I'm not one to brag on myself, but I'll be sure to stand behind what our team can do."

"Yeah, man," Gabe said. "We're the equivalent of the Veritas Center for investigators." He gave a mischievous grin and took a handful of potato chips.

Burke had been annoyed with this guy at first, but it was pretty hard to stay aggravated with someone who tackled life with such humor. He wanted to be more like Gabe. Maybe not as much of the sarcasm, but less of an intense approach to everything.

But the impact of his strict upbringing held him in check. That's why he was so drawn to law enforcement. He liked the black-and-white rules and laws to abide by. If a person violated them, they had to pay. End of story. His other motivation—his brother Kyle's overdose and death—also contributed to his career choice.

Stop. Don't go there. Don't dwell on the painful loss.

He grabbed the file and ignored the surrounding conversation about Blackwell Tactical. He would like to learn more about their organization, but finding immediate leads to locate the crown and keeping his job motivated him more.

Victor had given them permission to review his will, so Burke dug it out of the folder and laid it next to his plate. He alternated eating and reading. One cookie left to eat and he'd reached the end of the will.

At a break in the conversation, he swiveled toward Abby. "Victor's will is pretty straightforward. Everything goes to his son, except for gifts of cash and specific collectibles to his daughter and grandchildren."

Abby set her water bottle down. "He didn't mention having grandchildren. Maybe the daughter knows about the will and feels like she's not getting her share of the property. A perfect motive for stealing the crown."

"Sounds plausible," he said. "Of course the will doesn't mention the crown, but one thing's for sure. Unless Victor stole it, someone else *must* know about it."

Abby gave him a thoughtful look. "Even if Vidal's in the know, what motive would he have for stealing it when he would inherit it?"

"Maybe he needed the money now," Gabe joined in the discussion.

"A good possibility," Abby said. "When we meet with the team, I'll ask Hayden to do a deep dive on Vidal too, including his finances." She glanced at her watch. "We need to meet Sylvia and Ugo at the ferry. We should get going."

"I'd like to scan their fingerprints before you do get started with them." Sam dumped her plate into a garbage can.

"We'll bring them to you in the library first thing," Abby said.

"Thanks. And before you go, I should tell you that I think the samples of the oil in the hallway are gun oil."

"Gun oil?" Burke looked at her. "How sure are you?"

"I can't be one hundred percent certain until I analyze it, but I'm over ninety percent sure."

Abby started packing leftovers into the cooler. "Why would someone have gun oil in the hallway?"

"If you're a gun owner," Gabe said, "it makes sense to use the oil, especially after cleaning or when stored in less-than-ideal conditions to protect it from rust."

Abby paused, potato salad in hand. "Less-than-ideal, like the high humidity from a house located at the beach."

"Exactly. But still, you don't oil your gun in the hallway. Or at least I've never known anyone who does."

Abby closed the cooler. "We need to ask Victor if he owns any firearms and go from there."

"I can also determine how long the oil has been there," Sam said. "It's time-consuming, so it would be good to first determine if it's an important lead and should take precedence over other items I recover."

Burke appreciated her ability to look at forensics recovery and processing like a detective might and not just gather the evidence and believe it all had equal weight "Once you finish the scene, we can sit down and evaluate the evidence together to set priorities."

Sam nodded and stepped out the door.

"I'm off to meet the ferry unless anyone else has questions," Abby said.

Gabe picked up the bag of journals from the table. "I assume I'm still tasked with babysitting these for the rest of the day."

"You are," she said. "But if we keep them with us, you should be able to accompany us in many of our tasks."

He dramatically swiped a hand over his forehead. "Thank goodness. Babysitting them all alone was like watching paint dry. I wanted to poke my eyes out by the time you got back."

Abby laughed, and something in Burke's chest twitched. She got to him more than he would like. Not that he'd ever admit it. Yeah, she was easy on the eyes for sure, but it was more than that. She was sharp. Solid. Ethical. Just like him, always in control, always had a plan. No drama. So why was he trying so hard not to feel anything?

Then *her* face came to mind. *Tiffany.* The one who

screwed him up good. Messed with his head. He hadn't let anyone close since then. He didn't know if he could. Not again.

He shook himself from his daze and bolted out of the dining room to catch up with Abby. He caught up to her at the front door and held it open for her.

Outside, Burke scanned the area. Deputy Cunningham remained on duty at the crime scene tape, keeping a watchful eye on the ferry. Burke kept tabs on the ferry, too, as they descended the remaining stairs. A handful of people stood near the vessel's back gate. Three of them were young, two were older. Had to be Sylvia and Ugo. From this distance, Burke couldn't tell if they were eager or dreading their arrival.

With a nod of approval for his deputy, Burke held up the crime scene tape for Abby, and they slipped underneath. The ferry's crew had secured heavy ropes to the dock and the tailgate groaned toward the dock.

The older couple hurried down the ramp. The woman was short and wide as if someone had pressed down on her when she was growing up. Her hair was a warm shade of gray, and waves softly framed her face. She wore black pants and a green rain slicker. The guy, on the other hand, was tall and thin. He had coal-black hair liberally laced with gray, and wore a similar slicker with brown pants.

Head down, she walked faster than he did, but he limped and seemed as if he was trying to keep up with her. He suddenly grabbed her arm. They stopped. She cupped a hand over her eyes, staring ahead. She suddenly shook her head, then said something to him. The pair turned and bolted back toward the ferry.

"What in the world?" Abby blinked rapidly. "I was sure that was Ugo and Sylvia. Why would they be turning back?"

A good question. One Burke intended to answer before

the ferry departed with them on board. Even if the couple weren't Victor's workers, they had to have a reason for laying eyes on the bright yellow tape fluttering in the breeze and the uniformed officer standing guard, then reversing course.

"Come on," he said to Abby. "People don't run away unless they have something to hide, and we need to find out exactly what they don't want the police to know."

12

Abby held out her newly acquired shield and introduced herself and Burke to the couple. They didn't reply with names, so Abby took a stab at their identity. "Sylvia Bass and Ugo Morell, we need you to come with us to answer a few questions."

Ugo backed up, but Sylvia pointed her chin at them. "Tell us now before we agree to anything. Is Victor hurt?"

"He's fine," Abby said.

Sylvia studied Abby, her gaze wary. "You wouldn't be lying just to get me up there and grill me for answers?"

"I'm not lying, and I don't plan to grill you for anything." Abby smiled, hoping to disarm the older woman's suspicions. "So let's do this the easy way and head up to the mansion without any fuss."

Sylvia continued to stare at Abby, deep brown eyes tight and distrustful. Thankfully, Abby had been able to flash a shield at them, or they might not have taken her authority seriously.

Sylvia shifted the canvas grocery bags in her hands. "Badge or no badge, you can't arrest us. We haven't done anything wrong."

Following her lead, Ugo raised his goatee-covered chin. "We don't even know why the police are here."

Burke eased closer, his presence intimidating. "We'll be glad to explain all of it inside."

"Come on, people." A chunky dock hand left the gate controls and stormed over to them. "Make up your mind. You coming or going? Captain's getting mad. He has a timetable to keep, and I need to cast off."

"They'll be staying on the island." Burke moved behind them as if he intended to herd them like cattle up the stairway.

Neither of them budged an inch.

Abby rarely lost her patience, but she was coming close with this couple. "You can answer our questions now or we'll stay on the ferry and escort you to an interrogation room in town for questioning."

Sylvia gritted her teeth. "Fine. We'll accompany you, but under protest."

"Noted," Abby said. "Can I help carry your bags?"

She huffed and started ahead, her steps urgent now as if she wanted to get this over with. Ugo trailed her, but his feet shuffled over the wooden planks, and he fell behind. Both of them seemed beyond retirement age and still working. Why? One of the questions Abby intended to pose.

Perhaps they were hoping when Victor passed away they would receive something in his will. She knew such hopes wouldn't come true. Victor hadn't left a single thing to them. She wasn't really surprised. Not with his aristocratic air, where he thought domestics were beneath him.

At the crime scene tape, they stopped to record their names on the duty officer's entry log, then started upward toward the mansion. Sylvia continued to move quickly, her groceries swinging at each tread. But Ugo, latching on to the handrail, climbed with extreme effort.

Abby glanced back at Burke and signaled her plan to stop Sylvia from entering the mansion ahead of them. She rushed up the steps and brushed past her. Opening the door, she blocked the older woman. "Do any of your groceries require refrigeration?"

Sylvia shook her head. "Victor gets those items delivered from the grocery store. I go to the local farmers' market and bring him fresh fruit and vegetables along with my home-baked bread."

"That's a very kind thing to do."

"We're family." Her tone had softened, and a fondness for Victor lingered on her face. "We take care of each other."

Would that make her unwilling to answer questions that may put Victor in a bad light? They would have to tread carefully when questioning her.

"Since you don't need to access the kitchen, I'd like you to take a seat in the hallway while we talk to Ugo."

"I don't have time to waste sitting around. I have work to do."

"I'm sorry. The entire mansion has been designated as a crime scene, and there will be no work here until we release the scene."

Sylvia's expression turned hard and rigid, but she nodded her understanding.

Abby moved back to let her enter, and she stormed inside.

The men reached the top of the steps, Ugo was huffing and puffing.

Abby gave him a smile. "Have a seat next to Sylvia for a moment."

He cocked his head, but didn't argue, probably because he was too tired from climbing the steep stairway and needed to sit down.

He looked at Sylvia. "Why are you just sitting here instead of putting the produce away?"

She jerked a thumb over her shoulder at Abby and Burke. "Ask them."

"We can't have the crime scene disturbed until all evidence is recovered," Burke said.

Ugo shook his head. "I do not know the crime you speak of, but I do not like this."

"I'll tell Sam they're here." Burke headed to the library.

Abby faced the couple on the bench. "We'll be collecting fingerprints from around the house. Our forensic tech will scan your prints so we know which recovered prints belong to you."

"And if we don't want our fingerprints taken?" Sylvia asked.

"I'm afraid it's not optional, and we can get a warrant for them, but then we'll have to take you to the station and take them there."

"Just let them do it, Sylvia," Ugo grumbled.

"Fine," she said, but the deep sigh she let out proved she still wasn't happy about it.

Holding her portable scanner, Sam returned with Burke and knelt in front of Ugo. She gave him a big smile. "This will be painless and won't take long. I promise."

He held out his hand, and when it came to Sylvia's turn, she did as well.

Sam stood. "Thank you both for cooperating."

"Not like we had a choice," Sylvia muttered under her breath.

Ignoring the comment, Sam mouthed "good luck" to Abby on her way back to the library.

Abby turned to Burke. "I'll wait here with Sylvia if you'll send Gabe out to sit with her."

Burke gestured for Ugo to follow him to the dining room. "After you."

Gabe soon strode through the foyer looking all 'let's do this' as usual. If he approached Sylvia this way, they would soon be feuding.

"Stay put, Sylvia." She met Gabe where they could talk out of the woman's hearing. Still, Abby lowered her voice for good measure. "You need to tread lightly with this one. No sarcasm. No humor. She's feisty and distrustful. I don't want her all wound up by the time we question her."

He winced. "So, back to watching paint dry then."

"I really appreciate you taking on these menial tasks."

"Hey, we gotta do our part to keep the business going, right?" He squeezed her arm. "Now go charm the pants off Ugo. Or maybe make sure he keeps his pants on, but you know what I mean."

She rolled her eyes, something she did frequently around this guy, but her heart was filled with love for her teammate. For all of her teammates.

In the dining room, she found Ugo seated on the side of the table facing the fireplace. Burke poured a glass of water from a crystal pitcher and placed it in front of the older man.

"So tell us how long you've worked for Victor." Burke talked as he would to a friend, keeping things light to not spook the jittery guy more.

Ugo wrapped trembling hands around the water glass. "Victor was just turning twenty-one. His father, Valentino Lemoine, was disappointed in the way his son presented himself to the world, so he hired me to improve his grooming habits. I made sure he was dressed impeccably every time he went out in public. I was only a few years older, so we had a unique employee/employer relationship."

Abby slipped into a chair across from Ugo. "So you worked for him for over fifty years, then?"

He nodded. "I don't know where the time has gone, but yes, I've been in his employ for fifty-six years and three months to be exact."

In a stance she thought Burke meant to keep things light, he leaned against the sideboard, crossing his legs at the ankle. "You must have loved the job if you left Paris to come to Oregon."

"I enjoyed helping shape Victor's future. It was almost as if I'd come from money, too, and was living my life through him. Kind of heady for a young man. But I hadn't of course. What I did have was the premium salary his father paid me until he died several years after I moved here." A small grin crossed his face. "Victor has been even more generous, both with me and Sylvia." The grin evaporated. "If you expect me to say something negative about him, you've come to the wrong person."

"My only expectation is for you to tell the truth." A flicker of steel cut through Burke's casual expression. "Tell us about Estelle. What kind of person was she?"

"A wonderful wife and mother. The staff liked working for her. She was social and always having parties. Just the opposite of Victor. He's always been an introvert."

"What do you think happened to her?" Abby asked.

"I've wondered about that from the day she disappeared." His eyebrows drew together. "Like I said, she was well-liked, so I don't think anyone would want to hurt her. And she loved running this mansion, hosting parties. Living in Oregon in general. So I can't see her disappearing on her own. Which I guess leaves some stranger abducting her." He shuddered.

Abby thought it was time to move on before he fell apart. "Do you own a gun or does Victor?"

"A gun?" Eyes wide, Ugo stared at her. "Why would you ask that?"

"We just need you to answer the question," Burke said, his tone giving the guy no doubt he had to answer.

"Not me. I know Victor has an antique gun collection. He inherited it from his father, and it's in a locked cabinet in his bedroom. I've never seen him take them out. Besides, he would never shoot anyone, if that's what you're asking me."

"Do you have a key to that cabinet?" Abby asked. "Would you know if a gun was missing?"

"I don't have a key, and I've never seen the guns, so I wouldn't know if they were all there."

"You've been with the family long enough to have worked with Dominique," Abby said. "Do you know how to contact her?"

"I don't, but Sylvia might. The last and only address I had was the one I used to ship paintings to her parents' house outside of Paris."

"So she *did* receive the two paintings from the hallway?" Abby asked.

"I don't know if she received them, just that I sent them. Another example of Victor's generosity."

"I understand you like the job and the money, but why continue working at your age? Why not retire?"

"And fill my days with what?" He shifted his gaze between them. "When you find a calling in life, there's no reason to retire from it unless you can no longer perform the duties."

"I don't mean to cast aspersions on the job you're doing as the estate manager," Abby said. "But the property seems to be in great disrepair."

"Not for lack of trying." Ugo sighed. "I've wanted to get Victor to see the state of things and fix them. He's in savings mode. Or so he claims. And he's the one who fired Juan

López, the gardener, in a fit of anger. After that, I couldn't take care of it all, nor would Victor or Sylvia, so everything grew out of control."

"Do you know why he was angry at Juan?" Burke asked.

"My guess is he simply values his privacy and doesn't want repairmen around the property. I think he let the gardener go because of that, not finances. He has plenty of money and will never run out of it in his lifetime. Juan was hired by Estelle and lived in a caregiver's house on the property. After she disappeared, Victor not only lost interest in the garden, but he didn't want someone else living here."

Abby didn't understand it, but then she didn't have the phobias Victor seemed to have. "Victor mentioned you broke the basement window, and he thought it'd been fixed."

"I hit it with a ladder when I climbed up to stop a shutter from completely falling off the building. The window is on backorder. I told him that, but at our age we often forget things."

She had no reason not to believe him. "Have you noticed anything unusual around here lately? Like people on the property who shouldn't be. Things gone missing or even being moved in the house that didn't make sense."

"No. No. If I'd seen anyone other than our usual delivery service personnel, Victor would know about it. Why do you ask?"

"What about the cells in the basement?" Burke asked, thankfully changing the subject, so she didn't have to sidestep what was going on. "Have you been down there lately?"

A flash of surprise lit in his eyes. "No one goes down there. Why would we? It's a very depressing place that serves as a reminder of an equally depressing time in Oregon history. Imagine living without any real law enforcement and homeowners had to take the law into their own hands."

Abby couldn't even begin to imagine living among such lawlessness. Not when she liked things neat and tidy and according to plan. "Are you aware of any secret passages in the mansion?"

"There's a passageway leading from the library up to the master bedroom," Ugo said.

"Have you been in it recently?" Burke asked.

Ugo shook his head. "It's Victor's personal space, like his bedroom, and Sylvia and I don't ever use it."

"Do you know who has over the years?" Burke asked.

"Victor never really did, but Estelle used to."

"Did Estelle like to shoot guns?"

"Estelle?" Ugo's eyes widened. "She was far too much of a lady to touch a gun."

"Have you seen or found any hidden storage cubbies in the house?" Burke was on a roll, so Abby sat back for now.

"I've never come across anything like that," Ugo said.

"So you don't know about the hidden compartment in the floor by the office fireplace?"

"No. Is there one?" His surprise seemed legit.

"Have you visited the greenhouse lately?" Burke wasn't giving Ugo time to think, an interview method used to encourage him to say the first thing that came to mind.

Ugo raised his hands in frustration. "How would I even get to it? I'd need a machete, and there's no point in going there when it might collapse on my head."

"Have you seen anyone else in there?"

"Again, how would I see such a thing with the wall of greenery between it and the house?"

Burke took out his phone and displayed a picture of the locket. "Do you recognize this necklace?"

"Sure." Ugo continued to study the screen. "It belonged to Estelle. She wore it every day."

"So she had it on when she went missing?"

"I didn't see her that day, but it seems likely."

They needed a copy of the police files for Estelle's disappearance, not only to check for any mention of a locket, but for any other details they might need to follow up on.

Abby would mention it later, but now, her questions. "Do you ever spend the night here?"

He looked at his hands. "I did, back when we lived in the servants' quarters, but not since then."

Avoiding eye contact could mean he was lying. "So in all the years you've worked here, you never missed the last ferry?"

"I didn't say that," Ugo lifted his head, his expression blank. "The few times it *did* happen, Victor arranged a water taxi for me. Did the same for Sylvia so neither of us had to stay over. As I've said, he likes his privacy. He particularly likes to be alone in the evening."

She believed his last statement, but he seemed pretty wishy-washy about spending the night. Maybe his family members could further clarify. "Are you married? Have children?"

His eyes squeezed shut, brows knotting tight. "Was. Had a son. Both were killed in a hit and run three years ago."

Oh no! Poor guy. If only she could take her question back. "I'm so sorry, Ugo. It must have been extremely hard to lose them."

"Even more since I have no idea who hit them and got away with murder." He shook his head. "Daniel took my sweet wife to Portland to buy a dress for our fiftieth wedding celebration. That makes it even worse."

With such a terrible tragedy in Ugo's past, Abby didn't want to continue questioning him. He'd suffered mightily.

Was still suffering. But he'd also been acting evasive, and she had to do her job. Still, she could offer some support. "I'll pray for your comfort and peace, Ugo."

He waved a hand. "Don't trouble yourself. Walked away from God when He took my family. Your prayers won't matter."

She wanted to argue. Tell him no one could know God's plan in the loss of his family, but now wasn't the time to discuss his faith. But she would pray for him. Pray he was able to embrace his faith again and return to God. "Do you know of any extremely valuable items stored in this house?"

"Extremely valuable?" He stroked his goatee with twisted fingers. "I can only tell you about the items I've arranged to be insured. Most of the paintings would fetch a high price at auction. Victor owns a large assortment of watches, and he still has Estelle's jewelry. She had quite the collection of rare gemstones when she married him. Of course, there's the silver and crystal, and the limited edition and rare books. Most of the furniture is French antique, and it, too, would bring a good auction price."

Just as she expected. No crown. "Does Victor keep these items in a safe on the property?"

"There is a safe. It's in the hallway leading to his bedroom, but the thing is ancient. Was installed when the house was built. The island has been crime-free until recently, so he had no need to use it."

Extremely interested now, Abby sat forward. "You said recently. Why do you think it's changed?"

"Several of the homes are now vacant. The homeowners have taken their valuables, but the houses have been broken into and vandalized."

"What about here? Any unlawful entries?"

"No."

So the crown likely hadn't been stolen by someone

breaking in and discovering it as Victor had suggested. "Has Victor mentioned any recent thefts?"

"Now wait a minute." He shot forward. "If you're accusing me or Sylvia of stealing something from him, you can stop right there. We would never do that. Not only is he family, but it would violate the ethics code we both try to live by."

He might be hoping to eliminate her suspicion of his involvement in the crown theft, but she wouldn't let this go so easily. People lied. Especially people with a lot to lose. If Ugo was found guilty of stealing the crown, he would have a tremendous amount to lose, including his freedom for his last days on earth.

13

Burke took a frustrated breath and blew it out after Sylvia's latest response. He and Abby had fired questions at the woman for fifteen minutes, bringing up the same topics they'd asked Ugo, but she was even more difficult. Giving short, one-word answers if possible.

She'd been argumentative from the moment she'd arrived on the island, but now she barely cooperated. Not only was he certain Victor was hiding something, but Ugo and Sylvia seemed like they were as well. Perhaps the same "something," and they were trying to protect their boss or each other.

"Look." Sylvia crossed her arms. "If you're trying to get me to say something negative about Victor, I'm just not going to do it. He's been very good to me over the years, and he's a wonderful man. Like family. Whatever you're doing here, and whatever you think he might be involved in, I can assure you, he wouldn't break the law."

"Let me clarify," Burke said, trying to keep the irritation out of his tone. "If we find he's done something illegal, and I'm not saying he has, and you're willing to lie for him, you'll go to prison for obstructing justice."

Her arms dropped, and her face paled. "I'm not lying to you, so there should be no problem."

Brave words, but she was skating on thin ice with Burke. "Tell us about your family."

She arched a brow. "I'm not sure what they have to do with whatever is going on here."

"Background helps fill in missing pieces. So humor me and tell us a little bit about them."

She took a long breath. "I've been married for thirty-eight years and have one child. A daughter. She's twenty-seven and still lives in Seaview Hollow. She's a loan officer at the local bank."

Bank? Was it a coincidence that she worked where Victor banked? She wouldn't have access to his safety deposit box without his key. But could Sylvia have taken his key so her daughter could open it, then returned the key to Victor?

"How long has she worked there?" He made sure to sound interested but not suspicious.

"Let's see." Sylvia cocked her head. "She was hired right out of college. She was twenty-two when she graduated, so five years. She started as a teller and worked her way up to a loan officer. Now she's in training to become the assistant manager. We're very proud of her."

"You should be," Abby said. "Sounds like she's determined to get ahead."

"Takes after me, I guess." Sylvia laughed.

So Sylvia saw herself as a go-getter. As a person who wanted to get ahead. Could such a plan involve stealing a crown? Certainly money from the sale would put her ahead in life.

"I suppose with a family, you've never spent the night here," Burke said.

Her shoulders tensed. She was bothered by the question, but why?

She met Burke's gaze head on. "Back in the day my husband and I lived here, but then we had our daughter and bought our own house. Since then, I've had no reason to stay overnight."

He forced a smile to encourage her to talk. "I didn't think you would have, but I'm sure in all these years your workday ran late and you missed the last ferry."

"Yeah." She visibly relaxed. "Happened to me and Ugo both, but Victor arranged water taxis to take us to the mainland."

"When's the last time it happened?" Abby asked.

Sylvia's eyes tightened. "I don't keep track of things like that, but I guess it was on Victor's birthday in September. He asked me and Ugo to have dinner with him."

"It's kind of you to join him," Abby said.

"Like I told you, he's family to us. We'd help him any way we could."

"What about Estelle?" Abby asked. "Tell us about her."

Sadness washed over her. "She was an excellent employer. Didn't treat the help like we were lower class. Asked us to do things instead of commanding it. And she had a great sense of humor, so we laughed a lot on the job."

The same story Ugo gave. Not helpful at all, but Sylvia appeared to be telling the truth.

At least Burke bought into her story, and he was the king of suspicion. "We were surprised to find locked cells in the basement."

Sylvia jerked back but quickly relaxed. "I thought that was odd too, but it made sense after Victor explained how law and order barely existed when this house was built."

"Do you know if the cells were ever used?"

"He never mentioned it, and I never cared enough to ask.

It's super creepy down there. Why would I want to know more about it?"

"I agree it's creepy," Abby said. "But I'd want to know everything possible about a house I spent so many years working in."

"Guess that's the difference between you and me." Sylvia leaned back and crossed her arms.

End of discussion, from her point of view anyway.

"What about firearms?" Burke asked. "Do you know if Victor owns any guns or do you carry one to work with you?"

Sylvia's mouth dropped open. "Me? A gun? No. I'm deathly afraid of them. Victor inherited an antique collection, but I've never seen him even open the cabinet to look at them, much less use one."

"So you wouldn't have brought oil here to lubricate a gun?" Burke asked.

She shook her head, but didn't speak as if she thought his questions were ridiculous.

Wouldn't stop him. "Do you have a key to the gun cabinet?"

"No. I've never even seen the guns." Her adamant tone seemed to confirm she was telling the truth.

Abby picked up her phone from the table and displayed the recovered locket. "Do you recognize this?"

She let out a slow breath and studied the screen, as if she was thankful the discussion had moved on, but why? What was she withholding?

She looked up. "The locket belonged to Estelle."

"Belonged, as in the past tense and Estelle is no longer alive?" Abby asked.

Sylvia cocked her head. "We don't know anything for sure, but even if no one else will say it, Victor's the only one who believes she's still alive."

"What do you think happened to her?" Abby quickly asked.

Sylvia shrugged. "My guess is someone took her. Obviously not for ransom because there was never a demand for money, but perhaps for something else. She was a beautiful woman. Could've been reason enough for some guy to abduct her."

"So you don't think she left here on her own accord?"

Sylvia shook her head. "She was happy here. Loved her new life in Oregon. In France, she was just one of many wealthy women. Here, she was exotic and stood out. Made her the queen of the social scene. Plus, she loved Victor. So I just don't see it happening."

"Say she did leave on her own," Burke said. "Do you think her former maid might have something to do with Estelle's disappearance?"

"Dominique?" Sylvia's eyes narrowed. "I don't think it's likely. Especially after Victor had her investigated and they couldn't locate her."

"She could've gone into hiding with Estelle."

"Nah. I don't buy it. One thing I know about Estelle is she liked the finer things in life. That takes money. If she left on her own accord, she would've found a way to take some of Victor's money, but he said nothing was missing. So, she would've had to get involved with a rich guy who was willing to lavish his money on her."

"Like a male suitor, you mean?"

Sylvia nodded. "But if she was secretly seeing someone who went away with her, no one else in the area was reported missing."

Could be the man waited to leave and not draw attention to himself. In case Sylvia was incorrect, Burke would check other missing persons investigations.

"Back to the locket," he said. "Do you know if she was wearing it the day she disappeared?"

"Not for certain, but she wore it every day, so it would've been odd if she didn't have it on."

"Have you seen the jewelry she left behind?"

"I didn't have a reason to and wouldn't have asked Victor to look at it anyway. The pain of losing Estelle has always been too raw for him, and I wouldn't knowingly inflict more."

This woman came across as strong and combative, but she really did have a soft spot in her heart for Victor. She really could be covering something up for him.

"What about a safe on the property?" he asked. "Does Victor keep these jewels in a secure area?"

"No. No safe. Well, if you don't count the one in the library hallway. That ancient relic has been there forever."

"But he doesn't use it?"

She shook her head.

"Do you know why?"

"I've never asked him, but shortly after we moved here, I barged in on his father opening it. He told me it'd been installed when the house was built. He said the combination had been shared so many times over the years that nothing would be secure in it."

Interesting. "Victor told us a far different story. He said his father warned him to keep the combination a secret, implying not many people knew about it."

She shrugged. "All I can tell you is what his father told me. But I should also mention his dad was pretty dramatic and was suffering with dementia by then."

Was she right? Was it a matter of an elderly man's dementia? Or had the combination been shared multiple times in the past? One of them could be lying, he supposed. A question worth asking Victor again.

"Did you learn the combination?" he asked.

"No, he didn't come right out and share it with me. Just said others knew it."

"And you didn't look over his shoulder? I mean, if I was there, I'd have a hard time not looking."

"Why would I?" She eyed him. "Oh I get it, you think I stole something from there. He said they never kept anything valuable in it, so what good would it do me to know the combination?"

"Then you didn't open it and put journals inside?" Abby pressed more.

"Journals? Estelle was the only person who kept journals here, but no, I never put anything in that safe or took anything out of it. Do her journals give you any idea of what happened to her?"

No way Burke would answer that question. "So if the jewelry isn't kept in a safe, do you know where it is?"

"Finally something I know the answer to. It's in the bottom drawer of a large chest of drawers in Victor's room."

"In all these years, you must've cleaned his room many times. Never been tempted to take a peek at it?"

"Why?" She lifted her chin. "I saw everything when Estelle wore the different pieces to social events. No need to look. Besides, you may think of me as a lowly housekeeper, but I do know how to respect my employer's privacy. If Victor wanted to share them with me, he would have."

With such force behind her words, Burke believed her. "Do you know if the detective who investigated Estelle's disappearance asked to see the jewelry?"

She nodded. "Victor mentioned the police inventoried everything she'd left behind."

Maybe the information was in the report he'd requested, and Ryder would get the staff to move quickly on finding it.

"We know about the recent break-ins and vandalism on the island. Have you experienced anything here?"

"Thankfully, no, but I'm surprised. The house looks abandoned. Maybe we've escaped any problems because we convinced Victor to put lights on timers in the office and library. They go on and off at night and make the place look occupied."

"Sounds like a good plan," Burke said. "I don't suppose you installed security cameras."

"We wanted to, but Victor thought they would spy on him. Not true, but he doesn't understand how it works."

Burke finally got to the point. "So you don't know of anything that's been stolen here?"

Her expression went cold, and she sat forward, intertwining her hands and resting them on the table. "No. Nothing. If this is what your investigation is about, and if you think Ugo or I had anything to do with it, you're wrong and wasting time. Now, if you're not going to charge me with anything, I'm done talking to you."

She stood and challenged him with a narrow gaze. "I have work to do, and I need to get to it."

Burke got up. "As Deputy Day told you, there'll be no work here until the forensics are processed and I'm satisfied we've recovered everything we need for our investigation."

"But I... but what will Victor do if we're not here to support him?"

"We'll make sure he's taken care of until we're finished with the investigation. Maybe even find him other accommodations."

"Hah. Shows what you know. There's no way Victor will leave this house for any reason."

Abby got to her feet. "Actually, he went to the bank with us today and did very well."

Sylvia's mouth fell open. "If he left this house for the first time after all these years, this must be far bigger than the theft of Estelle's jewelry."

If she only knew, but there was no way she'd hear about the crown from him.

"Please don't try to come back here until we notify you it's clear. A deputy will be on duty twenty-four/seven and will turn you away." Burke picked up his notepad.

Sylvia crossed her arms. "I want to know where Victor is so I can make sure he's okay."

"Right now he's taking a nap in his room, but I'm afraid it's not possible to disclose any future plans." Burke held out his pen and notepad to her. "Please write down your address and phone number so we can contact you. Stay in town. No sudden trips anywhere."

She jerked the pen from his hand and wrote furiously. When she finished, she dropped the pad and pen and turned to leave. Burke picked up the notepad to make sure her writing was legible. It was. Barely.

She stormed out the door, and Burke looked at Abby. "I don't know what to make of her. When she talks about Victor, she seems so sincere, but then her attitude about everything else is suspicious."

Abby nodded. "She had full access to this place for over forty years. She would know it inside and out. While cleaning, she could very well have discovered the crown and kept the information to herself."

"Yeah. Coupled with the possibility of having gotten the safe combination from Victor's father, this currently puts her high up on my suspect list."

Abby gave him a thumbs up. "Let's catch up with my team to see what they've discovered, and I'll ask Hayden to run background checks on both Sylvia and Ugo."

"I was hoping you'd suggest that." Burke looked out the door and watched Sylvia take furious strides toward Ugo. "There's something not right about her. Hopefully, Hayden can tell us what it is, and if she is indeed our thief, we can arrest her."

14

Abby wanted to call the team right away. First she escorted Sylvia and Ugo down to the dock to wait for the ferry. She didn't trust either one of them to actually leave without an escort. Burke stayed in the dining room to call Sheriff Ryder and ask him to look up missing persons investigations occurring around Estelle's disappearance. He also agreed to keep an eye on the journals to give Gabe a short break.

The ferry churned through the water, the motor rumbling as the vessel pulled up to the dock. The ferry staff jumped onto the dock and started tying ropes to large metal cleats.

Abby turned to the couple who'd been silently standing by. "Thank you for your help and have a safe trip to the mainland."

Sylvia eyed her. "And thank you for your trust in believing we would leave on our own without needing someone to babysit us."

Abby didn't take the bait and respond to Sylvia's sarcasm but watched them walk the short plank to the gate and then stop at a card reader. They each swiped passes.

Passes? Duh! Why hadn't Abby remembered seeing

passengers use them on the ferry? She didn't have to take Sylvia and Ugo's word for whether or not they'd spent the night on the island. She just had to get eyes on the ferry logs. Sure, if they'd taken a water taxi home, there wouldn't be a record of their return trip to the mainland for that day, but the program would've recorded one back to the mansion the next time they worked. If they'd stayed on the island, that trip wouldn't be recorded.

These logs should be a piece of cake for Hayden to get, and if Ugo or Sylvia lied about staying the night, Abby would have facts to call them out on their lies.

Abby remained in place until the ferry departed with the couple aboard, then jogged up to the house to share her lightbulb moment with Burke. She burst through the door, planning to jog to the library, but Gabe remained in the foyer, his phone in his hand.

He looked up. "I didn't think you were coming back."

"Why would I leave?"

He shrugged. "Maybe the creep factor of this place. The belligerent employees. The detective you seem to have a thing for."

She rolled her eyes, but didn't comment. "Are you coming to the team update?"

"Okay, ignore your feelings for him, but they won't go away."

She bit her lip to keep from gaping at her teammate. Gabe never talked about feelings.

"I know," he said. "I don't talk about this stuff, but I figure you should recognize when you're fighting a losing battle. You two have something between you. It'll eventually overcome your resistance."

"You mean like you and El?" El—Elaina—Lyons was the local detective working for Mina. Anytime the two of them were in the same room sparks flew and shields went up on both sides.

Gabe glanced sideways before meeting Abby's eyes. "Exactly like that, which makes me an expert on the subject."

"Wow! I can't believe you actually admitted your feelings for El."

"Figured it'd help convince you that you were losing the battle."

"This is a battle I think I can win," she said, but wasn't at all certain she was right.

"Then go for it and see how it works out for you." Gabe got up. "As always, should you give this information to anyone else, I will disavow any knowledge of our interaction." He laughed and headed for the door, his laughter trailing behind him.

She chuckled at his Mission Impossible reference, but he was serious about her keeping this information to herself. She would never betray his confidence, and she hoped she hadn't discouraged him from sharing personal information in the future.

She caught up to him just as he stepped into the dining room and followed him through the door. Burke stood at the far end of the table, his phone pressed to his ear.

"Of course," he said. "You got it." He swiped his finger up the screen and set his phone on the table.

She grabbed her iPad and sat near him. "Everything okay?"

"Fine. Ryder wants to be sure I keep him updated. FYI, no other missing person's investigations occurred when Estelle disappeared, so we can cross that off our list of items to follow up on." He handed the journals to Gabe.

Gabe gave the stack of books a sour look. "Guess this means I'm still on babysitting duty."

"Sorry," Abby said. "But think of the potentially interesting reading you're going to do."

"Yeah, right. The most exciting thing I've read so far is about the ball Estelle hosted. She goes into crazy detail about what everyone's wearing." He rolled his eyes. "But hey, I get it. Someone has to do the job and why not me?"

"We appreciate it for sure." Burke glanced at his watch. "We're late for the three o'clock team update."

Abby opened her iPad case. Telling him about the ferry computer passes would have to wait until after they met with her team.

"Wouldn't be the first time we started late." Gabe retrieved a laptop from his backpack.

She looked up at Burke. "Do you have a tablet or computer with you? If not, I'm glad to share my screen."

"I could use my phone, but I'd like to look on with you if it's all right."

She tapped the chair next to her, ignoring Gabe's raised brow and told-you-so look, to log into the session already in progress. Pictures of the remaining four members of their team popped up on the screen, and Gabe's photo followed.

"Thanks for meeting with us," Abby said. "I'd first like to introduce you to Detective Burke Ulrich."

Burke leaned closer until her camera caught his face, and the screen displayed it next to hers.

Abby introduced everyone else and ended with Hayden. "He's doing the deep background checks on Victor and Estelle Lemoine."

Hayden stared into the camera, his gaze intense as usual. "I handle techie things for the team. Most often writing algorithms to find information not readily available to the average internet user."

"Thanks for your help," Burke said. "Did you locate anything we need to know about?"

Hayden confirmed the basic information Abby and Burke had already learned about the Lemoines. "The most interesting thing I found relates to Estelle's missing person investigation. The detective in charge told me there were rumors she'd had an affair shortly after they moved to Oregon. Orman couldn't prove it, so you won't find it in the files, but he heard it more than once."

Abby tamped down her excitement at the lead to focus more carefully. "Did he say who told him?"

"No. Not even when I pushed him." Hayden's gaze intensified. "He said if we investigate her disappearance, ask everyone we interview about the affair, and press anyone who mentions it for more details."

"Did he seem willing to talk with us about the investigation?" Burke asked.

Hayden rubbed a hand over his face, dragging his fingers down slowly. "Not open at all. He wouldn't discuss any other details and basically said to leave him alone. This investigation had already ruined his life once, and he didn't want to go there again."

"Any idea what he meant by that?" Abby asked.

"When Orman didn't find Estelle, Victor threw his weight around with his wealthy friends and basically burned the detective's reputation. That ended any chance he had to advance in the department. He quit right after that and left the investigation in his rearview. He doesn't want to bring it all back up, and I was lucky I got him to say anything at all."

"I don't blame him." Burke gripped the edge of the table. "Politics and policing have no business being bedfellows."

"Amen to that." Gabe's rigid expression solidified his opinion. "But it's often a bigger factor than anyone in law enforcement wants to admit."

Abby didn't want them to continue down this path and forget their mission. "Did you learn anything else?"

Hayden shook his head. "I still have algorithms running. They might pull something up on some obscure website, but I wouldn't hold your breath."

"Can you look into Sylvia Bass and Ugo Morell?" She told him about their jobs. "Ugo started working for Victor in France, and I need you to go back that far if possible. We definitely want their financial information. I'll text their addresses to you."

"No problem, but don't count on me finding the old information. Very few files that old made it to the internet."

"Just do your best." Abby told them about the computerized ferry passes and how they might help determine if Ugo or Sylvia spent the night on the estate. "Can you also get recent logs for their pass numbers? I'd like to see their movements around the time we think the crown was stolen."

"No sweat," Hayden said. "Consider it done."

"Also, get a list of anyone who took the ferry to the island in the last month. I doubt our thief would've been dumb enough to take public transport, but it's possible."

"Is that all, Your Majesty?" He grinned.

"Actually, no," Abby said. "We need background on Victor's son, Vidal, and Victor also has a daughter, Viviane, and three grandchildren. We'd like information on them as well. They're named in Victor's will. I'll forward a copy of it."

"Can you be sure to include a look into their finances too?" Burke asked. "We need to know if money motivated them to steal the crown."

Abby waited for Hayden to comment on being overworked, but he simply nodded.

"Hey, thanks, man," Burke said. "I know we've piled a lot on you, but we really appreciate your help."

Hayden shrugged. "When you're the only one who can find hidden information, you get used to it."

"So one more thing then," Abby said. "Sylvia's daughter works at the bank where Victor rents his safety deposit box. It's probably just a coincidence, but I'm wondering if there's any way she could've accessed the box and discovered the information on the crown."

Hayden scratched his chin. "Would be difficult to do without a court order, and even then they would have to drill the box open and change the key. But if she somehow got Victor's key, she could do it. Any possibility of that happening?"

"Her mother could've taken it from the mansion and brought it back," Abby said.

"Then let me do a deep dive on her. See if there's anything to indicate she's involved in shady things and might need money."

"When can you get to all of this?" Burke asked.

"Starting right now." He flicked a hand in the air and looked down.

Abby couldn't see his fingers but she heard them clicking on his keyboard. "Anyone else have anything to report or ask?"

Nolan sat up straighter. "I had an interesting conversation with Leonard Shaw. He's the antique dealer in Seaside Harbor I told you about. Obviously, I couldn't straight-up ask about the stolen crown, so I played it off like I was asking about some 1800s artifact. He said a thief wouldn't be able to move something like that around here—not in the small towns, or even in Salem or Eugene. They'd have to go to Portland to fence it. Unfortunately, he didn't have any names to give me."

"So this is a dead end?" Abby asked.

Hayden smirked. "No, Nolan has me doing his job for him. I'm searching for potential fences in Portland."

Nolan stared at Hayden and shook his head. "I showed Shaw the locket but kept the inside pics hidden like you asked. He said he'd need time to verify the authenticity, but it's probably French from the late 1800s and was custom-made for an aristocratic family. Shaw also said it would fetch a pretty penny and mentioned jewelry like the locket is hot right now, and he'd pay top dollar for the piece if it checks out."

"So even without Estelle's picture, the guy's statements suggest it could've belonged to Estelle," Burke said.

"But what was it doing half buried in the greenhouse?" Abby wondered aloud. "She sure didn't lose it or bury it herself."

"So who did?" Jude squinted his eyes. "The only reason I can see to bury the necklace of a missing woman where she lived is if you're trying to frame the property owner. But if that was the case, the person who buried it would've told the police where to find it."

"Maybe there's more than the necklace buried there," Reece suggested. "Maybe Estelle's body is buried there too."

"Good thought," Abby said. "We either need to get a cadaver dog to search the property or call the Veritas Center's anthropologist."

"No cadaver dogs in the local area," Burke said. "But the state police K9 team has them."

Abby looked at Burke. "You can call them in, but if their dogs locate something, they'd insist on using their own forensic anthropologist to excavate the remains. It could take days, maybe weeks, to get on her calendar."

"Then I'll call Kelsey Dunbar at Veritas," Nolan said. "Not only does she have the latest technology for locating remains, but if she discovers a grave, she can immediately begin unearthing them."

Abby shifted her attention to Burke. "Does that work for your department?"

"I'm good with it. If Ryder has a problem, I'll make it work."

She smiled her thanks and turned her attention back to Nolan. "Let me know if she's available as soon as you find out."

"I hope we don't find a grave," Burke said, "but it would be good to close the mystery of Estelle's disappearance."

"But unless the murderer screwed up and left some obvious evidence, it won't tell us who killed her without further investigation." Abby paused to gather her thoughts. "It's even more important to hunt down those rumors about her having an affair."

Burke nodded. "I should have her file by morning, and we can review the interview list. Maybe we can figure out who thought she was two-timing Victor."

Abby looked at her teammates. "Anyone have anything else to report?"

"I located several experts who can date the torn velvet you found in the greenhouse," Reece said. "I'll text them to you."

"Perfect." Abby smiled at her teammate.

Jude swiveled in his chair to face the camera head on. "Ditto for me on finding experts. Well, close anyway. I only found one person in the area who can authenticate an antique certificate. Turns out he's the same guy Nolan spoke to in the antique shop. Seems like everyone thinks he's the big cheese of antiques around these parts. I could expand my search to bigger cities if you want."

Abby thought for a moment. "At this time, I don't think it's worth the effort to pursue. That could change when

Victor approves us to show the actual certificate to an expert."

"With his paranoia, it doesn't seem like he'll agree." Burke frowned but his negative expression quickly cleared. "Hayden, I'm expecting the registration details for the boat that tried to ram us. Could you look for anything that might connect the owner to the investigation?"

"Of course," Hayden readily said. "Abby can give you my phone number so you can text it to me."

Abby hoped Hayden would find something to add to the leads they were already pursuing.

Now, on top of tracking down a missing crown, they were racing to solve an attempted murder—and praying they could stop another attack on Victor before it happened.

15

While Abby and Gabe signed off, Burke sat back to evaluate what had transpired in the meeting. An impressive meeting. Her team's help and research made his job easier. If only he had such a professional team on his side every day. He'd save so many hours.

Gabe closed his laptop. "You two really think Victor is involved in this theft?"

"Not really." Abby looked up. "But even without a motive we can't rule him out. Especially not until we figure out how someone learned about the crown and got into the mansion."

Burke agreed. "Maybe we should take another look at those blueprints. See if we missed an entrance."

"I left the plans on the table in the office," Abby said.

"I'll get them. Been sitting around far too long today." Gabe hopped up and tapped the journals. "Keep an eye on my babies while I'm gone."

He laughed and bolted through the doorway.

"I liked your team," Burke said. "Even Gabe's growing on me."

She chuckled. "He's an acquired taste. But he's an excellent investigator, and the most loyal person I've ever known. *If* you're a law-abiding citizen. You break the law, he doesn't have the time of day for you. All stems from his family. He comes from a long line of lawbreakers, and he managed to escape their way of life."

"That's impressive." Burke was about to ask for additional information, but Gabe charged back into the room with blueprints in hand. He unrolled them with a flourish and laid the open pages in front of Abby as if it were game time and his team just needed one terrific play to take the lead.

She picked up a pen. "I'll put an X on each exterior door we've checked."

Burke tapped the main door, and she drew a large black X over it.

"Nice one, Captain Obvious." Gabe laughed.

Burke did too, grateful for some humor when the stress of this investigation was getting heavier. She drew an X through the french doors in the office and the door leading from the dungeon.

"Wait a minute." She looked at Burke. "Remember the door covered with ivy? I don't see it on the plan."

He ran his finger over the prints to find where the door opened inside. He tapped the paper on a hallway at the right side of the library. "It should be right here, but it's not indicated on the blueprints."

"Let's check it out." She shoved her chair back and shot to her feet.

Burke fell in beside her, and they sprinted down the corridor. At the far end, an interior door loomed, its frame catching the dim light.

She came to a sudden stop. "We already checked that door. It's just a closet."

"Maybe, or maybe it's a closet with a false back." He brushed past her and jerked open the door.

Shelves ran deep, stuffed with every kind of linen you could think of—tablecloths, napkins, towels. A mountain of fabric.

He reached past them, having to strain over the depth of the shelves until he touched the back wall. "There are gaps in the plaster."

"Hurry!" She bounced on her toes. "Let's empty it and get those shelves out of there."

He began to remove the items, whipping them out of the way until a huge mound formed beside him and the shelves were bare. He scanned the back wall. Spotted cuts in the plaster. "Looks like a door all right, but doesn't look like an exterior one."

"The plaster could just be covering it up."

"Could be. I'll remove the shelves, and we'll see." He struggled to free the first one, but then quickly removed the others. Feeling along the wall, a catch came loose, and the wall popped open. The opening was door-sized, likely the reason for such deep shelving. He held up his flashlight, revealing what appeared to be another closet, this one bigger and deeper.

"What is that?" Abby slipped into the opening before he had a chance to determine if a threat existed.

Just in case, he lifted his sidearm, but the closet contained only an old steamer trunk.

Abby put on disposable gloves and dropped to the floor to tug on the tarnished metal hasp. "It's locked. Can you get something to break it?"

He'd love to comply, but... "We don't have permission to open the trunk or a search warrant giving us carte blanche."

She flashed an irritated look up at him. "Victor said to do whatever we had to do."

"In regard to checking the doors. Nothing more. Technically, we shouldn't even have lifted up the loose board by the fireplace or opened the closet door."

She stood and planted her hands on her hips. "Thankfully I'm no longer a sheriff. Private investigators don't have to abide by those rules."

"You're forgetting. You're a deputy now, and you *do* have to abide by the rules. So we do nothing but wait for Victor."

"Wait for Victor to do what?" The deep male voice came from behind Burke.

He spun to find Victor watching them, his eyebrow raised. "What's going on here?"

"Sorry for the mess." Abby shifted her weight, but continued to hold the older man's gaze. "We remembered seeing an outside door covered in ivy and couldn't figure out where it went. Today we realized it led to this closet and discovered a hidden door."

"Sorry for tossing everything aside," Burke said. "I got caught up in the hunt and was in a hurry to find out what was behind the shelves."

"And what did you find?" Victor's pointed gaze burrowed into Abby's eyes.

She didn't back down. "An old steamer trunk. It's locked, and we need your permission to open it."

"Let me look at it first." He slipped past them, his limp more pronounced and his weight heavier on the cane. He stopped in front of the trunk and released a long, drawn-out sigh holding a good measure of sorrow. "Belongs to Estelle. I last saw it in the attic. When she disappeared, I searched up there, but it was missing just like she was. I assumed she took it with her. Looks like she simply had it moved down here."

He ran a hand over his head, and his whole body shuddered. "Do you think because it was left behind, it means someone *did* take her, and she didn't leave voluntarily?"

"Could be." Burke rested his hand on Victor's shoulder for a moment. "Abby and I can move the trunk to the library, and we can look through it together."

Victor gave a solemn nod. "There's an extra key for the lock with Estelle's jewelry. I'll get it while you move this."

"Thank you." Abby smiled at him. "And thank you for agreeing to open the trunk. I hope the contents give us answers."

"After all these years, I've about given up on learning what happened to her." Tears formed in his eyes. "And now the time is here when I might actually learn something, and my feet feel like they're made of lead."

Abby moved closer to him. "Would it help if we prayed about it with you? I know you really don't believe in prayer, but remember we prayed in the boat, and we weren't harmed."

He rubbed his hand over his mouth. "You have a point. Maybe there *is* a God, and I should look into this more. For now, go ahead and pray."

Burke respected Abby for offering to pray with Victor at this time, especially when the guy once told her he didn't believe in prayer, calling it mumbo-jumbo. But maybe, just maybe, she'd planted a seed of faith and was nurturing it to grow.

Could he apply this to his life? After Tiffany left him at the altar, he'd figured he could only trust himself. He learned to rely solely on logic and intuition to see him through. But maybe he should try to strike a better balance. Seek God's direction first and *then* utilize his own abilities and strength.

Was it time to end this impasse with God once and for

all? He sure thought so, but it wasn't as simple as just realizing what he needed to do. He had to let go of her betrayal and trust again. That was the tricky bit. The hard part. The part he still didn't know if he could manage.

∽

Sitting on the sofa next to Victor, Abby held her breath as Burke knelt by the trunk and lifted the lid. A pungent mothball odor wafted from inside the fabric-lined leather trunk. Victor reached out to clutch her hand. All three of them had put on disposable gloves so they wouldn't disturb any evidence Sam might recover, but even through the latex, his hand felt cold.

The trunk revealed women's clothing from the past. At the top lay a lightweight cotton dress, soft taupe in color, with a small floral print. And a big rusty brown blob stained the chest.

"Blood! Is that blood?" Victor whipped his hand to his heart and clutched his dressing gown.

"Looks like it," Abby said, though she didn't want to confirm it to a grieving husband.

"Is this one of Estelle's dresses?" Burke asked.

Fear radiated from Victor's eyes. "Her favorite for casual day wear. Does this mean someone killed her?"

"It would be odd for someone to kill her, then take off her dress, and put it in the locker," Burke said. "But anything's possible."

"So maybe she was just injured." Victor's voice was filled with hope. "And she was still able to change clothing and pack her trunk to go wherever she was headed."

"Again," Burke said, "possible, but we're looking at a lot of blood. She would've had to seek medical attention before going anywhere."

"Did law enforcement check with your family doctor when she disappeared?" Abby asked.

Victor nodded. "They wanted to be sure she hadn't been suicidal. And as I told them over and over, Dr. Roach confirmed she wasn't depressed in any way."

"We'll need to talk to him," Burke said. "Is he still practicing?"

Victor shook his head. "Passed away about two years ago."

Another dead end.

"Do you mind if we continue to search the trunk?" Abby asked.

"Go ahead, but unlike the things in the closet, please respect her items."

A sheepish look crossed Burke's face as he gently removed the dress, revealing a similar one, but in a bright floral fabric. Next came a luxurious ball gown made of green silk. He gently took all three dresses to the end of the sofa.

But Abby's eye caught on the next items. Small, framed family photos.

Victor sighed. "Many of those pictures are of her family in France. She kept them on her nightstand and her little writing desk in the corner of the bedroom. I knew they were missing, but thought she'd taken them with her too."

"You said her family didn't approve of her marrying an American and definitely didn't approve of her moving to the United States," Abby said. "What if she was leaving you and returning to France, but someone in the family didn't want her to come back?"

"I know all of her close family members. They loved her too much to hurt her, so I don't have a clue who would want to keep her away."

"Was she in line to inherit property or money in France?"

"I don't think so. She has two older brothers who would inherit the family's estate and other properties. Though I do believe her father would've left one of their six homes to her."

Burke carefully placed the dresses on the couch. As he moved the ball gown, polaroid pictures fell out of the folds and fluttered to the floor at Victor's feet.

He tried to snatch them up, but he was having trouble with hands that seemed stiff.

"Let me." She dropped to the floor to gather them together, then returned to her seat next to him. Burke moved behind them.

The first photo showed Estelle in front of the mansion. She held the crown in her hands, posing with it as a model might do when displaying something for sale. A broad smile beamed from her face.

Victor gasped. "She knew about the crown. Even took it outside. But how? When? And who took the picture?"

"Let's check the others out." Abby shifted the top one to the back, revealing another shot of Estelle. She wore the same dress, once again with the crown in her hands, but in a different pose. Abby continued to the next one, and the next. Each one a different pose, but still featuring the crown.

"I don't understand this." Victor collapsed against the back of the sofa. "It just doesn't make sense. If she knew about the crown, why didn't she tell me? Or why didn't she ask questions about it?"

Abby was equally as baffled. Maybe they missed something. She flipped through the photos again.

"Wait," Burke said. "Is there something written on the back?"

Abby turned it over. "A date. September 28, the year before she disappeared."

"Does that day mean anything to you, Victor?" Burke asked.

Victor shook his head. "Absolutely nothing, except it was the fall before she disappeared. But that's her handwriting. I'd recognize her scrolling S anywhere."

Abby flipped every picture over. None of the others held a date. "I don't see why the dated one is more unique than the others. But the way she's displaying the crown is almost like she's holding something out for sale, like an item on eBay."

"I don't know what this eBay is, but how could she even be thinking about selling such a valuable part of my past?" Victor sorrowfully swung his head side to side.

"That would assume the photos were taken to give to someone else," Burke said. "If so, why did she still have them?"

"Maybe they took more," Abby suggested. "Then gave the better ones to whoever they were taking them for, and she kept these as a memory of the day."

"Such an event doesn't seem very special," Burke said.

"It doesn't, does it?" Abby let thoughts race around her head and finally settle. "Could it be because of who took the pictures?"

Victor shot her a horrified look. "Are you thinking Estelle was having an affair with the person who took these pictures?"

"Does that seem possible to you?" Abby asked.

"No. No." Victor shook his head so hard she imagined his brain rattling inside. "Absolutely not."

Burke perched on the sofa arm beside Abby, his attention remaining fixed on Victor. "I'm sure Orman asked you the same question."

"Repeatedly." Victor spit the word out as if it were

poison in his mouth. "But each time I told him it wasn't true."

"Yet he'd heard the rumor about an affair from several sources." Burke's intense gaze didn't waver. "So, humor me. Pretend she was having an affair. What man might it have been with?"

Victor crossed his arms. "I don't even want to go there."

"I know you can't believe your wife could've been unfaithful," Abby said gently. "You could very well be right. But if you provide us with names, we can look into them and might locate other information to help us find out what happened to her."

"Fine. I have a twin brother."

Abby gasped and waited for her shock to settle down before she could speak. Something he'd withheld from them this entire time. Something big! "Why didn't you ever mention him?"

Victor's mouth tightened. "His name is Vincent. He lived in Paris, but frequently stayed with us here. We had a falling out, and I haven't heard from him since. He was paying too much attention to Estelle. Always flirting with her, asking her to do the things with him she enjoyed doing and I didn't. It'd been going on for years, getting progressively worse, until he crossed a line I felt he shouldn't cross." He paused and gnawed on his lip. "I didn't like it and was extremely jealous. I asked him to leave."

"When was the last time you saw him?" Burke asked.

He rubbed his brow, as if trying to remember. "Christmas the year before she disappeared. He sent a few letters to Estelle after that. I intercepted and destroyed them. He was trying to get her to leave me and move back to France. Eventually, he stopped writing."

"Did she seem receptive to his advances?" Burke asked.

"I could tell she was flattered, but she would never have

entertained cheating on me. I know that as much as I know my own name."

"Did you talk to him after Estelle went missing?" Abby asked.

He grimaced. "I tried. Left messages on his home phone. He never returned my calls. If he was still bitter about our falling out, he may have been more interested in taking it out on me than he was in hearing about what happened to Estelle."

Burke cast Victor a sympathetic look. Did he believe Estelle had indeed cheated on Victor? Had he experienced what Victor was going through? Maybe that was the reason for his trust issues, causing him to control everything around him.

He stood and shoved his hands into his pockets. "You said after Estelle went missing you had a private investigator look into Dominique. Did you also ask the PI to check on Vincent?"

Victor nodded. "He discovered my brother was simply traveling a lot and ignoring me. He found zero indication Estelle had gone to live with him."

Burke turned to Abby. "Any more questions?"

"No." Her heart had grown so heavy with everything Victor had gone through, but all she could do was offer a quick prayer for him.

"Okay, then," Burke said, returning his attention to Victor. "If you want to touch anything in this trunk, be sure you wear gloves so you don't disturb any evidence."

"You can put it all back and close it as far as I'm concerned." His eyes were glassy. "Estelle might not have cheated on me, but she clearly kept her knowledge of the crown a secret. And I can't help but believe the pictures indicate she was hoping to somehow gain from it."

Abby agreed. What else could be the point of the

pictures? Maybe Estelle simply took them as souvenirs of having found it, but honestly, such a thought didn't make any sense.

No, when it came to the crown, Abby had to believe Estelle was up to no good, and it could very well be the reason for her disappearance or murder.

16

Burke walked beside Abby toward the dining room, pondering this recent find on the way. He didn't want Victor to be disappointed over a wife who cheated on him, but he believed she'd done just that. He understood how the man was feeling. Tiffany had not only fallen in love with his partner, she'd let her deception go on until their wedding day. The worst kind of trust break ever.

On top of it, having a falling out with a brother and never speaking to him again? Burke couldn't even comprehend that. Not when he would do anything to have his little brother back. If he hadn't been so eager to escape his strict parents, he would've stayed at home and seen his brother's struggles. Seen his drug addiction. Could've prevented it all, and his brother would be alive today.

But Victor didn't seem to have such qualms about being separated from his brother. He was allowing his anger over Vincent's interest in Estelle to let this rift continue even after all these years.

Would he have the same outcome as Burke? A deceased brother and extreme guilt over failing him? Burke wouldn't wish such pain on anyone.

Abby glanced up at him. "Do you think Victor's right about Estelle not having an affair, but was just hoping to profit from selling the real crown?"

Burke drew his thoughts away from his brother and back to the investigation. "I'd like to think he is, but my past experience says it's not likely she wasn't having an affair."

"Personal or professional experience?"

"Both, but mostly on the job," He quickly glossed over the subject he still wasn't ready to share with her. "And I have to believe Detective Orman was on to something when he'd heard the rumors."

"Who do you think was spreading those rumors?"

"Probably people they socialized with. Maybe a woman scorned by the man having an affair with Estelle."

"Or could be hotel staff," she said. "If she met a man there."

"Problem is, it happened too long ago to find out unless we can get Orman to tell us."

"His files might hint at who it is, and we can follow up with them. If not, we can talk to everyone he interviewed."

"Agreed, but I think Estelle's journals are far more promising. I want to dig into those first."

"I could have someone on my team do the interviews."

He shook his head. "I'd want an official deputy to handle them, so it'll have to be Gabe."

"I'm sure he'll be glad to give up his babysitting duties." She laughed.

Burke smiled, but his phone chimed, and he whipped his attention to the screen. "A text from Deputy Mullen. She has boat registration details."

Abby got out her phone and held it out to him. "Hayden's number."

Burke quickly entered Hayden's phone number and fired

off the owner's name. "Not that I'm overly optimistic, but let's hope this gives us something to go on."

"Sometimes the things you least expect to come through are the ones that do."

Her melancholy tone hinted at something else beneath her comment, but she didn't say anything and entered the dining room.

Gabe sat in the same chair, a journal open in front of him. "I thought you two got lost."

She told him about the trunk and the conversation with Victor.

He tapped the journal he was reading with a gloved finger. "So far nothing here mentioning an affair."

Abby moved to the end of the room and took the other books from the evidence bag. "Are these dated?"

He nodded. "I'm reading the oldest one, two years before she disappeared. Nothing of interest, but she does mention Vincent flirted with her. She liked it but said it wouldn't go anywhere."

"It'll be interesting to see if her thoughts changed over time." Burke grabbed disposable gloves from a box on the table. "How many of these books do we have?"

"Eight," Gabe said. "She doesn't make a daily entry. Just enters things that seem important to her. Each book covers roughly a third of a year. It's not consistent though. The last one is May of the year she went missing."

Abby picked through the journals and retrieved the final book. "I've got the last one."

Burke chose a book and took it to a chair. "I'll split the difference. This one's in the middle."

They sat silently, paging through the books. Estelle's handwriting with flourishes on her capital letters was neat and not difficult to read. And very distinct, making it easy to tell if someone else had made an entry, but so far no one else had written in the book.

As Burke read, he soon formed a picture. "She once enjoyed living in Oregon, but was getting frustrated with the lack of culture and arts, and seemed interested in moving back to France."

Abby narrowed her eyes. "Just the opposite of what Victor, Ugo, and Sylvia said."

Burke nodded. "She also says she needs to get the courage to discuss it with Victor. She doubts he would ever agree to move from this home. No mention of the crown, though. Or of an affair, or someone she was even interested in. And no mention of any letters or contact from Vincent."

"That all goes along with what Victor told us," Abby said.

Burke flipped the page and stared at her next entry. Not only was it in capital letters, but it made no sense.

BGYRWPIAAYDYRGAIDACONELCRDMSFNBYROIINLCWREIAUTIDUEFG

"Got something odd here." Burke looked up. "She suddenly starts writing in gibberish. My guess is it's some sort of code."

"No one ever mentioned her being proficient in code writing," Abby said. "But I suppose she could've been."

"I've been known to figure out a puzzle or cipher or two." Gabe held out a hand. "Let me take a look."

Burke slid the journal to him.

Abby stood behind her associate. "How does it make any kind of sense?"

"It's a cipher for sure," Gabe said. "Odds are good she would've used one of the easiest ones out there. Give me a few minutes, and I'll figure it out.

She squeezed his shoulder, then picked up a new journal. "This one starts in September. Estelle doesn't disappear for another year."

"The month she took those pictures with the crown." Burke wished she would've left that one for him to review.

"Exactly why I chose it." Abby went back to her chair and opened her book.

"Not a Caesar or Atbash cipher or even ROT13," Gabe muttered. "And clearly not Pigpen or Morse Code either."

"I assume what you just said is helpful." Burke laughed.

"I'd call these the top five most common ciphers out there," Gabe answered without looking up. "Which narrows it down to one she could've used."

"Good news then," Abby said.

"Paper!" Gabe shouted. "I think I've got it, but I need a pen and paper to be sure."

Tearing out a page from her notepad, Abby took it to him along with her pen.

He grabbed them and scrawled *Rail 1, Rail 2,* and *Rail 3*, one phrase above the other.

Burke had no idea what a rail had to do with codes, but he wouldn't disturb Gabe to find out. Next he began writing the letters from the message, starting with Rail 1, then moving down and plotting the letters next to the different rails.

He entered the last letter and pumped a fist up in the air. "Yes! This is it. A Rail Fence or Zigzag Cipher."

"I don't see a message yet," Abby said as Burke slid his chair down the table to them.

"It's simple if you know what you're looking at," Gabe said. "Follow the letter pattern."

He tapped the letters, alternating between the three rails. He figured out the first word was *big* and the second word *day*. Then, writing in large print across the bottom of the page, he transcribed the note:

Big day. Crown replica ready. Must find buyer for original.

"Replica?" Abby dropped into the chair next to him. "Estelle had a replica made?"

"Could be why she was posing with it." Burke fought to keep his enthusiasm in check. "It wasn't the real thing, and she was proud of it."

"We need to look at those Polaroids again." Abby pushed to her feet. "If she's holding a fake, she could've put the replica in Victor's cabinet back then and disappeared with the real crown years ago."

∽

Abby made quick work of retrieving the old Polaroids from the evidence inventory bin and returned to the dining room to spread them out on the table.

"We can compare these to the picture of the crown Victor gave us." She found the photo on her phone and held it out so Burke and Gabe could see the real one too.

"Try to stop me." Burke circled the table to come stand behind her.

She looked back and forth between all the photos, not seeing any discrepancies. "It's almost like the pictures you see on social media where you have to find the differences. I can do those, but I don't see any variations."

"It might be just me or maybe it's the lighting," Burke said, "but the jewels on the crown Estelle is holding don't reflect the light the same way."

"Maybe." Gabe glanced up. "Like you said, it could be the lighting."

Abby studied the jewel placement on each Polaroid picture. "Does the ruby on the right side look like it's in the same place? It appears further spaced from the emerald to me."

Burke leaned over the table and picked up one of the pictures. "She's holding this one in almost an identical direction as Victor's photo, and I think you're right. It's different."

"Agreed," Gabe said.

Abby leaned back. "So Estelle might've stolen the real crown and our current-day thief has a fake."

Burke frowned. "It wouldn't take long for a jeweler to identify the fake gems and tell the thief the crown was worthless."

Gabe took a seat across the table from them. "If you were the thief, what would you do when you heard that?"

"I'd think Victor tricked me," Burke said. "That he'd hidden the real crown for safekeeping. So I'd come back to search for it."

"Could've actually happened that way," Abby said. "And we need to search the house."

Burke nodded. "I can assign deputies to do that."

"If it really did happen like this, we could use it to identify the thief." Gabe shifted to face Abby. "We could catch him in the act of coming back, but we'd have to stay here twenty-four/seven or install cameras."

"Might work," she said. "Not knowing when the crown was stolen, we have no idea how long our thief might've known it was fake. He could've already come back to check. Or he might not have found out it's not real yet."

"Or we could be wrong about the jewels," Burke said. "He could have the real crown, and he's not coming back at all."

"In any event," Abby said. "Staying here would require so many of our resources when we need to put all of our effort on the investigation, not babysitting this place. So I say we're better off installing cameras."

Burke nodded. "We'll need Victor's permission. Might not be easy to get."

"Actually," Abby said. "He's so down after finding the trunk, I think he might agree."

"It's a long trek to and from the inn to get our equipment," Gabe said. "We could have someone on the team deliver it. Still would take a couple hours."

"No worries," Abby said. "Gage will not only have cameras, but they'll be top-of-the-line."

Gabe rubbed his hands together. "If you need someone to go to his compound, I'm your man. I might get a look at the other gadgets they have to add to our team wish list."

Abby rolled her eyes. The team had zero dollars to buy additional gadgets, but Gabe could always dream.

She glanced at her watch. "There's another ferry scheduled to arrive in half an hour. You could get to the Blackwell compound and back here on the six o'clock ferry."

"Give Gage a call." Gabe jumped up. "I'll go meet the ferry, and you can let me know if I should get on it or not."

"No question he'll say yes," Abby said. "He's one of the most generous men you'll ever meet so you might as well plan on leaving."

"Looks like I'm off babysitting duty." Gabe gave a crooked grin as he slid the journals down the table toward Abby. "Officially handing over the most thrilling assignment on the island. Hope you're up for the challenge."

The deep rumble of his laugh as he exited put a smile on her face.

Even Burke's mouth quirked up on the side. "I'll keep looking at this journal while you make the call."

She nodded and dialed Gage to give him a quick rundown of their needs, mentioning they needed Victor's permission before installing the cameras. Just as she expected, he readily agreed. She counted herself blessed to know him. To know his whole team. On her many visits to Sam over the years, she'd had a chance to interact socially with the entire team, and they'd come to her aid professionally a few times as well.

And, of course, she and her deputies had attended many of their trainings. The LLL team had been wanting to attend them too, but they'd been too busy to fit any classes into their schedule. Maybe being here and needing their help was God urging them to get going on developing additional safety skills.

"We're good to go with Gage." She set her phone on the table. "How many cameras are you thinking we need?"

Burke placed his finger on the journal page and looked at her. "One on the steps down by the dock. One for every entrance to the building, including the one covered in ivy. One for the greenhouse too."

"I think we should also place one in the library facing the crown's hidden cabinet."

"Agreed, and if Blackwell can spare enough cameras, one in the foyer."

The plan was really shaping up. "We need Victor's approval, but we can't leave him here tonight knowing the thief might return."

"Which means not only convincing him to leave but finding a safe place for him to go," Burke said. "Our department doesn't have an actual safe house. No surprise there. I hate to waste valuable time hunting down a place."

She agreed. "He can come with me to the Blackwell compound. If they don't have a cabin for him, he can have mine, and I'll bunk on Sam's couch."

"What about twenty-four-hour protection for him?"

"The compound is one of the most secure facilities I've

stayed in. I'm confident he'll be safe there, but I can arrange for someone to stay with him when I'm not there."

"I could take night duty."

Burke was the last person she wanted in a nearby cabin or even worse, in her cabin. "I think we've got it covered. Let's go talk to Victor."

She scooped up the pictures to maintain the chain of custody.

He reached for the journal he'd been reading. "I'll bookmark the pages we're reviewing and bring all of them with me."

She didn't wait for him to gather the books, but took off, spotting a light on in Victor's office. She found him sitting in an easy chair, staring at the fireplace. When she entered, he looked at her, his expression so forlorn she wanted to offer him a hug. Not a professional thing to do. She felt for him, but she needed to maintain her distance. He'd never been ruled out as a suspect, though she honestly didn't believe he stole his own crown anymore.

He clasped his hands together on his lap. "Don't tell me you have more bad news for me."

She sat in the matching plaid chair next to his and shifted on the faded cushion to face him. "We don't know if it's bad news or not, but Estelle wrote a cipher in her journal, and Gabe cracked it. She mentions having a replica of the crown made."

He gasped. "Impossible."

She waited for him to process the information. "I'm sorry, but it seems likely. We compared the photos from the trunk to the one you showed us of the crown, and we believe she's holding a fake."

He blinked slowly, shock flashing in his eyes. "Do you think she replaced the real crown and disappeared with it?"

"Seems likely."

"I can't believe it. I can't believe she would do such a thing to me." He twisted his hands together, rubbing them over and over as if trying to wash away the pain of betrayal.

"In one of the last journal entries in the year she disappeared, she mentioned being unhappy here and wanting to move back to France, but she was afraid to approach you about it."

"No! I refuse to believe such a thing." He gave a weary shake of his head, eyes clouded with emotion. "She never said anything to me. Not a word. How was I supposed to know? I love this place, but if I'd known she was so unhappy I would've gone to France with her. Anything, not to lose her."

A silent ache grew in her chest as she watched him. "I wish she would've told you."

"If she had, maybe she'd still be with me." He hung his head and began sobbing.

She couldn't ignore his pain anymore. She knelt on the floor and took his hand. "Let's pray."

She didn't give him the option this time, but offered a sincere prayer on his behalf.

He lifted his eyes to her. "I want to believe in prayer. Want to believe it will make things easier, but I just can't. Not after all of this."

She squeezed his hand and leaned back. "I understand. I'll continue to pray for you to find the faith to believe."

Burke stepped into the room, the bag of journals tucked under his arm. "We good to go on the cameras and safe house?"

"Cameras? Safe house?" Victor blinked at Abby. "What's he talking about?"

She didn't want to add to his worries, but she had no choice and explained the situation to him. "We can't let you stay here and risk your life."

"But I..." He clapped a hand over his mouth, then dropped it to his knee and shook his head. "Today's trip to the bank was brutal. I can't leave again so soon."

"We'll be with you and will take precautions on the transport." Abby tried to sound confident, something she didn't feel quite yet, but would once they'd made a game plan.

"I don't know." Victor scratched the back of his neck, eyes darting away.

"I need you to trust me. Trust us." She put force behind her words to get his attention. "We have your best interest at heart."

His stern expression wavered.

"Think of it as an adventure," she said, trying to make it sound exciting. "You'll be staying in a top-of-the-line law enforcement training facility. A tour of the place alone is worth going, and you'll be protected by tight security."

"Such a tour might appeal to you," he said. "It's not my cup of tea."

"Then think about being safe." She plunged ahead. "You won't have to worry about anyone breaking in here while you're here alone."

"I guess I have no option, and I'll have to try." He sighed. "I have sleeping pills I can take with me to knock me out overnight. But you *will* bring me back tomorrow, correct?"

"I would like to say we will, but it'll depend on what happens tonight," she said. "We'd like your permission to install video cameras in the house and on the property to record any events that might occur tonight."

"Cameras." He narrowed his eyes. "What difference does it make if I'm not here? So go ahead. Let's catch this thief. Do we need to leave right away?"

Abby shook her head. "Gabe is headed to the mainland to get the cameras. After he returns, we'll need time to install them. While he's gone, we'll arrange secured transport for you."

"If only you had a helicopter." He let out a long breath through his nose. "It would make me feel a lot better than crossing the bay in your boat again."

Burke stared at Victor, his lips parted in stunned silence. "You're good with riding in a helicopter?"

Victor bobbed his head, firm and assured for once. "I like how it's enclosed, cocooning. And it's above all the danger we faced this morning."

Abby liked the idea too. It was not only safer, but faster. "Is there a helipad on the island?"

"There is. One of the remaining families here maintains it for their comfort, but any homeowner on the island can use it."

Finally, something positive in Abby's day. "Then let me look into securing a helicopter."

Burke flashed her an incredulous look.

She smiled at him. "Follow me if you want to know what I have planned."

They went in search of Sam and found her in the library, kneeling under the display case where the crown had once been stored.

"You must've read my mind." She stood. "I was just going to come find you."

"Did you locate something?" Abby asked.

Sam held out a vial holding a pale greenish-gray item.

Abby squinted at it. "What is it?"

"A lichen someone must've tracked in on their shoe. I can't be certain until I analyze it, but I did a quick internet comparison and it looks like a *Cladonia* species, specifically Cladonia arbuscula."

Abby rolled her eyes. "Well, that clarifies it for me."

"Sorry." Sam laughed. "A lichen partners with a fungus

and a tiny plant-like organism, like algae. They thrive on rocks, tree trunks and branches, and soil."

"Okay, I'll pretend to understand that part. But what does this lichen have to do with our investigation?"

"First of all, this particular lichen isn't common in Oregon, but can be found in the coastal areas, so it likely attached to someone's shoe while walking the property and was brought inside."

"And that's important, why?" Burke asked.

She gave them an all-knowing look. "One thing I didn't mention is it can commonly be found on gravestones."

"Gravestone?" Abby let the idea settle in. "You're thinking about Estelle."

Sam nodded.

Burke tilted his head. "But if she was murdered and buried on this property, it's not likely the killer would've put up a gravestone for her."

"Agreed," Sam said. "But the lichen also frequently grows on wood chips over a grave."

"Then we need to get this analyzed ASAP to find out if it really is what you think it is."

"I couldn't agree more." Eagerness burned in Sam's eyes. "My assistant and I'll be here at least another four hours, and then we'll pack up and catch the ferry. I can start analyzing it the minute I get to my lab."

"Speaking of leaving..." Abby explained about needing the helicopter for Victor. "Do you think Gage would be agreeable to such a big ask?"

"Of course he would, as long as the helo isn't in use and Riley or Coop are available to fly it."

"Perfect," Abby said. "Let me know what Gage says. Then after we get cameras installed, I'll have Gabe stay here until you're ready to go, in case you need anything."

"I'd appreciate that." Sam got out her phone. "Let me call Gage to arrange your flight."

Abby squeezed her friend's arm in thanks.

A quick call to Gage, and hopefully they'd soon have Victor in the air, safely winging his way to Blackwell Tactical's secured compound and out of danger.

17

Abby settled back as their pilot, Cooper Ashcroft—Coop—flew her, Burke, and Victor over the ocean toward the compound. Long bench seats ran on each side of the chopper in the opposite direction of most commercial aircraft seats. Coop said they'd customized the helicopter to fit as much equipment and as many team members inside as they could.

Victor and Burke sat across the aisle from her, and everyone wore headsets so they could communicate over the loud rotor thumps. The moment they'd taken off, Victor had swiveled toward the window, his face nearly pressed against the acrylic pane. He'd been wound tight, searching through the setting sun around them as they made their way to the helicopter, and while waiting for Coop to explain safety rules. His unease ended the moment Coop had them winging away from the island.

Victor let out a deep sigh, and his shoulders dropped. This was the most relaxed she'd ever seen him.

Burke, on the other hand, tapped his foot rapidly and had fidgeted since they'd taken off. He didn't mention being uncomfortable in a helicopter, but with his need to control, he was no doubt displeased with having no control over their mode of transport. Or maybe he was second-guessing his demand to stay at the compound tonight. She'd tried to talk him out of it, but even though he said he trusted her and the Blackwell team to keep Victor safe, he wanted to be on site just in case.

She didn't like his decision, especially when she learned Gage didn't have an extra cabin. Not when he'd already assigned one to her and one to Gabe. The option was for her, Victor, and Burke to bunk in one cabin or she could share a cabin with Gabe or sleep on Sam's sofa. Out of every decision she'd made since starting this investigation, this one was the easiest. Even more so since Gabe snored like a wild animal. Sofa it was for her.

As much as seeing Victor relaxed was wonderful, this would be the perfect time to ask him questions they hadn't asked. She got out her phone and scrolled to the picture of Estelle's locket. "Victor, could you look at this picture a minute and tell me if you recognize it?"

He turned, the peace evaporating from his expression. She held out the phone.

He took a quick look and gasped. "Why do you have that picture? It's Estelle's locket. Did you find something out about her disappearance?"

"No." She pocketed her phone.

He sighed, his breath seeming to go on and on. "Then why show me the picture?"

"We found the locket half buried in the greenhouse on your property," Burke said.

Victor shifted his eyes to Burke. "Why was it there? Why were you there?"

"The night we arrived at your property, my deputies saw

a light in the greenhouse. Abby and I went to evaluate it. No light and no one in the greenhouse, but we did locate a fresh footprint and the locket."

Victor shook his head. "Why on earth would it have been buried there? I gave Estelle the necklace on our wedding night, and I don't believe a day went by when she didn't wear it. Sure, when we went to formal events, she would change it out for any one of her many jewels, and she took it off to sleep, but otherwise it was around her neck.

"Do you think…" He paused and glanced between Abby and Burke. "Do you think this means someone attacked her in the greenhouse and left her locket behind?"

"We don't have any theories yet." Burke's tone was gentle. "Who used the greenhouse when Estelle was alive?"

"She did. She loved gardening, and it was her happiest place. With the help of the gardener she'd hired, she grew flowers and vegetables. After she disappeared, Sylvia continued to grow vegetables for our cook while Juan took care of the landscaping."

"And then?" Abby asked. "How did it fall to ruins and the landscaping become overgrown?"

Pain lanced Victor's eyes. "Back then, I couldn't deal with it—or anything for that matter. Sylvia took over Estelle's duties, but after a couple of years said she no longer had time to garden and keep the house unless she worked more hours. Her family needed her, and she didn't want to put in the hours she'd been working. She was just doing it for me. So we compromised. She would quit raising vegetables and buy them instead from our local farmers' market when she shopped for her own home. The greenhouse hasn't been used since then."

"And the landscaping?" Abby asked even though they'd gotten Ugo's version of what had transpired. "What happened there?"

"I got tired of someone else living on the property. Especially Juan. I think he blamed me for not doing enough to find Estelle. Plus, the guy was half in love with her. So one day he made some unreasonable demand or other, and I got angry and fired him. Simple as that."

Ugo had told them Victor didn't want anyone else living on the property, but hadn't even suggested Juan might have feelings for Estelle.

Abby didn't know what to make of that, but would be on the lookout for any connection to the theft. "I hate to ask you this, but let's assume finding the locket means someone hurt Estelle. Do you have any idea who that might've been?"

Victor fixed his sorrowful gaze on Abby. "I can't think of anyone. Everyone loved her."

"It would be rare for *everyone* to love someone," Burke said.

Victor whipped his head toward Burke. "You didn't know my Estelle. She was an amazing woman. Kind to everyone she met. Sympathetic to those in need. And willing to help them in any way she could."

Abby still doubted there wasn't at least one person who didn't like Estelle, but it was clear Victor wouldn't be the one to provide the needed information. Time to try a different approach. "What if someone loved her too much? Someone like Vincent. Maybe, when he learned he couldn't have her, he didn't want anyone else to."

Victor's eyes widened. "Maybe. Yes, could be. It would explain why he disappeared not long after Estelle went missing."

Burke's gaze intensified. "He disappeared, too, or you just didn't hear from him after he left here?"

"I guess I misspoke. As far as I'm concerned, he disappeared because after the private investigator tried to contact him and failed, I tried calling him at our family residence.

He's probably still living there, but the phone number was disconnected. My father left the French estate to Vincent and the estate here to me."

Abby nodded, but made a mental note to have Hayden follow up on Valentino's will.

"Sylvia told us something interesting. She claimed your father said the combination had been shared often."

"What?" Victor scrunched his eyes together. "That's not what he told me. So I guess she could've been the one to put those journals in there."

He seemed to be telling the truth, and hopefully the fingerprints from Sam would confirm it. Until then, Abby needed to ask one more question. "What about guns? Do you own guns?"

"No," he answered. "I mean, not really. At least not any I'd ever touch. I have no need to. But my father left a display case of antique ones locked up in my bedroom. I haven't looked at them since the day he showed them to me."

"Are you the only one with a key to the cabinet?"

"As far as I know." His eyes narrowed. "Since my father told a different story about the safe to Sylvia, maybe he gave cabinet keys to someone else too."

"Will you give us the key and allow our forensic expert to process them?" Abby asked.

"Sure. No reason she shouldn't look at them." He pulled a ring of keys from his pocket and removed one for her.

"Just an FYI." Coop's deep voice boomed through their headset. "We'll be beginning our descent to the compound soon. If you look to the right of the aircraft, you'll see the lights in the thick stand of trees. Any questions before we land?"

"I'm good, and thanks for such a smooth flight," Abby said.

The others didn't speak.

"Since there aren't any questions, I'm Cooper Ashcroft, your pilot for the evening and at your service. I hope you've had a pleasant flight and will fly with us again, but for now sit back, relax, and enjoy the remainder of your flight." His deep laugh rumbled through the headsets.

Abby laughed along with him, even more so, because much like Burke, Coop was often extremely serious. He'd mellowed a lot since he'd married Kierra, and they'd had three children.

Abby glanced at Burke. Would he chill out too if he got married and had kids? The smiling faces of a little boy and girl popped into her mind. The boy, a spitting image of Burke, and the girl looking like her. She quickly shook her head to erase the picture from her mind and looked out the window.

Stars sparkled in the distance as the lights from the compound lifted up to welcome her. The site was breathtaking at night. She'd only ever arrived at the compound via ground transport, and breathtaking was the last word she would have used to describe the secured entrance. More like alarming.

The helicopter slowed and began a gradual descent, soon engulfed in a layer of clouds.

"It's quite the sight, isn't it?" Victor glanced over his shoulder at her. "At least until we got stuck in the clouds, but it's even impressive."

"It's interesting you feel so at home in a helicopter," she said.

"I know it seems odd because I'm not the pilot and in control, but for some reason when I'm in a helicopter, I feel like I have control over my life."

Burke mumbled something she couldn't make out. She glanced at him, giving him a questioning look.

"It's nothing," he said, his tone warning her not to ask any additional details.

"It's clear you don't agree, Detective," Victor said. "Like I said, it doesn't make much sense. But it's like being in a dream for me. It has the same floaty, ethereal feeling. We're insulated inside a small, comforting space, and it seems like I could direct the pilot to go almost anywhere. No restrictions."

She nodded, but she wasn't quite sure if she understood what he was going for. Considering Burke's skeptical look, he had no clue.

The helicopter made a sharp descent, and Victor swung his focus back to the window.

Burke continued bobbing his knee, but he tipped his head at Victor, then gave her a pointed look. Maybe he was thinking about Victor's answers to their questions. Instead of finding closure, his answers had given them more questions to ponder. But then, that's how investigations worked.

She prayed that the new set of questions would indeed give them answers before someone tried to make another attempt on Victor's life.

∽

The helo settled on the ground with a bump. Burke took off his headphones and released his seatbelt. He didn't know what to expect in the compound. He hadn't taken any classes with Blackwell Tactical, but a couple deputies in his department had, and they'd come back almost glowing from the visit. He'd wondered if their descriptions had been over the top in an effort to make their fellow deputies jealous. He was finally going to find out.

The door slid open, and Coop waited outside as refreshingly cool air rushed in.

Burke waited for Abby to unbuckle and move to the door. Coop offered his hand. She took it without hesitating.

What? Any time Burke offered his help, she'd rejected it. He didn't know what to make of that, but he didn't have time to ponder it. He wanted to get outside ahead of Victor so he could help him down.

Victor got up slowly and limped his way to the door. He hooked the end of the cane over his arm, then let Burke and Coop take his elbows to heft him safely to the ground.

Victor looked around, his gaze searching. "You're sure this place is safe?"

"It's too dark to make out the fence." Coop pointed toward the perimeter. "But it's there, along with an exceptional alarm system. Trust me, if anyone tries to enter, we'll be alerted. You can be sure our team will immediately intercept the intruder."

"Sounds perfect." Victor gave a nervous smile.

"I'll get your bags." Coop jerked a thumb over his shoulder. "But Gage should be here any minute to take you to the cabins."

As if he'd summoned Gage to the location, an all-terrain vehicle pulled up to the helipad, The man Burke assumed to be Gage jumped out from behind the wheel. He was tall, buff, and had super dark hair. Burke put the guy in his early forties. Burke knew everyone on the Blackwell team had served in the military, but had been discharged due to injuries. He wasn't familiar with Gage's injury, but he didn't move with any obvious residual effects from it.

"Welcome," he said as he approached and held out his hand. "I'm Gage Blackwell. I hope you enjoy your stay with us."

Victor eyed him. "Will you keep me safe?"

"You have my word on that." The self-assurance in Gage's tone gave Burke confidence in his abilities.

They made the introductions.

"I can give you a ride to the cabin," Gage said. "Or maybe you want to stretch out and walk after your flight."

Abby turned to Victor. "It's up to you."

"A walk might be good. It will give me a chance to look around."

"Then a walk, it is."

"Don't stray off the road," Gage warned. "Coop and I'll deliver your luggage to your cabin."

Burke and Abby flanked Victor as they set off down the paved road. In the glowing light of a street lamp, they caught sight of a small town made of cutout storefronts.

"What is that?" Victor pointed at it. "Looks like a Hollywood movie set of a city street."

"You're almost right," Abby said. "False fronted buildings were created to mimic an urban street for close combat and tactical training for law enforcement officers."

His eyes lit up, and his pace increased. "I've got to see this."

They reached the tree-lined street holding a bank, post office, grocery, and various retail stores. Everything was top-notch. The realism of all the details left Burke believing he was on an urban street. Looked like the deputies who returned from training here weren't exaggerating.

Victor turned in a circle. "This is amazing. It feels so real. Reminds me of Disneyland's top quality."

Abby nodded. "Gage doesn't do things halfway. It's only the best for him and his team. Which also includes the compound security. No one is going to hurt you here, so you can relax."

A broad smile crossed his face. "I honestly believe you now. Thank you for arranging such a sanctuary for me."

"Of course."

They continued down the street, Burke taking everything in. Just ahead stood a large, steel, barn-like building about the size of a basketball court.

"This is their training facility and the team's armory," Abby told him. "Since you're staying the night, you might want to ask Gage or Coop for a tour of their armory. I've never seen anything better."

"I'll ask." Burke wasn't really into weapons, but as a professional in law enforcement he needed to carry one and be prepared to use it. It could mean his handgun or a long gun. Plus, as a detective he needed to stay up to date with what was on the street, and he'd be interested in seeing the variety of weapons they chose to buy.

"Sam's lab is also at the back of this building," Abby said.

Burke looked to the left where six small log cabins were lined up in a row along the road. They were identical rectangular boxes, but further down he spotted six additional cabins, each one a different design.

"The first cabins are used by trainees and where you'll be staying," Abby said. "Further down you'll see the founding team members' cabins they designed and built. Everyone but Sam has moved out for more space for their expanding families, and the cabins are occupied by new team members."

Victor stopped, staring ahead. "Looks like they got pretty creative in their designs."

"They did," Abby said. "The buildings fit the team member's personality. If you know them, it's easy to determine which person designed which one."

Once again, Burke was impressed. Not by the quality of the build, he couldn't see the cabins well enough to determine that, but by the way Gage had included his original team members in his organization. Burke kept seeing hints of a strong leader and could understand why this team was so successful.

"You're in cabin three." Abby led the way and opened the door to a small, rustic log-lined box.

"Oh my," Victor said. "I know you said cabin, but this is really primitive. I don't know if I can stay here."

"It has everything you need," Abby said. "There are two beds in the bedroom, and the bathroom is newer and well-maintained. There are snacks in the cupboard. No food for meals, but then I don't think you'll be here long enough to need to cook."

Victor's forehead knotted. "I guess that's good, because I don't have the faintest idea how to."

"You can't count on me either," Burke said. "Toast, coffee, and sandwiches are about the extent of my kitchen skills."

"Perfect! I make a mean bowl of cereal, so between the three of us, we have Michelin-star potential." Abby laughed freely, more relaxed than he'd ever seen her.

His heart gave a kick. He jerked his gaze away.

"I'll just pack up my things," she said, "and head to Sam's place. I'll see you both for dinner tonight."

"About that." Victor cast her an uncertain look. "I appreciate her husband offering to cook for all of us, but I'm way too tired to socialize."

"You have to eat," Abby said.

"Would it be possible just to get a sandwich?"

"My specialty." Burke chuckled. "I'd be glad to make one if Sam has the fixings at her place."

"I'm sure she does, and I can handle it." Abby's good mood disappeared, why, he didn't know. "Let me get my bags, and I'll be back with the sandwich."

Burke watched her stride toward the bedroom, catching something in her expression she probably didn't mean to show—something uneasy, maybe even vulnerable. She didn't fully trust him yet. Her expression made it obvious. Maybe trust anyone. Still, he was sure she believed he'd do the right thing, even if she wasn't totally sure she could rely on him for everything.

He'd take anything he could get from her right now—it was a start anyway. A start of something he shouldn't even want to pursue.

18

Sam's daughter, Ellie, and her son, Hudson, raced to Abby at the door. Ellie flung her arms around Abby's legs. Abby had visited Sam enough for Ellie to get to know her, but not true for Hudson. He screeched to a stop and hung back, his thumb popped in his mouth.

"C'mon, Aunt Abby." Ellie, a precocious, blond-haired five-year-old and spitting image of her mother, grabbed her hand and dragged her into the house. "I wanna show you the castle I built with my MAGNA-TILES."

Hudson jerked out his thumb, creating a sucking noise. "I helped."

The two-year-old was Griff's Mini-Me with startling sapphire eyes and dishwater blond hair, and he puffed out his chest with pride.

"Not much," Ellie said.

"Now, sweetheart." Griff gazed at his daughter, pure love in his eyes. "Remember that your brother is three years younger than you and doesn't have the same skills you have, so be kind to him."

"If I haveta." Ellie pouted and continued dragging Abby across the room to a pastel colored castle.

Abby dropped to the floor. "You did a beautiful job, sweetie."

"I know," she said. "I've been tested, and I'm advanced."

"We really have to work on self-worth." Griff laughed.

A knock sounded on the door, and he strode across the room to answer it. Abby heard Gabe introduce himself before stepping into the room.

"You're here already." Abby tried to stand, but Ellie took hold of her hand and held her in place. "Sorry, sweetie. I've got to make a sandwich for a guest I brought along and get my friend settled in his cabin. Then I can come back and play."

She peered up at Gabe. "Is he your boyfriend?"

Abby chuckled. "We just work together."

"Too bad." Ellie let go of Abby's hand and wrinkled her cute little pug nose. "He's pretty."

Griff snorted. "Out of the mouth of babes."

"What does that mean, Daddy?" Ellie asked.

"I'll explain it to you later."

"I've never been called pretty before, but I'll take it." Gabe laughed heartily.

Abby shook her head. "Where's Sam?"

"She went straight to her lab to test the lichen."

"Then I need to get over there." Abby turned to Griff. "Victor appreciates your invitation for dinner, but he's pretty tired and wants to stay back at his cabin. I promised I'd bring him a sandwich. Could I impose on your hospitality even more and ask you to make one, then take it to him?"

"Sure," Griff readily agreed. "If your buddy here can watch the kids while I deliver it."

"Watch the kids!" A look of sheer terror widened Gabe's eyes. She'd never seen him express fear before. Not in the many dangerous situations they'd found themselves in, and here he was afraid of two little children. "No. No. Not a good idea. For any of us. I assure you. You don't want me to be in charge of children."

Griff laughed. "No experience with kids, huh? Then maybe you can deliver the sandwich."

"Take a short hike, sandwich in hand. Knock on the door. Hand it over. Yeah. I can handle that mission for sure. If I can resist the sandwich." Gabe's panic receded, and he grinned.

She didn't let him relax for one second before asking another favor. "Burke will want to meet with Sam too. Can you babysit Victor while we're gone?"

"Yeah, an octogenarian who doesn't move at the speed of light like little kids is in my wheelhouse too."

"Then I'm off." Abby opened the door.

"Tell Sam not to be late for dinner," Griff called after her. "When she gets in her lab, she doesn't want to leave."

Abby nodded and quickly exited before Ellie could try to stop her. She paused outside to text Burke about meeting her at Sam's lab after Gabe got to his cabin, then she set off.

"Hold up," Gabe yelled, catching up to her. "I thought you might want to know. I had quite the conversation with the ferry captain on our way back to the mainland tonight. I asked if he knew of anyone out of the ordinary recently visiting Lemoine."

"And did he?"

"Yep. He said over the years he got to know Lemoine's regular visitors. He thought we should know about one woman, though she's a regular visitor. She's a local botanist. He said something seemed off about her."

"Botanist?" Where could this be going?

"The captain said her name is Dr. Melanie Shore. He got the feeling she initially came to answer questions Victor had about the island, but then they became friends."

Could she have something to do with the lichen found

in the library? "Did he mention how long she'd been coming and when she last visited?"

"He wasn't certain when she last visited, but he said she's been a regular since he'd taken over as captain. That's twenty-five years. The captain before him said she was already a regular. It seems odd to me that no one we questioned has mentioned her. I think she's worth looking into. Maybe she knows something more about the lichen Sam found."

"I'll mention it to Burke to see how he wants to proceed."

Gabe let out a long breath. "Now, back to my babysitting duty, right after I fulfill my role as a DoorDash delivery guy."

"I'll try to find something more interesting for you to do, I promise."

He shrugged. "It is what it is."

As he walked back to the cabin, she hurried to the training facility and skirted around the building to the back. The lab started out as a tiny room in this building, but quickly outgrew the space. Gage built an addition not only to provide a bigger lab but an exterior entrance too.

Abby pulled the thick metal door open, revealing expensive equipment on stainless steel shelves ringing the room. Tall, stainless steel tables stood in a row in the middle. Wearing a white lab coat, Sam sat on a barstool at the nearest one while she looked into a microscope.

When the door closed behind Abby, Sam jerked her head up. "Abby. Thank goodness. You scared me."

"Sorry, I should've told you I was coming or knocked on the door." She joined Sam. "Burke is coming too."

"Good," Sam said. "Because I can't share anything without his presence."

"So you *did* find something."

Sam nodded.

Abby's interest piqued, she shoved her hands into her

pants pocket to try to control her building excitement. "Two interesting things I should mention before we get started."

She retrieved the key to the gun cabinet from her pocket and handed it to Sam, asking her to process it. "Also, the ferry captain told Gabe a local botanist has regularly visited Victor for over twenty-five years. The captain thought her first visit was for business reasons, but then they became friends."

"That *is* interesting." Sam's eyes narrowed as she pocketed the key. "Maybe she was discussing the lichen with him."

"If it's the one found by graves, do you think she has something to do with Estelle's disappearance?"

Sam shrugged and opened her mouth to speak, but a knock sounded on the door.

"Must be Burke." Abby crossed the room to answer.

Burke, his jaw tight, stood darkly handsome in the shadows. "I wish you would've waited for me for the results."

"Don't worry," Abby said. "Sam's a professional all the way, and she wouldn't tell me what she found without you being here."

"Doesn't mean you wouldn't have let her give you the information if she was willing, right?"

Really? He was going there? "Well sure, but it's not like I'm trying to hide anything from you. I did text you and ask you to come over here, so you would've heard it a few minutes later."

He cocked his head and studied her with an intensity he'd never trained on her. "True, but what happens in the future if I'm not by your side?"

The same distrust he'd previously expressed came back to his eyes. Man, she thought she'd made progress with him on the trust issue, but clearly she hadn't.

Did it really matter? She wasn't sure she trusted him either.

Two people falling for each other, and yet not trusting each other. Made them quite the pair. It also made this investigation harder.

But if she tried to alleviate his distress, things could go better for them. "Would it help if I promised never to ask Sam for information without you present?"

His shoulders visibly relaxed. "Yes, and if you forget, I'll try my best to give you the benefit of the doubt."

Good. He was willing to try to change, and that's all she could ask at this point. "Then you have my word. Now let's get to Sam's findings."

Burke moved past her and crossed the small room to Sam. "Thank you for honoring our contract."

"Of course," she said. "I wouldn't violate it no matter who asked for information." She bit her lip. "Well, I might consider it if someone's life was in immediate danger and I had information that could save them."

"I would understand sharing it then and wouldn't have a problem."

"So what did you find?" Abby asked, anxious to hear the information.

Sam crossed her long legs. "I've confirmed the lichen is Cladonia arbuscula."

"The one found near graves," Burke stated, his tone low and somber.

Sam folded her gloved hands in her lap. "I know discovering the locket made you question if Estelle is buried on the property. This lichen could mean there's a clandestine grave there. Maybe Estelle's. Seems like the next step is to find someone skilled in finding such graves."

"Say we do find a grave," Burke said. "We have to

connect the lichen to our suspect to prosecute them. Can you figure out who tracked it into the house?"

Sam's eyes narrowed. "Yes, but only if I have your suspect's footwear and it still contains traces of the lichen."

"Aren't we missing the obvious here?" Abby glanced between the two of them. "Just because someone picked up the lichen, doesn't mean they had anything to do with killing and burying a body. For that matter, they could've picked it up anywhere, couldn't they?"

Sam leaned back on her stool. "It's possible they tracked it in from another property, but it's highly unlikely. With this lichen being so unusual in this area, I doubt we would find it on another property around here."

"Also," Burke added, "if we find the grave with the lichen on the surface, without footwear supporting our theory, it could just be coincidental."

"Agreed," Sam said. "But before wasting too much time discussing this, we can either search for the lichen in the morning, or we can get someone to the property to do a professional search."

Abby connected gazes with Sam. "Nolan told us he would call Dr. Kelsey Dunbar at the Veritas Center to see if she might be available if we need her. She's their forensic anthropologist. Do you know her?"

Sam nodded. "She's the best."

"Let me see what he learned." She dug out her phone and tapped his icon. When he answered, she put him on speaker and explained their thoughts about the lichen. "Did you talk to Dr. Dunbar?"

"I did," he said. "I just have to let Kelsey know if we need her, and we'd become a top priority in her schedule."

"Then let's get her out to the property as soon as possible. The first ferry tomorrow arrives at six."

"No need to depend on the ferry," Burke said. "I can bring her over in my friend's boat."

"Good. I'll let you know when to expect her." Nolan ended the call.

Excitement burning in her gut, Abby looked at Sam. "I'd hate to put Victor through watching Kelsey search his property for a body, especially not his wife's. I would like to leave him here."

Sam covered her heart with her hand. "That would be cruel. He can stay here. No problem."

"But we do need to tell him what's going on," Burke said. "And get written permission to search his property. You seem to have the best connection with him, Abby. Can you talk to him? I'll be there for support."

"Of course." She didn't want to be the one to break the news that his wife might be buried on his property, but delivering bad news had always been part of her job as a sheriff. Meant she had plenty of experience, and maybe she could help him move closer to believing in God.

"Victor doesn't need protection here," Burke said. "Still, I'd like to leave Gabe here with him. Never know when Victor might freak out and demand to leave."

Not an idea Abby much liked. "I'm sure Gabe would agree, but I've basically only given him grunt jobs. Let's let him finish reviewing the journals, then he can interview the people Detective Orman talked to. I can call Nolan back and ask him to send someone else from our team."

"Hold up," Sam said. "Why make them drive all this way? I'm sure Gage would assign someone to stay with Victor."

Abby liked the idea, but... "We've already asked so much of you guys."

"You know we're happy to help in any way we can. Helping others is our calling."

Abby smiled at her. "If you put it that way, then sure, and we really appreciate all of you. Gage needs to know Victor is temperamental, and it would be good to have someone with plenty of patience staying with him."

Burke grimaced. "She says as I'm about to spend the rest of the night with the man in a tiny cabin."

Sam chuckled. Abby wanted to join in, but Burke just highlighted another personality trait. Impatience. Something else he had in common with her family. Control their surroundings and people to help them achieve their goal, and along the way, if the person didn't fall into place, lose patience.

She couldn't think about that now. She had to prepare herself for breaking the bad news to Victor.

Burke smiled at Sam. "I guess we'll see you at dinner unless you keep working and discover something else before then."

"I'll take another look at the oil sample. I already took a quick look at it on my other microscope. Dust and debris has settled into the sample, suggesting it's been there for some time. I can further analyze the layering of particles, which might offer a rough timeline."

Burke's expression didn't change much, but the respect in his eyes said enough. "I'm way beyond impressed with what you can do."

"Actually, this is nothing. Next, I'll use gas chromatography-mass spectrometry to analyze chemical degradation." She paused and looked at them. "Your blank expressions say this means nothing to you, but trust me. It's specialized equipment, so not *every* forensic tech uses it, but it's the gold standard in forensic trace evidence analysis."

"Then I'm thankful we have you on our side." Burke smiled.

He might be tough and impatient, but he readily praised

solid work, which Abby's family didn't do. A characteristic in his favor, but did it outweigh the negative ones?

"Thanks again, Sam." Abby turned toward the door. "No time like the present to talk to Victor."

Burke caught up to her. "One of the pleasant parts of our job I'm sure you don't miss."

She didn't stop walking, but continued toward the cabin. "I don't, but in my current line of work, I always face the possibility of informing families their loved ones are deceased."

"Has it happened often?"

She shook her head. "Thankfully, no. We've had good success so far, but we know every rescue can't turn out positively."

"I've got a lot of respect for what you do. Looks like you've got a solid crew—tight-knit, good chemistry."

"We do. Makes facing challenges easier." She reached the cabin and knocked on the door, then pushed it open.

He sat in an easy chair, a book in his lap, an empty plate on a nearby table. He shot a quick look in their direction and released a deep breath. "It's just you. Good."

"Relax. You don't have to worry about any danger here." She took a seat on the chair next to him.

"Then why send him to babysit me?" He jerked his thumb at Gabe, sitting at the dining table, lost in his phone.

Victor was right. She'd be wound up in his position too, but she wouldn't explain their reasons when they had something far more difficult to talk about.

He glanced at Burke and then back at her. "With the somber looks on your faces, you must be here to give me bad news."

"We are." She shared the information about the lichen. She'd caught Gabe's attention, but she had to focus on Victor.

Victor sat forward, the book on his lap sliding to the floor. "And you're just telling me this now?"

"We wanted to see if it was important to the investigation before upsetting you."

He clutched his hands together on his lap. "The thing you're not saying is you think Estelle is buried near this lichen."

"It's a possibility we have to explore," she said. "We'll need your permission to search your entire property."

He scratched his unkempt facial hair, but didn't answer. She fell silent, waiting for his response.

"Seems like I don't have any choice." The defeat in his tone broke Abby's heart. "Where do I sign?"

"I'll get the necessary forms together for you in the next few minutes," Burke said.

Victor shook his head. "I thought this day might come, but it will be hard to watch the search for Estelle."

"About that," Abby said, dreading sharing the next thing she had to tell him. "We can't have a civilian present during the search, so you have to stay here for the day. But that's good news. You'll be safe and not have to worry."

"Not worry? Of course, I'll worry." He messed up his hair, then clutched it as if wanting to pull it out. "The only way I'll agree to remain here is if you call me immediately when you have information."

Delivering negative information by phone wouldn't be Abby's first choice, but if she had to do it to keep him here, she would. "I'd rather wait until I see you."

"Because you think you'll find Estelle." His eyes glistened with unshed tears. "But, okay. As long as you come to see me as soon as you can."

"I promise." She took his hand. "God can be by your side through all of this, Victor. You just have to ask Him."

"I don't know." He shifted in his chair. "Maybe I can try it."

She seized the opportunity to help bring God's peace to his life. "Let's do it together."

She offered a heartfelt prayer. Surprisingly he offered a halting one of his own. It wasn't pretty. Not eloquent. But it was music to Abby's ears.

She squeezed his hand. "Just keep praying. I promise it'll help."

"Couldn't hurt, I guess." A faint smile appeared on his face. "Thanks for showing me how important it might be."

She smiled back at him and stood. "We'll arrange for someone to stay with you tomorrow to ease your security worries."

Gabe cocked his head in question. She shook hers, letting him know he was off the hook from another unexciting day of babysitting.

He slashed a hand in front of his neck and smiled.

Burke gave Victor what she knew was one of his rare comforting smiles. "We want to make this process as easy for you as we can."

"I thank you for that." Victor relaxed back in his chair.

Abby's heart, already warm from Victor's attempt to return to God, heated even more over the kindness Burke had just shown. Another positive characteristic in Burke's favor. He could empathize with people in difficult situations and didn't seem afraid to show his compassion.

Confusing. Which guy was he really? The one who reminded her of her family, or the one who'd just comforted a stranger in need?

Did it even matter? She wouldn't give in to her feelings, especially not when they could possibly find Estelle's body tomorrow, changing everything.

Abby would once again find herself working with Burke

on a stressful murder investigation. Such an investigation would take over everything else in her life right now, leaving her feelings for Burke on the back burner.

～

Enough. No more tossing and turning for Burke. He gave up on trying to turn off his brain to sleep. He hadn't been counting sheep because his thoughts were filled with the investigation. No. It was Abby of course. She occupied every inch of his mind, coupled with visions of a future with her. Like tonight. Sitting across from her in a casual dinner setting, relaxed and animated. A side of her he'd never seen before, and he liked it. Every bit of it.

"Argh." He pushed out of the twin bed, making sure he didn't wake the snoring Victor.

He stepped into his boots and grabbed a jacket, then moved outside. His breath puffed white in the cold, and he tugged Griff's loaner jacket tighter around his body. Griff had offered casual clothing, but Burke opted to stay in his suit. He thankfully accepted the loan of the jacket though.

No destination in mind, he strolled toward the fake small town. Looking up, he stopped to stare at the millions of stars glistening above, and the moon, bright and full, beaming down on him.

If he didn't believe in God, the beautiful creation before him would certainly make him question. But he'd believed in God—had for as long as he could remember and still did —learning to live for Him from his family.

But living for Him now? Not so much. Now he felt the need to blame someone for Tiffany's betrayal, and God was convenient. Always there. Always the same. Always reliable. He never changed. Only Burke had changed.

"So what do you plan to do to fix that?" He continued to

stare at God's mighty display overhead as if he could find his answers in the stars.

"Couldn't sleep either?" Abby's voice came from behind. She was wrapped up in a fuzzy-lined coat, her face red from the cold, but looking toasty warm. "My mind's been racing all night, and I couldn't get it to quiet down."

"Same."

"Is it the investigation?"

He didn't want to tell her the truth, but he wasn't a liar. "No. Something about you is."

"Me?" She blinked. "What about me?"

"I think you know. All those sidelong glances, and that not-so-hidden attraction."

Her smile wobbled a little, awkward. "So it's that obvious, huh?"

He nodded.

She released a quiet breath. "I'm surprised Sam didn't say anything. She usually doesn't miss that kind of stuff."

"Oh, she noticed. She was watching us during dinner. She just didn't comment."

Abby shook her head and wandered over to the bench outside the fake Starbucks. She sat, and he took it as a quiet invitation to join her. They needed to talk. Maybe he was reading everything wrong, but even so, it was time to stop dodging whatever this was between them and talk it through.

He shifted on the cold metal to face her. "You're not loving this situation any more than I am."

"It's not the feelings I don't like. I do like them. Maybe too much. I'm just..." She paused. "I'm not ready for a relationship."

He shouldn't care. He wasn't ready either, but her answer still knifed him in the chest. "You said something about being too busy with work."

She nodded. "I dated before I became sheriff. Not much time then, and even less now. But honestly, that's not the real reason."

Say what? "And the real reason is?"

"Did I tell you my mom passed away recently?" She rubbed her palms over her jeans. "I'm not close with my family. They're all high-powered defense attorneys—super polished, super judgmental. When I didn't follow in their footsteps, they didn't get it. Didn't respect it. The pressure to 'fix' my career path never let up."

"Sounds exhausting."

"It was. Still is. Eventually we stopped talking altogether. They didn't invite me to family events anymore. I stopped fighting it and just let the distance grow. I figured I had time to fix things later. But then my mom died. Just like that. No warning. No chance to make things right."

He didn't know what to say, but he did know he had to resist the urge to reach for her hand. "I'm sorry, Abby."

Her eyes shimmered in the moonlight. "Yeah. How do you deal with never getting to say what mattered most to someone you love? I thought my faith would get me through it, but it hasn't. Not yet."

"I'd like to help," he said quietly. "But I'm not exactly in a good place with God right now."

"That's okay. I'll pray for you anyway. Want me to do anything else?"

He shook his head. "I'd say I'll pray for you too, but honestly, I don't feel like I can."

"It's alright. I've got to work through this by myself anyway."

He nodded, but the words didn't sit right with him. They were both trying to carry the pressure alone when maybe they needed to lean on something bigger—God—and maybe each other.

"There's another reason I've hesitated," she said. "You."

"Me?"

She looked at him with all sincerity. "I've been struggling with who you are. One minute you're controlling like my family. The next minute you show me a side in direct opposition to my family." She caught her breath and let it go. "Which one are you, Burke?"

Now it made sense—all the mixed signals, the guarded looks. "I don't want to be controlling. I really don't. It's just—my fiancée, Tiffany, cheated on me with my partner, then left me at the altar. Trusting anyone has been hard since then. Staying in control feels safer."

"But control doesn't protect you. I know. My family tried to control everything. They lost me in the process." She paused, searching his face. "If you keep going that way, who are you going to lose?"

"You." He swallowed. "And I don't want that. Don't want to lose the possibility of us. You can tell I care for you, right?"

She didn't answer right away, but kept her eyes pinned to him. "Most of the time. At least in the way you look at me, the way you react when I'm close. In all the ways that count. I feel the same way too."

He reached up, fingers threading gently through her hair. "I'm going to kiss you unless you tell me not to."

She glanced around, eyes wide and vulnerable, like a cornered animal. He didn't like the idea of pushing her. Not one bit. She needed space to choose.

He removed his hand. "You can walk away right now, or you can let me kiss you."

She stared at him. "I can't say no. I have to know. I need to feel it. To see what this is."

She pulled his hand back into her hair, then her arms wrapped around his neck, tugging him close.

He wasn't sure who moved first, but suddenly their lips met. The world melted away. The kiss wasn't just heat and chemistry. It was everything. Emotion. Longing. Hope.

Something real.

He didn't care about the investigation. Didn't care about Tiffany. For once, all he wanted was this.

This kiss.

This woman.

A future.

He didn't know how he could make it happen, but he had to find a way.

19

Under warm morning sunshine, Burke walked up to Dr. Melanie Shore's front door, Abby by his side. In his friend's boat as they'd traveled to the mainland and again on the car ride to the doctor's house, they'd both been self-conscious and somewhat high-strung. No doubt it was because of the kiss last night, but neither expressed regret over letting it happen.

He wished another person had been with them to ease the tension, but Kelsey wouldn't arrive for another two hours. Thankfully, the botanist needed to be interviewed, providing a neutral third person.

She wasn't hard to find. She'd retired ten years ago, and for forty-five years she'd been living in the same small bungalow near a local forest reserve in Seaview Hollow.

Burke pounded on her door and stepped back.

"Cute cottage," Abby said. "And she couldn't live any closer to the reserve. Probably a great location for a botanist."

The lock snicked open, and a thin, almost frail-looking woman stood in the doorway. She had long gray hair and wore a *Leave Me Alone* T-shirt. Hopefully, her shirt didn't indicate how the questioning would go.

"Dr. Shore?" Burke asked.

One of her thick eyebrows shot up. "Who are you?"

Ah, the suspicious type. He got out his shield and introduced himself and Abby. "We have a few questions for you regarding your visits to the Lemoine Estate."

"Victor and I are friends. What questions could you have about that?"

Abby smiled widely. "Could we come in and explain it?"

She took a few deep breaths, then nodded. "But only for a few minutes. I have an appointment soon."

She led them into a cozy kitchen that opened to a combined dining and living area. Sunlight poured through the windows, flooding the space in warmth and highlighting the lush greenery filling nearly every surface.

As if used to being obeyed, she pointed at a floral sofa. "Sit."

Burke waited while Abby took a seat, then settled next to her. "We were told you first visited Victor for professional reasons."

"And if it was?" The same eyebrow went up again. "Is informing someone on the local flora a crime?"

Burke hadn't expected this much hostility from their innocent questions. "What exactly was Victor interested in learning about?"

The doctor crossed her arms. "That's between me and him."

Burke wouldn't be put off and back down until he got a straight answer. "When did you first meet with him?"

She shrugged. "I don't remember the exact date."

"Give us an approximate one."

She raised her eyes to the ceiling. "I'm not sure on the year, but it was a few months before Estelle went missing."

A few months before? Could she be connected to Estelle? He schooled his expression to hide his interest. "Did you meet Estelle back then?"

She shook her head. "He said she was a naturalist and the one driving his questions, but she wouldn't be interested in any details."

"And what questions and details are those?" Abby asked, as her phone chimed, indicating a text. Thankfully, she ignored it and didn't break their rhythm.

The woman sighed. "You people don't give up, do you?"

"You seem like you don't want to answer our questions," Abby said. "We're not here to accuse you of anything, we're just gathering background information on Victor."

"But why?" She leaned forward. "What's this all about?"

"All we can tell you is a crime was committed on his estate," Burke said. "We're trying to find the perpetrator."

The doctor's mouth fell open. "You don't think it's me?"

"We're too early in our investigation to know who it could possibly be." Abby smiled at the woman. "So if you'd please answer our questions, you'd be helping Victor."

Her anger melted like a chocolate bar on a hot dashboard, but she quickly squared her shoulders. "He wanted to re-create the garden his wife left in France. His gardener told him some of those plants wouldn't grow on the Oregon coast, so he wanted information about landscaping on a coastal property."

"But after his wife disappeared, you continued to visit him," Burke said.

She held Burke's gaze for a long moment without speaking. "I lost my husband to a freak car accident, so I knew the pain he was going through. True, Victor hadn't actually lost his wife, she was just missing, but the grief's the same. So I stopped by to see if he wanted to talk about it. Our time together helped him, and we met weekly after that. Eventually, we became friends."

Her explanations seemed logical, but her underlying tension and argumentative behavior said she was hiding something or giving them half-truths.

"When's the last time you visited him?" Burke paused for a moment, keeping his gaze on her. "And before you answer, please know we have the ferry logs with dates and times people arrived on the island."

"It was last Friday. In the afternoon."

"Can you be more specific on the time?"

"I arrived on the one o'clock ferry and left on the six."

"Did Victor seem upset about anything at this visit?" Abby asked.

"Upset? No. Nothing unusual." Her words were relaxed, but her posture remained stiff. "We had tea and spent most of the time comparing the aches, pains, and trials of aging."

"You mentioned a gardener," Burke said. "Do you know where we might find him?"

"All I know is Victor fired Juan, and he took off in a huff. I'm not sure where he went. He once mentioned moving here from California, but that was, what? Forty or so years ago, and he was in his fifties at the time. That would put him in his late nineties now. Or even over a hundred. He likely wouldn't still be living."

Unfortunately, Burke agreed with her. Still, they would try to find him, though his common name would make it harder. Hopefully, Abby would ask Hayden to look into him.

"Are you familiar with Cladonia arbuscula lichen?" he asked and watched carefully for her reaction.

Her face screwed up in a puzzled expression. "I am, but what does that have to do with coastal gardening?"

"I just wondered if you're familiar with it." Burke tried to look as innocent as he could.

She scowled. "Of course I am. I'm a botanist."

"Does it grow on Victor's property?"

"It does."

"Can it be found all over the property or just in specific places?" Abby asked.

"Not everywhere," she said. "You'll find it only in sunny open areas with well-drained soil."

Abby crossed her legs, but her gaze was intense. "From what I've seen, his land is predominantly wooded."

"It's sunny near the coastline."

Just what Burke needed to hear, and he was done here. He stood. "Thank you. Your information is most helpful."

Abby offered one of her comforting smiles she'd given to so many people during the investigation. "Thank you so much for your time, Doctor."

He'd spent months with her on the prior murder investigation, and he'd learned about her kindness. Or at least he thought he had, but this investigation was really revealing the depth of not only her kindness but her faith too. Made her even more attractive to him, if that was possible.

Burke cleared his brain of such thoughts and motioned for Abby to precede him to the doorway.

As soon as they were in the car and Abby closed her door, she took out her phone. "I got a text from Kelsey. She didn't want to waste the day driving to the island. She had Coop fly her, and they'll land in thirty minutes."

"Perfect. It'll take us about that long to get out to the island." Burke fired up the engine and pointed his department vehicle toward the marina.

Abby swiveled on her seat to face him. "Do you think Dr. Shore has anything to do with the theft of the crown?"

"I don't know. She seemed to be hiding something. I just don't know what. She *did* visit Victor last Friday, which would be within the theft timeframe."

"When she said she was there all afternoon, I kept thinking how Victor said he napped every afternoon, no matter what."

"You think she might've swiped the crown while he was sleeping? Maybe put it outside until he woke up, so when she left he wouldn't see her take it?"

"It's a possibility we should consider. She could even be the one who tracked in the lichen."

"We could try for a warrant to search her house so Sam can process her footwear. Could be tough to get one before we actually have a body though."

Abby nodded. "If there *is* a body on the island, Kelsey will find it. You can be sure of that."

Burke had read articles about the anthropologist on the internet last night and everyone spoke highly of her, but could anyone be so good? He was about to find out.

After weaving through heavy traffic, they finally boarded his friend's boat. He started to push it full throttle, but the sunshiny day had brought people flooding to the bay. He had to take it easy to maneuver through the other boats. The typically thirty-minute trip took an hour. Abby notified Kelsey of their delay, who said she would start an initial search on the sunny, coastal area mentioned by Dr. Shore.

When they arrived, she was exactly where she said she would be, controlling a drone. Abby had said it was how Kelsey would likely locate the body. Burke could hardly believe it. Using a drone to find a body? Science fiction as far as he was concerned, and he couldn't wait to find out how it worked.

Kelsey had brought along a skinny guy with thinning hair and an average-height woman with reddish brown hair pulled back in a ponytail, looking more like a teenager than a forensic scientist. All three of them wore protective white suits, but a camera hung around the other woman's neck.

He and Abby approached the trio. No recognition of their arrival from Kelsey. Her focus stayed on the controller in her hand.

"Hey, Kelsey." Abby stopped next to her.

"Oh, good. You're here. I'll take a quick break so we can talk, then re-launch the drone." She maneuvered the controls until her drone landed, then she turned to them.

She didn't look anything like Burke expected a hardcore forensic anthropologist might look. A sparkly clip held back her curly dark hair, and her Tyvek suit, open above her waist, revealed a frilly floral blouse. Her fingernails were coated in a pastel pink, matching her lipstick. A girly girl.

She shoved out her hand to Burke. "Kelsey Dunbar, forensic anthropologist, Veritas Center."

"Detective Burke Ulrich." He took her soft hand, surprised at her strong grip.

She shifted her attention to Abby. "Good to see you again, Sheriff—I mean, Abby." She shook her head, her curls bouncing. "I didn't think you'd ever leave law enforcement, but I've heard wonderful things about your new team."

"I am most blessed to be on it."

Kelsey gestured at her team members. "This is Shawn Fortune, my assistant, and Ainslie Houston, one of the center's forensic photographers." She returned her attention to Abby. "Thank you for texting the information from the botanist. I'm concentrating on the area she suggested, and it should move things along faster."

"So I assume you haven't located anything so far," Burke said.

"Nothing, but I just got started."

"I don't want to delay you or question your methods, but this is all new to me, and I'm dying to find out how you locate graves with a drone?"

"No worries. I've explained this to any number of law-enforcement officers since I started employing it." She gave a quick smile. "The drone uses infrared imaging. Works both above and below the ground. If for some reason the body has been moved, the infrared technology can also find both locations for up to two years after the removal."

"No offense." He squinted at her. "But that almost sounds unbelievable."

"Doesn't it?" Kelsey chuckled. "But I assure you the drone works. If I didn't have it, I could pass by a clandestine body and not realize it's there. In fact, the drone doubles my chance of finding one."

He wanted to know more. "So would an explanation of how it technically works be above my head?"

"I don't know you well enough to say that." She grinned.

He laughed as did Abby. It impressed him that a person who found and unearthed victims for a living could have a positive attitude on anything.

"But seriously," she said. "When bodies decay, they release carbon and nitrogen that first kill plants, then fertilize the soil. The change alters light reflection, which near-infrared drones detect, and I confirm with ground-penetrating radar."

"Wow!" Burke had to work hard not to shake his head. "Impressive."

"I agree," she said. "Not because it's something *I* do, but because researchers figured it all out for me. I can process not only this whole area today, but if we don't find anything here, I can complete other areas of the property before the day is out."

"Then we'll step back and let you get to it." For the first time in this investigation, Burke was filled with a solid hope. This one based on forensic science, which rarely let them down.

20

Although Kelsey's process was faster than ground penetrating radar alone, Abby wanted the process to go even faster. After taking a few minutes to say hello to Coop, who was at the helicopter dealing with some sort of mechanical issue, she'd stood next to Burke for nearly an hour. The tension between them was even more pronounced after the kiss last night, and each moment Abby hoped Kelsey would call them over with a hit. No such luck, and she was running out of lichen area to search, but Abby wouldn't lose hope.

At least Burke finally stepped away to make phone calls, one to ask his sheriff to apply for a warrant to search Dr. Shore's house to look for the lichen.

The ferry horn sounded from below, cutting through the quiet and drawing Abby's attention. Sam and her assistant should be arriving on this trip to finish processing the mansion's interior. Once finished, they would head back to her lab and start sorting through all of the recovered fingerprints.

Unless Kelsey located a body. Then Sam's full attention would be on the grave.

Gabe strode up the hill toward her. Burke was hot on

Gabe's heels. Gabe's determined stride and the journal clutched in his hand seemed to indicate he'd located something of interest.

She went to meet them. "Did you find something?"

"He did," Burke said. "But he wouldn't share it unless you were with us."

She wanted to smile over her teammate's loyalty, despite Burke's frustrated tone, but she didn't want to irritate him more. "So spill, Gabe."

"Read this." He opened the journal and pointed to the bottom of the right-hand page.

She leaned closer, and Burke came to stand behind her, and together they studied the page.

"Whoa!" He jerked back. "Estelle really *was* having an affair."

"Not simply an affair," Gabe said. "But one with Victor's brother."

Abby's heart raced as she skimmed ahead in the reading. "And she was pregnant and planning to run."

"She didn't want Victor to know about the baby," Burke said. "She was going off somewhere to have it on her own."

"What I don't get," Gabe said. "If Vincent was the father, why go off on her own? Why not stay with him?"

"Doesn't make sense, and it doesn't match what Sylvia said about Estelle needing money for the 'finer things of life.' Unless..." An idea hit Abby. "Unless she somehow embezzled money from Victor all along."

"We need financial records from the day they got married until she disappeared," Burke said.

Abby agreed, "We can ask Victor for them, but what's the likelihood he'll have the files readily available?"

Gabe shrugged. "We can hope records for part of their marriage are computerized, but accounting software was just introduced for home computers in the early eighties."

"Victor an early adopter of computers? Not likely." Burke scowled. "But if he uses an accountant, the accountant might've been."

"We should definitely ask." Abby jotted in her notepad to follow up.

"Abby! Abby!" Kelsey's voice broke through Abby's concentration as she frantically waved them over.

Abby and the others bolted toward Kelsey, but carefully picked their way over rocky soil.

"What do you have?" Abby asked and resisted dancing in place as she waited for the answer.

"Looks like a clandestine grave." Kelsey's voice lacked Abby's excitement.

To be fair, Abby shouldn't be excited about finding a body, but she was glad this might bring Victor some closure on Estelle's disappearance. "Is there lichen in the area you located the grave?"

Kelsey nodded. "I'll start marking off the coordinates with flags. Shawn is getting the GPR from the helo. A quick scan, and I can confirm the presence of remains."

"Do you need any help?" Burke asked.

"Shawn's getting equipment from the helicopter, but he might need help to move it over this rough terrain."

"I'll do it." Gabe shoved the evidence bag for the journal in Abby's hands and took off before either of them could argue with him.

Kelsey picked up small red flags and strode to a section near the cliff. By the time she had the suspicious area marked out, Shawn and Gabe returned carrying what looked like a lawnmower. The machine had wheels with a yellow box mounted close to the ground, and the top of the handle held a video device.

They set it down in front of Kelsey.

"Perfect," she said. "Thank you for working so fast."

"Mind if I tag along to watch?" Gabe asked.

"I don't mind at all, as long as you stay behind me."

Abby looked at Burke. "The question I was about to ask, but he beat me to it."

"Me too," Burke said. "I could always order him to step down, but you're right about him. He's done a lot of grunt work and deserves something more exciting."

Okay, that did it. Her heart flip-flopped. Burke showed he cared about others. Her family didn't do that either, and wasn't that, along with faith, really the basis of a person's motivations?

"That's kind of you," she said.

"Only fair. But I'm not hanging back here and waiting." He headed toward the cordoned off area.

She didn't linger behind, but took long steps to keep up with him.

By the time they reached Kelsey, she'd completed walking one length. Questions raced through Abby's brain, but as much as she wanted to know what was going on, she didn't want to interrupt Kelsey's concentration. Instead, she tapped her foot.

Burke's phone dinged, and he glanced at the screen. "Estelle's missing person files are on my desk."

"Then we need to make a point of picking them up as soon as possible so we—"

"Hey, wait," Gabe called. "Is that something on your screen?"

"It is," Kelsey said. "I can't be certain it's human remains, but one more pass will help with that."

Abby listened to the machine hum, counting down the moments in her head until they would know if a body had been buried on this cliffside. She wanted to clutch Burke's arm, but restrained herself.

At the end of the last pass, Kelsey looked up. "Something the size of human remains is buried here."

Abby's heart sank for Victor. He would be devastated when he learned Estelle was on his property this whole time.

Kelsey turned off the machine and closed the short distance to Abby and Burke. "Although the size suggests human remains, I won't be able to confirm my suspicions until I unearth them."

"When can you get started?" Burke looked like he'd lost all patience and wanted to push her into action.

"Give me five minutes to get some water, and we'll begin the dig."

"How long will it take?" Abby asked.

"The remains aren't buried terribly deep so we should be able to do it fairly quickly."

"What is 'fairly quickly' for you?" he pressed.

"If the GPR is correct on the depth, and I have no reason to believe it wouldn't be, just a couple of hours," Kelsey answered, not seeming to be bothered by Burke's pushy behavior. "But you'd be wasting your time to stand here and wait. Pay attention to your phones and I'll contact you the minute I find anything."

She stepped to her team, who'd taken a seat around a large cooler, each of them drinking bottled water. Kelsey grabbed a bottle for herself and settled on a nearby rock.

Abby changed her focus to Burke. "If you're able to obtain the search warrant for Dr. Shore, we'd have enough time to serve it now."

"If we succeeded, it should be in my inbox." He took out his phone and swiped his finger over the screen several times. "Got it. Let's grab Sam to process the forensics and head for the mainland."

Abby didn't have to be told twice but hurried toward the

house. Their investigation had just changed. Or had at least *likely* changed. And it was time to find out if Dr. Shore had anything to do with the theft of the crown and Estelle's death.

∽

Burke had wanted to race to Dr. Shore's house, but it made sense to pick up Estelle's missing person file on the way. To ensure things moved faster, he left Abby in the car where he wouldn't have to introduce her to everyone. Or maybe he left her behind because his feelings for her weren't under control. Either way, he ran in, grabbed the file, and bolted for the door before anyone tried to talk to him. Then he raced over the speed limit to Dr. Shore's house.

Since Sam knew the evidence she was looking for, he and Abby left her in the entryway to do her thing and escorted the doctor into her small office.

"Take a seat," he instructed.

"I thought I answered all of your questions before." Sitting, she looked up at him. "What's this about?"

She twined her hands together in her lap. "And why do you have the forensic tech here? What could I have possibly done?"

Abby sat next to the doctor, and Burke perched on the corner of the wooden desk holding neat piles of paperwork.

He took a slow breath, pushing down the accusatory edge in his voice. She was older, and everyone had moments where memory faltered. He would try to be more gentle in his questioning, even if she could be a murderer. "When we last talked, I don't think you told us everything about your visits to Victor."

She swallowed hard. "I don't know what else there is to say."

"Maybe it helps if you know we've located a clandestine grave on the property," he said, hoping to shock her into revealing anything she might know.

She gasped. "Estelle?"

"Could be. We hope to know more in a few hours."

Abby scooted forward on her chair. "If you had anything to do with her disappearance, tell us now, and it will go better for you."

"I didn't." She flashed her gaze between Abby and Burke. "Honest. I'd even take a lie detector test to prove it."

"But there's something you're not telling us, isn't there?" Burke pressed harder. "Maybe something that could've contributed to Estelle's death, but you don't see the connection yet."

"Okay, fine." She slumped in her chair. "That first visit to Victor. It was for a specific reason. His gardener was having problems with garden pests. Estelle didn't want him to use synthetic pesticides, and he'd read that botanical toxins worked well."

Now they were getting somewhere. "And did you share the information with him?"

"I did, but first, I educated him on the limitations of botanical toxins and warned him about their safety issues. Then I gave him the names of the three most common toxins he could use."

Finally! "Toxins that could potentially be deadly to humans?"

"It's possible, if not managed properly. You're not..." Her eyes widened. "You're not thinking the toxin was used to kill Estelle, are you? Because Victor would never hurt her. He loved her. And his gardener wouldn't either. That man was in love with her too." She spit out the final statements with disgust.

Abby got out a notepad and pen. "Tell us the names of the toxins you gave Victor."

"Rotenone, Ryania, and nicotine. All are derived from plants."

Abby's pen raced across her pad before she looked up. "Did he hope to grow them and make his own pesticide?"

"Manual labor for Victor?" She snorted. "No way. But he'd have Juan take care of it."

Abby held her pen over her notepad. "Can all three of these plants be grown in Oregon?"

"Could be, but the first two wouldn't survive without extra care. They're tropical plants, which would have to be raised in a heated greenhouse here. Nicotine, of course, comes from the tobacco plant most often grown in the southern United States. You might be surprised to learn it's also been successfully grown in Oregon for years. Since this is the easiest one, we worked together to come up with a way Juan could grow it and extract the nicotine."

"Seems like a lot of trouble to go to for a pesticide." *Unless someone was doing it for a poison.*

"I thought so too, but he said his wife was a naturalist and refused to let Juan use anything artificial. Victor was passionate about getting this garden just right for her. I suggested that instead of growing the nicotine, it would be easier to take tobacco from cigarettes. Finely ground tobacco is steeped or boiled in water to let the nicotine leach into the water. It's then strained and used directly as a spray."

"And this is poisonous to a person too?" Abby asked.

"Oh yes, very poisonous. Which is why the USDA eventually banned its commercial use and cautioned small gardeners against using it."

Abby scribbled another note. "And did Juan make the pesticide? Did it work?"

"Yes, they had glorious flowers that spring and summer. But then Estelle disappeared, and Victor lost interest in everything outside of locating her."

"But you continued to visit him?" Abby asked.

"I told you. The loss of a spouse brought us together."

Sam poked her head into the room. "Can I have a word with you two?"

Her expression didn't give anything away, but she wouldn't interrupt them if she hadn't located something. Abby must've thought so, too, as she lurched to her feet and marched out the door.

"Stay here." Burke went to the doorway, but by the time he got there, Sam and Abby had moved down the hallway, likely making sure they were out of the doctor's earshot.

"What is it?" he asked, trying not to sound demanding. "What did you find?"

"The lichen in question is on the doctor's boots."

A flash of excitement sparked in Abby's eyes. "Can you tell if it's fresh?"

Sam nodded. "Once detached from their host, lichens dry out, can't photosynthesize properly, and may die within days to weeks. The sample I located is still viable, so it can't be very old. But we still can't be certain of the location she picked it up or even if it's from Victor's property."

"But you said it wasn't common in this area, right?" Abby asked. "And odds are great if we're already looking at her as a possible suspect, and she has it on her boots, she *did* pick it up at the mansion."

Sam frowned. "Yes, odds are good, but scientifically, I can't say it attached to her boots in that location."

Abby fired a look at Burke. "We have to make her think we know she picked it up there and find out why she was recently walking Victor's property."

"Let's question her again." Burke headed for the office.

Abby kept up with him. "Sounds like you think Victor might've used the nicotine to poison Estelle."

He glanced at her. "Don't you?"

"It's a possibility, yes, but Victor is displaying a tremendous amount of grief over her disappearance, and the average person can't fake something like that."

She had a point, but... "People can kill other people and still grieve their loss."

Abby tipped her head and thought. "And he could've found out about her affair and pregnancy, a reason many people commit murder."

"We'll table this for now and see what we can find out from the doctor first." Burke gestured for Abby to enter the room before him.

Neither of them sat, but peered down at Dr. Shore. She cringed in her chair.

Burke didn't attempt to hold back his frustration this time. "We found fresh lichens on your boots. The lichens we discussed. The Cladonia arbuscula."

His statement didn't seem to faze her. "Like I told you earlier. I'm a botanist. I may be retired, but I still spend as much time as I can in nature. It wouldn't be unusual for me to track all sorts of things into the house."

"It's funny you mention tracking into the house." Abby crossed her arms. "Because we found the same lichen on the floor in Victor's library near a cabinet where something valuable was recently stolen."

"And since Victor doesn't leave the house, he wouldn't have tracked it in," Burke added.

The doctor crossed her arms. "Could've been Sylvia or Ugo."

She could be right, and if she didn't admit to being near the clandestine grave, they would have to branch out and ask Victor's employees the same question.

But, Burke would continue trying to get an admission from her. "Neither one of them have a reason to be tramping around Victor's property. Plus, Ugo doesn't seem steady enough on his feet for such a trek."

"Sylvia, then."

"Do you remember our earlier conversation when I said things would go better for you if you would admit what you'd done?" Abby eyed the woman. "If you've done nothing wrong, then you can admit to taking a walk on Victor's property and tracking the lichen into the house."

She growled under her breath. "Okay, so I went for a walk the last time I was there. Big deal. Victor needed to take a nap, and I was bored. But all I did was hike out to the cliff and come back to the library to talk to him."

"The lichen was found by the bookcases, an odd place to have a conversation with Victor," Burke said. "Do you always wander the room when you talk to him?"

"Sometimes."

"Why?"

"What difference does it make?"

"Because I'm asking you," Burke said, trying hard to keep his growing irritation under control. "Give me a direct answer, or I'll have my deputy take you in for formal questioning."

If looks could kill, Burke would be dead. "I often pace when talking to him so he can't see how I really feel."

"Feel?" Abby asked, coming across much softer than the testy behavior Burke had barely controlled.

"I developed feelings for him. All right? I was drawn to him immediately, but he doesn't return them and never will. He'll spend the rest of his days mourning the loss of the love of his life." Her eyes misted. "And now I sound like a lovesick teenager. But it's more than infatuation. I really do care about him."

Abby glanced at Burke. He caught the implication in her eyes and gave an almost imperceptible nod in response.

Dr. Shore had just given them a motive for murdering Estelle.

Burke's phone rang. Seeing Kelsey's name, he quickly answered. "Have you found something?"

"I've unearthed human remains," she said, her tone ominous. "You'll want to get over here right away. It's not what you expected. It's not what you expected at all."

21

Sour acid burned in Abby's stomach. She wished the trip back to the mansion had been faster, but even though Burke had done an excellent job of navigating around other boats, it was still thirty minutes before they reached Kelsey.

Crime scene tape had been strung around the clandestine grave, marking the shape of the dig. Mounds of soil now lined the edges of the hole. Kelsey knelt on the far side facing Abby, Shawn on the other. Five-gallon buckets sat next to each of them. They scooped soil in strainers then moved the shifted soil to the buckets.

"Kelsey?" Abby approached the forensic anthropologist, Burke by her side.

She stood. "You're probably not going to like this, but I've exposed enough of the remains to know this isn't Estelle."

"But how can you tell?" Burke asked before Kelsey could continue.

"You're looking at a male, not a female."

Burke and Abby swiveled in unison to stare at the grave. She hadn't wanted to look at the remains, but it couldn't be helped. Inside the half-dug grave lay a fully skeletonized body.

"Are you sure it's a guy?" Staring into the grave with unblinking eyes, Burke crossed his arms.

"Positive."

He shook his head. "How?"

"The male pelvis is structurally different from that of a female. In simple terms, it's narrower. Facially, males have more pronounced brow ridges and a larger, squarer jawline, evidenced by this skull too."

Abby turned her gaze back to Kelsey. Their theory of what was going on at this property had just been annihilated. "We've been working under the assumption that if we found a body buried on this property, it would be Estelle. It's hard to shift gears."

"No kidding." Burke gave a short, dry laugh.

"He could be the gardener or even Victor's brother," Abby said, but they needed way more information to positively identify him, other than her hunch. "Is there any sign of cause of death?"

Kelsey shook her head. "I'll need to examine the remains back at my lab. It could take some time to figure it out. Teeth are the hardest substance in the human body, and they remain intact, so if you have a potential victim in mind and can get dental records, that would expedite your answer."

Burke frowned. "No idea of his identity at this point, but what about a wallet? Or driver's license? Did you find either of those?"

"Sorry, no. The only extraneous evidence were portions of his decomposed clothing. He most likely wore blue jeans and a cotton shirt. I also found the remains of a leather belt and a large silver buckle, which was tarnished and corroded, leaving a blackened and crusty surface."

"Do you think this buckle could be helpful in identifying him?" Burke asked.

Kelsey looked away briefly, as if weighing her answer. "Possibly. Even with the corrosion, I can tell it was intricately carved and has two sapphires mounted on the surface."

"If they're real, it could mean he had money," Abby said.

Kelsey nodded. "You'd have to get the jewels authenticated. They survived intact, but imitation sapphires would also be virtually unchanged, so I can't say if they're real or not. I'll email pictures for now, but once the buckle is taken into evidence, you could bring it to a jeweler for confirmation."

Abby looked at Burke. "We could show it to the antique dealer Nolan spoke to. He might be able to tell us when and where it was made."

"I haven't picked it up yet," Kelsey said. "I might find a maker stamp on the back that could help you identify him too."

Burke nodded, his frustrated expression gone. "We should first show it to Victor. If he recognizes it and can identify the owner, we won't need to do anything else."

"Good point." Abby smiled at him.

He was still looking at Kelsey and didn't notice. "Anything else you can tell us about the remains or any other evidence buried with him?"

"He was wearing leather shoes. The stitching has disintegrated, but you can still see the shape of the shoe, and it looks to be a formal dress style. I could see remnants of leather soles, though quite degraded. Could indicate his footwear is expensive."

"Interesting." Abby let the information work through her muddled brain. "So he had on basic jeans and cotton pants, but his footwear and his belt were likely higher-end items."

"Exactly," Kelsey said. "The only other thing I can tell you at this point is this man was between five-foot-ten and six feet tall. The catch is that without knowing ancestry or population, my estimate could be off by more than two inches."

"Still, this is all helpful information." Abby wanted to speculate on the victim's identity, but she didn't want to waste Kelsey's time and would wait to talk to Burke about that. She shifted to their interview with Dr. Shore and opened her notepad. "One of our suspects, a botanist, gave Victor botanical toxins supposedly for pest control."

"And you wonder if they were used to commit murder?" Kelsey frowned. "Depending on the toxin used, it could well be poisonous to people. I can't visually detect that. Did she give you the name of the toxins?"

Abby consulted her notes. "Rotenone, Ryania, and nicotine."

"Oh, well then it's not very likely it'll help in this investigation. These poisons are organic and biodegradable. They aren't known to bind to bone or deposit in detectable ways. It's possible we could find them in the bone marrow, but I hate to even mention it because the possibility is very slim. Still, I'll see what I can do."

"One more thing," Abby said. "Since we really believed Estelle was buried on the property, can you continue to search the remaining areas with your drone? We found her necklace in the greenhouse. Might be a good place to look."

"Sure. I can use GPR in there." Kelsey glanced at her assistant. "In fact, if it's a priority, I can leave Shawn to recover the rest of these remains and begin the search immediately."

Abby cast a questioning look at Burke. "Your thoughts?"

"Splitting responsibility to finish the property search would be good."

"Then that's what we'll do," Kelsey said.

Abby gave Kelsey's arm a gentle squeeze. "I'm so thankful you and your team are here."

Kelsey beamed. "Glad to help. I'll have Ainslie send the photos of the belt buckle to your email right away."

"Thank you," Abby said. "Any idea how long it will take you to complete recovering these remains?"

"Barring any unforeseen circumstances, Shawn should have them ready for transport in less than two hours, and I can probably finish the property search in the same amount of time. Gathering the evidence will take longer. In fact, since I won't be working the recovery, there'll be room for Sam to work alongside Shawn right now and may reduce the time she'll need after we've departed."

"I'll send her right out," Abby said. "Is there anything else I can help with?"

"If it isn't inconvenient, it would be great if you could provide lunch for us. I hate to waste time traveling somewhere to get food, but I want to make sure my team is fed."

"I'll take care of that," Burke said.

Now that was a surprise. Abby would never expect him to offer to get their lunches.

"Thank you," Kelsey said. "And you don't need to be concerned about any food allergies, but in general, we prefer to eat light at lunch."

"Understood," Burke said. "Anything else we can do for you?"

"Not that I can think of right now," Kelsey said. "But as we get further into the dig, we'll likely come across something we need your help with, so it would be great if I can reach you by text or phone at all times."

"We'll be available," Abby said. "Now we'll take off and let you get back to work."

Kelsey stepped over to talk to Shawn, and Abby and Burke took long strides to the path.

Abby looked up at Burke. "This certainly changes everything."

"You can say that again," Burke said. "Big question is whose remains did we find? Only one male we know of who spent much time here. The gardener. I don't mean to stereotype, but Hispanic males are typically not six feet tall, and he probably wouldn't have had money to spend on expensive clothing items, so I doubt it's Juan."

"I would agree, but we can't rule him out yet. If Victor can't identify the belt buckle, we can ask him about Juan's height."

"Only other guy we know of who hasn't been seen in a while and that's Victor's brother."

"You think it's him?"

Burke shrugged. "The detective Victor hired didn't actually see him so it's possible."

"Possible, but a long shot." She got out her phone and woke it up. "I'm texting Hayden to look into Vincent to see if he can locate the guy." She fired off a quick text, then looked back at Burke.

"Something else we need to consider." He ran a hand over his hair. "These remains might not be related to the crown theft at all."

"Let's hope Victor can shed some light on the victim's identity so we know what to make of this murder." Abby was already dreading having to tell the older man a body was found on his property. Not because she didn't want to question him, but she didn't know how he would react. At first, he would be thankful they hadn't found Estelle, but then what?

Maybe Victor wouldn't be surprised at all. Maybe he'd killed a man, his brother even, and buried him by the cliff. If so, he wouldn't readily admit it, and they had a challenge in front of them to identify this victim. Hopefully Sam would locate additional evidence in the grave to help.

They picked their way through the overgrown path to the mansion and found Sam in the library on her knees in front of the fireplace. She was dusting the lid to the hidden storage space with a fingerprint brush. Her hand stilled, and she looked at them. "Did Kelsey find any remains?"

Abby nodded. "But not what we expected. She located a male who appears to have been buried since the eighties."

Sam's eyes widened. "Oh wow. Any thoughts on who it might be?"

"We're considering a couple of guys, but nothing definite enough to mention," Abby said. "That's why I'm here. Kelsey said you can begin recovering evidence from the grave. We're hoping you can locate something to identify this guy."

"As soon as my assistant finishes dusting the exit doors, she can take over here. Then I'll get right on it." Sam picked up a large roll of clear tape and ripped off a three-inch piece.

"I'd like you to start by collecting the victim's belt buckle," Burke said. "We want to show it to Victor. Hopefully he knows who owned it."

"No problem. Give me fifteen minutes, and it'll be packaged and ready for you to sign out." Sam pressed the tape over the dusted prints. "By the way, you left this morning before I could give you an update."

"What do you have?" Burke asked.

"First, I got up early this morning and ran the prints from the boat and the Tylenol package. Bad news is, I searched AFIS but didn't return a match for any of them."

Bummer. Not what Abby wanted to hear. The Automated Fingerprint Identification System database managed by the FBI contained fingerprints from known criminals. No match, no suspect.

"So they're all a dead end, then?" Abby asked.

"The ones for the boat, yes, until you have a suspect and I can compare their prints to the ones I lifted."

"But what about the Tylenol?" Burke asked.

She smiled. "The prints were a match for Sylvia and Ugo."

"Kinda skipped over the best part, didn't you?" Burke grinned.

Abby wasn't in the mood to laugh. She looked at him. "So Sylvia and Ugo were in the cellar at some point when they both lied and said they weren't."

Burke's smile vanished. "They obviously need to be called on their lie."

"While we meet with Victor, Gabe could interview them. He can also ask Ugo about Estelle's and Victor's financial records." Abby looked at her watch. "But before we do anything, I'd like to get a quick status update from the team. They could've learned something to help determine our next priority."

"Sounds like a plan, but we can't lose sight of talking to Victor. He could very well know who the belt buckle belonged to."

She nodded, excitement burning through her. Not long and they could know the murdered man's name. Whether or not his identity had any bearing on locating the missing crown remained to be seen, but it could very well be the answer to Estelle's disappearance.

∾

Burke sat next to Abby in the dining room and waited for her team members to arrive in their conference room and connect to the call. He assumed they would be as surprised as he and Abby were about not only locating remains, but that they were for a man whose identity they didn't have a clue about.

Gabe yawned and set aside the ferry logs Abby had received last night from Hayden.

"Thanks for monitoring the cameras we installed here last night," Abby said. "Especially when there was nothing on them."

"Not nothing. The deer who set off the French door camera was interesting to watch." Gabe laughed and stood. "I'll do the rest of these logs when I get back from Ugo's and Sylvia's interview."

"Anything so far?" Burke asked.

"I'm compiling a log of swiped data for Dr Shore, Ugo, and Sylvia so you can compare them to their stories and decide if they told you the truth."

"Looking forward to seeing that," Abby said. "Hopefully it'll give us the answers we need, and you won't have to move on to other visitors."

Gabe nodded. "Unfortunately, it's a long shot when we can't determine who a visitor came to the island to see. I'll have to further investigate. It's tedious work but far better than babysitting."

He laughed and strode to the door, his usual confident posture in place. He had that macho man, law-enforcement-officer look and attitude at times, but Burke had discovered there was much more to him.

Gabe looked back at Abby. "Be sure to update me on the meeting highlights, and don't talk too badly about me." He grinned and left the dining room.

Burke shifted to face the laptop screen. "I really didn't like Gabe when I first met him, but he's grown on me."

"A lot of people feel that way about him, but it usually

doesn't take long to see he has a heart of gold. Not that he would ever willingly admit it."

Burke understood the guy. He didn't wear his emotions on his sleeve either, but he thought he had a far different reason than Gabe. Still, Gabe showed his affection for Abby, and Burke suspected he wasn't doing a very good job of hiding his feelings for her either.

The team's individual photos appeared on screen, and Abby clicked to enter the meeting. "We're pressed for time. Can we quickly go down to your follow-up items? Hayden, let's start with you. What have you found on background information for the people we asked you to look into?"

He grabbed something from the table. "I'll send you the official reports, but the short version is Sylvia and Ugo seem to be on the up and up. Sylvia has lived in the same house since working for Victor. Ugo lost his family in a car crash, but he still lives in the house he bought when he got married."

"Oh, man." Abby shook her head slowly, almost in disbelief. Recently having lost her mother, she probably could sympathize with him. "The poor guy. He didn't mention it, but it's probably too hard to talk about."

"Yeah, it was an unfortunate accident—drunk driver." Hayden took a deep, shaky breath and exhaled sharply. "But moving on, both of their mortgages are paid off. Their finances might not be perfect, but neither one of them are in any serious debt. However, looks like Sylvia is living paycheck to paycheck. Her husband has cancer, and their insurance is through Victor. Could be why she hasn't retired."

"Makes sense, and for the first time, I'm feeling bad for Sylvia," Abby said. "What doesn't make sense is that she didn't mention the cancer. Could be too tough for her to talk about too. Did you uncover anything about their daughter?"

"She's twenty-seven and a loan officer at the local bank. She still lives at home with her parents." Hayden looked directly in the camera. "I couldn't find anything to suggest she did or even might do something unethical with Victor's safety deposit box. I did, however, discover Victor gave her a reference to get the job."

Burke was impressed with what this guy could find. "So you don't think there's anything there?"

Hayden shook his head. "And nothing suspicious about Vidal and Viviane either. All three grandchildren belong to Viviane. Vidal is an engineer, married to a highly successful defense lawyer. Viviane is a stay-at-home mom, her husband a highly respected financial planner. Neither family lives beyond their means, and their finances are in excellent shape."

Since that line of questioning was a bust, he moved on. "Did you find anything about their relationship with their father?"

"I located a few internet stories connecting them together, but nothing showing if they got along with one another. Of course, with as private as Victor is and never leaving the house, it would be pretty hard for a reporter to do a story on them."

Abby sighed. "On the surface, it doesn't seem like either child would need to steal the crown."

"Exactly," Hayden said. "I do have some additional algorithms running. They might tell us more, but I don't think there's anything to find here. Also, I haven't located any information on Vincent except for a few articles in French newspapers scanned from the eighties.

"Odd," Burke said. "A guy from such a prominent family might not have an online presence in social media, but I find it hard to believe he hasn't appeared in more current articles too, unless he's a hermit like Victor or deceased.

"Me too," Hayden said. "I didn't find an obituary either."

"So with Victor's hatred of his brother, Vincent could be our victim," Abby said.

Murmurs of agreement traveled around the table.

"Anything else you have for us?" Abby asked.

Burke held his breath, hoping Hayden's extensive research would turn something up to move the investigation forward.

"I'm still working on compiling a list of potential fences in Portland. This isn't the sort of information you find on the basic internet, so I've been searching the dark web. Not as easy. I'll let you know as soon as I have anything." Looking frustrated, he sat back. "That's it for me, but knowing you, you have something else for me to do."

"You know it!" Abby laughed. "Do a deep dive for two people. Juan López first. He served as Victor's live-in gardener for many years until Victor fired him. The only thing we know about him is that he came from California forty or so years ago and was in his fifties when he worked for Victor."

"Hmm." Hayden frowned. "This one could be tough. His name is extremely common and without any other information, it could be a challenge to find something. I can start by searching for an obituary for him. Might narrow things down."

"I actually hope you don't find one," Burke said. "If he died, we won't be able to interview him."

"You said he was a live-in gardener," Jude said. "Means he might've used the estate's address for his driver's license and other mail. Could help locate him."

"Good point." Hayden's eyes filled with determination, then he looked at Abby. "You mentioned a second person?"

She nodded. "Dr. Melanie Shore, a retired local botanist. She's been friends with Victor for many years and provided him with a biological toxin for pest control. It's possible either she or Victor used the toxin to kill someone. We discovered skeletal remains on his property today."

"Hold up!" Nolan raised his hand. "You casually drop the news of finding a body like it's nothing?"

"Sorry," Abby said, and told them about the lichen and grave Kelsey discovered.

"And you have no idea who this man might be?" Reece asked.

"Maybe López, but the victim is much taller than a typical Mexican immigrant back in the day."

Reece angled her head. "So because the doctor told Victor about this toxin it makes her a suspect too?"

"Not an official suspect," Burke said. "But using such organic and biodegradable pesticides that are hard to detect in a body is suspicious. Plus, she admitted to being in love with Victor and he doesn't return her feelings. Gives her a motive to do away with Estelle."

"And you'd like Hayden to get the 411 on her." Jude laughed.

"Yes," Abby said. "Everything he can find, including any sign she acted on her feelings for Victor and had an affair with him. Not only is it a motive for him to kill Estelle, but if she discovered his plan to kill her or his affair with the doctor—if he was having one—are solid reasons for her to take off."

"You got it," Hayden said.

Abby gave him an appreciative smile. "Sorry, but I have one more thing. Victor mentioned he inherited the mansion from his father, and Vincent inherited their family's French estate. I want to confirm his statement."

Hayden snapped his fingers. "Piece of cake. Anything else?"

"Isn't that enough?" Abby chuckled.

"Trust me, I'm not asking for more to do. Just don't want to let you down."

"I can almost see Hayden's shoulders, collapsing under all of these requests," Reece said. "Is there anything the rest of us can do to help?"

Hayden laughed. "Thanks for caring about me, Mom."

"It's what I do." Reece grinned.

"Don't worry," Hayden said, "it's a lot, but not more than I can handle."

Abby glanced at Burke. "Do you have anything to add for Hayden?"

He shook his head.

"I second Reece's thanks, Hayden." Abby gave her teammate a broad smile. "Get back to me as soon as you can. I'm especially interested in the list of potential fences."

He nodded.

"Then we'll sign off."

"Before you do," Nolan interrupted, "don't get so caught up in this investigation that you forget your deposition."

"I won't," she said, but sounded as if it had already slipped her mind.

After she ended the call, she turned to Burke. "The deposition Nolan mentioned is for our last case. I've had to put it off twice, and the defense attorney is threatening legal action if I don't show up. It's scheduled in two days, and I'll have to go."

"No worries. I get it—juggling several investigations is part of the job." And he did get it. He lived it—usually balancing multiple cases at once without blinking.

What he didn't understand was the heaviness creeping in at the thought of Abby not being there with him. Not just on the job, but in his life.

Three days. That's all they'd had together. And

somehow when he looked ahead, she'd become part of the picture.

Was that crazy? Maybe.

But real.

The thought of moving forward without her left a hollow space in his heart.

Still—was he really ready for something more?

Just as important... was she?

22

Abby knocked on Victor's cabin door but didn't wait for permission to go in. The empty smell of peppermint saturated the air, probably from a mug on the table next to him. He sat in an easy chair with a traditional plaid blanket over his lap.

Victor pushed to his feet faster than she imagined he could move. He bumped into the table, sending tea sloshing from the mug, but ignored it in favor of picking up his cane.

He hobbled over to Abby and grabbed her arm, clutching so tightly it hurt. "Please tell me you didn't find my sweet Estelle."

"We didn't." Abby gently loosened his fingers.

Victor sagged, looking weak and fragile. Burke rushed over to take the older man's elbow before he collapsed and helped him back to the chair.

Abby dragged a dining chair to sit next to him. Burke stepped back and leaned against the wall, his feet crossed at the ankle. His typical casual pose, but his expression was anything but casual. She raised a finger to tell him to hold off questioning. He arched a brow, but gave a subtle nod.

"I've been so worried and conflicted." Victor spread the

blanket over his legs again. "I want an answer to what happened to my sweet wife, but I sure didn't want you to find her in a grave. That would mean someone had killed her."

Abby gave him a compassionate smile. "I can see how you would feel that way."

"But now..." He picked at a loose thread on the blanket. "Now I'm right back where I started. Unanswered questions."

Time to give him additional information.

Abby laced her tone with sympathy. "I can understand how you must feel, but we're not actually back where we started. Before we get into that, did you keep your old financial records from when you and Estelle first married?"

One hand hovered near his mouth, fingers twitching like he might speak—but didn't for a long moment. "I'm not sure how that's relevant, but I don't know a thing about my finances other than the monthly report Ugo gives me. Money is his domain. He's extremely efficient and organized, so I would assume he kept records needed for taxes and discarded the rest."

"Then you don't know where he stores the records?" Burke clarified.

"He has his own office. Back of the first floor. I assume records are kept there, but you really need to ask him." He waved his hand dismissively. "Enough of this busy talk. Did you find something on the property? Something to tell us where Estelle is?"

"Unfortunately," Abby said, "the forensic anthropologist located a clandestine grave in the clearing on the cliff side. She recovered a man's skeletal remains."

"On my property? I can hardly believe it." Suddenly red-faced, Victor clutched at his chest and struggled to breathe.

Abby held his free hand. "Look at me, Victor. Breathe with me." She took slow, measured breaths in and out.

He seemed unable to calm down and follow her. She continued to breathe in this pattern, but exaggerated it even more. He closed his eyes. Opened them. Looked around, appearing confused.

"Something's wrong," he said, his speech slurred. He lifted his left hand an inch. It dropped to the arm rest. "My arm. It's wrong. Help."

He relaxed back, his eyes closed, and his mouth drooped on one side.

"He's having a stroke. I'm calling 911." Burke already had his phone in his hand. "Let Gage know to get the gate open."

She dug out her phone and dialed Gage. Before she could connect, Victor's eyes flashed open, his gaze vacant and unfocused.

"The crown is not the treasure," he said his words slurred.

Baffled, she leaned closer to him. "What do you mean?"

His eyes closed.

Gage answered, and she brought him up to speed then turned her attention back to Victor.

"Victor," she said softly, looking to make sure he was still breathing.

He was, but he didn't stir. She offered a heartfelt prayer for him.

"Doesn't look good." Burke came to her side.

"We have to believe God will get help here in time." She sat back in the chair and rested her hand on Victor's arm. She wanted him to recover for so many reasons, and she wasn't proud to admit one of them was so he could explain his cryptic comment.

Burke paced the floor in the emergency room waiting area. He and Abby had followed the ambulance and had been waiting for news for almost an hour. Victor hadn't regained consciousness, and his medics agreed his symptoms suggested a stroke. How severe, they didn't know, but remaining unconscious wasn't a good sign.

Burke ran a hand over his head. He hated hospitals. Hated the medicinal smell of cleaning chemicals. Of potential death lingering in the air. He'd only been to hospitals when a crime victim needed attention or was clinging to life. Never for any wonderful reason like a baby's birth. No. This was just another incident of a crime victim needing help.

The double door swung open, and a female dressed in blue scrubs stepped through. She glanced around the waiting room. "Family of Victor Lemoine?"

Burke and Abby shot to their feet to race over to her.

"How is he?" Burke asked, before the woman could introduce herself.

She cleared her throat. "He has indeed suffered an ischemic stroke caused by a blood clot. We were able to successfully remove the clot, and his prognosis is good."

Thankfully the woman whose hospital badge identified her as a doctor didn't ask their relationship to Victor or she might not be willing to share confidential information with them.

"Is he awake?" Abby asked.

She shook her head. "He still has altered levels of consciousness without resulting in a full coma. This isn't uncommon for elderly patients. They can be drowsy or confused shortly after a stroke. They'll drift in and out of consciousness, especially if there's brain swelling or metabolic imbalance, which he suffered. But he'll have brief moments of lucidity."

"And long-term?" Abby asked.

The doctor's mouth tightened. "The stroke could affect the right hemisphere, causing left-side weakness. His speech should be spared. He's right-handed and it's typically left-brain controlled. Once the inflammation has receded, he should regain full use of his left side." She tilted her head just a bit. "In fact, he woke several times and kept saying, 'The crown is not the treasure.' I imagine you know what he means."

Burke nodded even though after a lengthy discussion with Abby on the ride over here neither had a clue. "Can we see him?"

"He's being transferred to a room. We'll get the number to you as soon as we have it, and you can meet him there."

"Thank you," Abby said.

"He's lucky you recognized stroke signs and got immediate care. You certainly minimized the ongoing damage by getting him here so quickly."

"One question," Abby said. "Could sharing upsetting news with him have caused the stroke?"

"Short answer is yes. A physiological response to acute emotional stress can trigger the fight or flight response and cause a surge of stress hormones. That can increase heart rate and blood pressure, putting a strain on blood vessels. It can also increase blood clotting, affecting platelet function and making blood more susceptible to clotting."

Abby frowned. "If we were to share additional troubling news with him, could it cause another stroke?"

"It's hard to say, but we didn't find any evidence of additional blood clots. So he might be fine, or another clot could form." The doctor nodded her goodbye and used a key card to return through the same door.

Abby let out a long breath. "Thank goodness he's going to be okay, but I feel like we're the reason he's here."

"You can't think that way. The doctor said it could've

happened at any point. You were sympathetic when you broke the news to him, and as the homeowner, he needed to know what happened on his property."

"I guess." She chewed on her cheek. "But I don't like it."

"I don't either, but the best thing we can do now is let it go and update his son."

"And stay with him until his family arrives." Staring out the window, Abby got out her phone and updated Vidal on his father's condition.

She'd just completed her call, and a nurse approached. "Mr. Lemoine is in room 321. You're welcome to visit him there."

"Thank you," Abby smiled, but she weaved like she might fall down.

Burke looked her in the face. "You okay to go up there now?"

"Fine." She started for the elevator.

She still seemed unsteady. No way he'd risk her falling. He took her arm and got her aboard the elevator. She didn't argue. Surprising. Even more surprising, she leaned on him, reinforcing his impression of her state of being. He continued holding her arm until he settled her in a chair in Victor's room and sat next to her.

Victor looked pale and vulnerable in the bed. Wires and tubes led from his body to various machines. The constant beep reflected his heartbeat, straining the silence.

"I don't know why I felt so woozy." Abby gave Burke a wobbly smile. "Doesn't make sense. Hospitals don't bother me. Sick people don't bother me. I've even seen terrible accident victims on the job. This has never happened."

"Maybe you've come to care for him and this has become personal for you."

"You could be right, even though I try to be sure that doesn't happen on the job." Frowning, she sat in silence for a long moment before her phone rang. She glanced at the screen. "It's Kelsey."

She answered and greeted Kelsey, then listened intently, her foot tapping urgently on the floor.

"Okay, thanks for letting me know," she said, then listened again.

"Thank you so very much, Kelsey. I'd like to come by and thank you in person, but Victor had a stroke, and we're at the hospital with him."

As she listened this time, she nodded. "I will, and thank you again."

She ended her call and looked at Burke. "Kelsey finished searching Victor's property. Found nothing. She and her team also recovered all of the remains and are loading them on the helicopter. She'll get back to us as soon as she has a cause of death or any other information."

Burke hadn't wanted Kelsey to find another body, but he had to admit to disappointment. Locating Estelle might've led them to finding the person who'd stolen the crown. "So we're left with the belt buckle as our only lead on the guy."

"Sam's still working the grave. She might come up with something viable."

"Let's hope she does." Burke looked at Victor resting comfortably. "When he wakes up, it's definitely not a good time to show him the belt buckle. The stress might cause another stroke. Not to mention his grief if he knows the person who died. Even if he was estranged from his brother, if Vincent's the person who was killed, it will come as quite a shock."

"I agree. We should be cautious and check with the doctor again before talking to him."

"Sounds like a plan," Burke said. "If she says it's not a good idea, we wait for Victor's family to arrive and take the buckle to the antique dealer."

"But I won't leave until I'm certain Victor's out of the woods."

"Agreed." Burke's phone rang, sounding louder than normal in the quiet hospital room. "It's Sam."

"If she's calling you," Abby said. "She likely has results."

Hoping for good news, he answered. "Putting you on speaker, Sam. Abby is here with me too."

"Great," she said, her voice enthusiastic. "We've been working on fingerprints from the mansion. The bad news is, I don't have any matches in AFIS so far, so some of the prints remain a mystery. On the bright side, one unmatched print was located at several locations."

"Where?" Abby asked.

"The greenhouse, Estelle's locket, trunk, and her journals."

Burke's hope for a solid lead deflated. "Those are all things Estelle would've touched, so probably her print."

"Problem is," Sam said. "We don't have her prints on file, and we obviously can't take them, so there's no way to prove it's hers. If Victor could give us something he knew only she'd touched, we could make a match. We did lift another partial from the locket, but it didn't link to anyone. We're still comparing it with other prints."

"Did you find the same print on the crown hiding place?" Abby asked.

"No, but we recovered three sets there. One is Victor's. The other two unknown."

"And the safe?" Abby asked.

"Just Victor's prints," Sam said.

"Then he was likely the only one who could've put the journals in there."

"Likely," Sam said. "Unless someone else wore gloves. And before you ask, Victor's prints wouldn't be smudged and would remain intact even if someone wore gloves afterward."

Burke clenched his fingers. "So we really don't have a lot to go on here."

"We're not down for the count," Sam said. "My assistant is still working on the secret compartment in the office, the exit doors, and the cells in the basement. I hope she'll have results by the end of the day."

"Any other results for us?" Burke asked.

"I finished analyzing the oil in the secret passageway. It's definitely gun oil, but it's old. My estimate says it was deposited in the eighties. And I matched it to the oil in the antique guns in Victor's collection. It looks like there might be one gun missing."

"So someone could've stolen one of his guns, and the oil timeline of the eighties could put it at the time our victim was killed and Estelle disappeared." Abby's excited tone had returned. "Kelsey doesn't know how the man was killed yet, but maybe he was shot and the person who killed him used the secret passageway to hide the gun."

"It's possible, I suppose, but I don't think the gun would drip oil in that manner. It most likely came from a leaky can." Sam's enthusiasm had mellowed. "But if you think this is an important lead, I can get with the weapons expert at the Veritas Center and have him weigh in."

"Hold off until we have the cause of death for our victim," Burke said.

Abby looked at him. "I don't know. This guy might not have been shot, but Estelle might have been. Or if someone took her, her abductor could've used a gun."

"But until we have a weapon, I don't think there's really anything we can do right now."

"True," Abby said. "Everything is basically on hold until Victor regains consciousness."

"I'll be praying for him." Sam ended the call.

Burke turned to Abby. "This probably seems insensitive to bring up, but now that Victor will be okay, have you thought any more about his cryptic statement?"

"I still think it has something to do with the value of the crown. Likely something's more valuable than it is."

"He could be referring to the forged crown."

"He didn't even know about it until we showed him the pictures. Would that really come up in his mind after having a stroke?"

"He could simply be very good at lying, and he'd known all along."

"No." She shook her head hard. "No. You can't fake his shocked response. He didn't know."

"I suppose he could've discovered something on the property regarding the crown after we showed him the pictures, but he was never alone after that to go looking around."

She sat silently, peering at him for a moment. "What if he meant something totally different than the monetary value?"

"Like what?"

"Like money isn't what's important in life. Maybe the stroke caused him to think of his family and living to the fullest is what matters. Maybe he has regrets about the way he lived his life, and he wanted someone to know."

"Sounds plausible." Burke mentally chewed on her statement. "If only he'd wake up, since the doctor cleared us to ask him about it."

"No way I'll let you talk to him again!" The deep male voice boomed from the doorway.

The monster of a man standing by the door had dark hair, dark eyes, and dark complexion, but resembled Victor in the shape of his jaw and his nose.

He pushed back a long, black raincoat and clamped large hands on his waist. "You're not going to cause my father to have another stroke."

"I assume you're Vidal." Abby rose to greet him, her hand outstretched. "I'm Abby Day. We spoke on the phone."

He ignored her hand. "I figured as much, but how can you be talking about solving whatever he hired you to do when he just barely survived a stroke?"

"I'm Detective Burke Ulrich." He extended his hand, also ignored by Vidal. "We weren't going to talk to him until we got his doctor's approval. We located a hidden grave on his property and were required to tell him. That's when he had the stroke."

"So *you* did this? *You* put him in this position?" The pitch of Vidal's voice rose with each word.

Abby let out an almost silent breath. "A stroke isn't something anyone can predict. So, yes, we gave him the shocking news, but we had no idea something like this would occur. And it certainly isn't something we would want to happen."

"I'm not taking any chances, and even if the doctor says you can talk to him, I won't allow it." He crossed thick arms. "I don't care if you're a detective."

They could get a court order allowing Burke to talk to Victor with the doctor's permission, but that would upset Vidal more. Burke could still show the belt buckle to the antique dealer, and he would pursue that route before speaking to Victor. And maybe Sam would discover promising information.

But if it came down to zero leads and an unidentified body, he would have to follow the necessary steps to resolve the investigation. Even if that meant taking legal action to gain access to Victor.

"Just so you know, someone has made an attempt on

your father's life." Burke shared the boating incident. "We've kept him safe in protective custody. For his safety while in the hospital, I am assigning a deputy to watch his door twenty-four/seven."

Vidal shook his head. "What's going on here? Why were you even searching my father's property when you discovered the grave? What's he mixed up in?"

"He had a valuable artifact stolen from his home, and he called the authorities and me to investigate." She told him about the LLL team. "While investigating, we discovered information leading us to believe your mother might be buried on the property. So we brought in a forensic anthropologist who located the clandestine grave."

"My mother!" Vidal breathed in and out like a huffing furnace. "Did you think my father killed her?"

Burke wouldn't pull any punches. "With the body potentially on his property, he's a suspect."

Vidal's glare deepened. "Did he know you thought she was buried there?"

Abby nodded. "He said if her body was located, he didn't kill her."

"Of course he didn't." Vidal firmed his shoulders. "He still believes she's alive."

"And what about you? Do you believe the same thing?"

Vidal looked past them, staring into the distance. "I don't know. I was only fifteen when she went missing. Dad made sure to keep the details from me and especially from Viviane. She was three years younger. But of course we both heard rumors."

Burke couldn't even begin to imagine how difficult life was for them when they were younger. "Did you look into it when you got older?"

"Sure, I located Detective Orman even though he'd resigned from the job. He wouldn't tell me anything, and

Dad still won't talk about it." He scrubbed a hand across his face. All the bravado had drained from him, and he seemed tired. "What can you tell me?"

"I wish I could give you information about the investigation," Burke said, "but I can't."

Abby flashed him a frustrated look, then turned back to Vidal. "After our investigation is concluded, if we don't find your mother, I hope we can provide you with the information you're seeking. Or at least persuade your father to talk to you about her."

Vidal's expression softened. "Do you think you'll find her?"

"It's unclear at this point," Burke answered. He wasn't about to speculate on how his investigation would go when he didn't have a clue. And he wouldn't disappoint this man again. He'd already gone through the loss of his mother and years of torment wondering where she could be.

Burke had seen too many times what happened to families when missing loved ones were never found. He wouldn't wish such a fate on anyone.

23

The drive to Seaside Harbor passed in silence. Abby hadn't expected to have such a strong reaction to Victor's stroke. And it grew after seeing Vidal and catching a glimpse of who he'd been as a teenager when his mother vanished. It stirred up everything she'd been suppressing about her own mother's death and the reconciliation that hadn't happened in time.

If she didn't get herself centered, she wouldn't be any help to Burke or the investigation. The only place she knew to find peace was at her church.

She looked at Burke. "I know we need to get to the antique shop, but Victor's stroke has put me in a terrible place. Everything that just happened brought up my mom's death. Would you mind if I stopped at my church for a few minutes?"

"I don't mind." His agreement came easier than expected. She thought he'd protest—especially with his current distance from God.

She gave him directions to the church she attended, and they drove through the quaint seaside town in silence.

Normally she'd take in the oceanfront and the weather, but today, the world outside the windshield barely registered.

They pulled up to the church. It didn't look like much—just a modern building tucked between shops—but Abby didn't care. Church wasn't the building. It was the people and sometimes the quiet, like she so desperately craved today. She led him inside, and they took a seat in the worship center's front row.

"You know," she said softly, "I think we're both stuck in the same place with our faith. For me, I'm convinced I didn't honor my parents like the Bible says I should do. I failed at that and can't shake the guilt."

"You just need to confess it, and God will forgive you," Burke said. "I know, simple advice but not always easy."

"Exactly. God might forgive me, but will I be able to forgive myself?" She turned to him. "But your situation's different. You weren't in the wrong. Tiffany hurt *you*."

"Yeah." He gripped his knees. "But it still feels like punishment."

"You know that's not God, right? That it's the enemy lying to you, and there's something deeper." She paused. "What's the truth, Burke?"

He stared ahead. "I don't know. Maybe I don't believe I deserve happiness."

She didn't respond right away. He was being vulnerable, and she didn't want to interrupt and risk shutting him down.

"It's not just Tiffany," he added. "I never told you about my brother, Kyle."

He exhaled hard and ran a hand around the back of his neck. "We grew up in a strict Christian home—no TV, no internet, no music. When I turned eighteen I'd had enough and bolted. Kyle was younger, but I didn't think about what I was leaving him to deal with. After I was gone, he spiraled. Drugs. Eventually overdosed. If I hadn't been so focused on getting out, maybe I could've helped him. Maybe he'd still be alive."

She took his hand. "You can't carry that. You didn't abandon him, right?"

"No. I would've called or texted him, but he didn't have a phone or the internet. So I visited every chance I got. I just didn't pick up on any signs of what he was going through. I don't know." His voice cracked. "Maybe he was hiding it from me because he didn't want me to see it."

"Then your guilt is a lie." She hoped her assertiveness would get his attention. "I heard once that when strangers hurt us, we blame the world. But when someone close to us hurts us or is suffering, we blame ourselves—even if it's not our fault. That's what you're doing."

He looked down at their joined hands. "I wish I could trust that, but trust isn't easy after what Tiffany did."

"She was the fool. You're an incredible man. Someone any woman would be proud to marry."

He locked on her face, his eyes searching. "You really believe that?"

"I do."

"Even after what I told you?" He took a long breath and held it.

"Especially then, but it's not just about me. You need to believe it too. And the only way back is prayer."

He glanced toward the front of the worship center where a large bronze cross was mounted on the wall. "You're right. Whatever I'm doing on my own, it's not working." He squeezed her hand. "Let's start now."

She bowed her head, and though the silence between them stretched out, Abby's heart wasn't silent. For the first time since her mother's death, Abby poured out everything —her grief, her guilt, and her need to make things right. Then God made her path clear. She had to see her father.

Ask for forgiveness. Try to rebuild what was left of her family, even if they wanted nothing to do with her and rejected her again.

When she opened her eyes, Burke hadn't moved. She stayed beside him, quietly absorbing his strength, wondering what it might feel like to truly belong with him.

Finally, he looked at her. "It feels good to trust God again. I hope I can actually put it into practice and learn to trust people too."

"You can," she said softly.

"Maybe. But trusting a woman again? That's still the hard part."

"I'd never betray you."

He searched her face. "So you think we should give this a real chance?"

"I'm done listing all the reasons we shouldn't," she said. "Let's start finding the reasons we should."

He took both her hands, eyes locked with hers. "That's the best idea I've heard all day."

Her heart soared. She smiled, letting herself imagine a future that, for the first time, didn't feel so far away.

Then her phone rang. She groaned. "Whoever's calling, their timing is terrible. But it could be about the case." She looked at the screen. "It's Gabe."

"He probably has an update on his interview with Sylvia and Ugo."

She tapped the screen. "Hi, Gabe. You're on speaker with me and Burke. Do you have an update on your interviews?"

A sigh crackled through the speaker. "I do, but it's not likely what you want to hear. Ugo and Sylvia don't seem like viable suspects."

Burke's shoulders tensed as he leaned forward. "Tell us what you discovered, and we'll be the judge of that."

"Well, okay then." Gabe didn't control the sarcasm in his

voice. "I thought we were past that, but here goes. Both of them spent the night at the mansion before Victor reported the crown was stolen."

Burke ran a hand over his jaw. "And after such a confession when they lied to us, you still don't think they're suspects?"

"Hold on. They had good reasons." His tone shifted, more measured. "Sylvia's husband not only has cancer, but he's dying. His treatments make him too sick to be around, and he doesn't want her to see him like that. A nurse is with him around the clock, so he insists Sylvia takes off. She doesn't want their daughter to know how bad things are so she can't stay with her, but they can't afford lodging, so she stays in the dungeon, and makes sure Victor doesn't know she's there."

Abby frowned. "Why doesn't she just tell him? I'm sure he'd understand and give her a proper room."

"I asked. She's afraid if she tells him and he says no, she'll lose her job and the insurance that comes with it. So she keeps quiet."

Burke crossed his arms. "And Ugo? He just lets her sneak around?"

"No need for sneaking past him. He's sometimes there too. They both leave early in the morning and sneak down to the ferry together, acting like they just arrived. It's all a routine now, just in case Victor's watching."

Abby was honestly surprised. "So why does Ugo stay over?"

"He's a functional alcoholic. He started drinking when his wife and son died in that car crash. On the anniversary of their deaths, he drinks excessively and can't make it home on his own. Sylvia helps him down to the cellar to sleep it off so he doesn't lose his job."

Burke's jaw flexed. "I had no idea Ugo drank."

"He clearly hides it well."

"I'll say," Abby said. "You wouldn't notice unless you knew to look for it."

Burke sat back, brow furrowed. "So they both spent the night. Did either of them see or hear anything?"

"Nothing. No sounds, no movement. Neither had any clue who might be buried on the property. Sylvia did mention that back in the eighties, they had male visitors—none regular, and no one who ever seemed angry or threatening."

Abby leaned in, her voice tight with hope. "Do you believe their story?"

"Sylvia's attitude rubbed me the wrong way, but yeah, I do. Both of them genuinely care about Victor. Doesn't seem like either would want to hurt him."

Disappointment pressed into Abby's chest. She had hoped for a lead—something. But the door wasn't fully closed yet. "What about the finances? Did Ugo keep any records from the eighties?"

"Surprise, surprise, yes." Gage's animated tone cheered her up. "He's kept everything from the time he started managing the household finances. He has paper copies in a storage room near his office. He offered to walk us through them."

Burke straightened, the wheels in his brain clearly turning. "We might have to take him up on that."

"Did they say anything about Juan?" Abby asked.

"Just that he was barely over five feet tall—so he's definitely not our mystery man."

"Didn't seem likely anyway," Burke said. "A guy like Juan wouldn't have owned such an expensive belt buckle."

"Which means we're still without a victim ID," Abby said. "That buckle just became our best shot at identifying the man in the clandestine grave."

Who knew a small town like Seaside Harbor would have top quality and expensive antiques, but the place's name and fancy sign out front should've been Abby's first clues telling her she was wrong. The next clue appeared the moment she stepped through the door of The Gilded Gallery, and the price tags displayed on elegant pieces made her gasp. The highest she spotted was fifteen grand.

She shared a surprised look with Burke as they made their way through an aisle lined with antique furniture. She didn't know the era, but the furniture was seriously old.

An agile-looking older man with a receding hairline stood behind the counter, his back to them. He and a woman were in a heated conversation about the price of a painting on the counter. She looked up and met Abby's gaze, her mouth dropping open. She spun and raced for the back room.

Abby stopped in her tracks. This woman was a forty-year older image of Estelle. Was Abby seeing things?

She nudged Burke. "Did you catch a look at that woman?"

"Not really. Do you know her?"

"She looked like Estelle. At least what I would imagine her at this age."

"Are you sure, or are you just hoping it's her?"

Abby shrugged. "I'm not sure why I would imagine it, but you could be right."

"Or you could be right. It could be Estelle." He tipped his head toward the man standing at the counter. "We can ask a few questions. See if we can find out."

They stepped up to him. He gave them a broad smile, his cheeks rising. "Can I help you folks?"

Abby introduced herself and Burke.

"I'm Leonard Shaw, the owner," he said, his pleasant expression remaining in place.

Abby took the evidence bag holding the belt buckle from her backpack. "We were hoping you could give us an idea of when and where this buckle might've been made."

He picked up the bag. "Can I take it out to examine it?"

"If you wear gloves," Burke said.

"No problem." He grabbed a pair of white cotton gloves. "These were freshly laundered."

"Actually." Abby drew a pair of disposable gloves from her backpack. "We'd prefer you'd use ours so we can be positive there's no contamination."

"I can do that." He put on a pair of glasses and the gloves she gave him, then bent over the buckle. "Gorgeous piece. My first impression is it's French."

He flipped it over. "Ah, I was right. The maker's mark is for Hermès. I imagine you've heard of the very high-end French designer."

"I have," Abby said. "Do you have any idea when this was made?"

He pointed at a small circle holding the letter A engraved on the back. "Circles were used for Hermès designs from 1971 to 1996. The letter A corresponds to a specific year. I just have to grab my detailed Hermès date stamp guide to check what the A means."

He dug under the counter for a small binder, flipped a few pages, then paused and ran a finger down the plastic sleeve enclosing a piece of paper. "Ah. Here it is. The buckle was made in 1971."

"You're certain?"

"Yes," he said, a puzzled look on his face. "But here's the thing. I don't think Hermès was making such pricey buckles in those days. This was most likely custom-made."

"Pricey?" Burke asked. "Like how much?"

"I saw a recent Hermès Kelly diamond buckle with crocodile belt in 18K yellow gold go for over fifty thousand."

Burke let out a low whistle. "So the guy who wore it would've had money."

"Yes, or someone he knew who could've gifted it to him. And they'd have to be well-connected to get a custom piece made."

"Anything else you can tell us about it?"

He shook his head.

"How about the woman you were talking to?" Abby asked. "Might she know something about the buckle?"

"Her?" His face blanched. "No, she doesn't have a background in antiques."

"But she works here?"

"No. Just a customer."

Abby leaned closer to him. "I heard your conversation about the painting when I came in. She sounded pretty knowledgeable to me."

"Sorry, you're wrong." He stiffened.

"What's her name?" Burke asked, his tone more casual and less intense than Abby's.

"I don't give out customer information." He put the buckle back in the bag and ripped off the latex gloves. "Now if you'll excuse me, I have work to do."

"I'll just check with her." Burke moved to the opening in the counter.

"Now wait a minute. You're not authorized to go back there. Besides, she was leaving anyway."

Burke didn't listen but powered ahead. Shaw rushed after him. Abby couldn't stand around and wait. She put the buckle in her backpack and hurried after them.

"See, I told you." The owner's voice boomed through the backroom. "She left."

Abby reached them in time to see Burke glancing

around. He locked eyes with Abby then gestured for her to leave with him. On the sales floor, he took a long look at the place. "Thank you for your help, Mr. Shaw."

She didn't have any other questions, so she went to the door, Burke's footfalls sounding on the vintage wooden floor behind her.

Outside, he looked up and down the street, then back at the building. "Shaw doesn't have any security cameras. Most surprising with his high-end inventory."

Abby nodded her agreement. "I noticed a security system. Maybe he doesn't think he needs cameras too. Or for some reason, he doesn't want his dealings recorded. Maybe a customer privacy thing."

"Whatever the reason, it's time to take a better look at this street. Someone around here could have cameras that recorded the woman entering the building."

Abby's heart slammed against her ribs. Was this it? Were they finally about to find Estelle?

24

In her room at the inn, Abby put on fresh clothes. The long hot shower should've cleared her mind of their failure to locate any cameras, and it had. Mostly. The only thing she couldn't seem to erase—Burke's kiss last night. She hadn't had any free time to think about it until now and it played over and over like a popular song she couldn't forget.

It had been amazing. A kiss beyond all expectations. She could've walked away, but she'd wanted him to kiss her. She'd instigated her actions. And she didn't regret it. Not one bit.

Had her prayers given her peace about being with him—maybe the reason she couldn't let it go? She now felt free to daydream about a future with him.

But she didn't have time to keep thinking about it now. Not when the attorney for tomorrow's deposition had called and basically demanded she come in for a refresher. She didn't want to miss more of the Lemoine investigation, but she wanted to do her best to put a kidnapper behind bars, so she had no choice.

Taking the company's SUV, she settled in for the short drive to the lawyer's office in Seaside Harbor only to be told he wasn't ready for her. She took a seat in the waiting area, and her phone alerted her to a video call from Hayden. She answered and put in her earbuds for privacy from the receptionist.

"You got a minute?" Hayden seemed all business.

Her pulse raced in hope of good news. "Sure."

"I just found out Leonard Shaw knew Estelle back in the day. *More* than knew her," he said. "He's one of the men she was rumored to have an affair with. They shared the love of antiques, and apparently Victor could care less about them. Shaw accompanied her when Victor didn't want to go to social gatherings."

"How did we miss something like that?" Abby asked. "Why didn't Victor mention it?"

"I can't answer why Victor didn't tell you, but I only learned about it from a gossip columnist. I located an article where she speculated on the affair. You'd think if it weren't true, Victor would've insisted the newspaper print a retraction, but that never happened."

"Wow! Just wow! I'll ask Victor about it when he's well enough to talk, but who knows when that will be." Abby's excitement lessened. "His doctor said it's possible that asking him additional stressful questions could cause another stroke. I don't want to risk that."

"I discovered something else about Shaw that might mean you don't have to question Victor."

"You've got my attention—spill it."

"I was hoping you'd say that." Hayden shared a mischievous grin with her. "Shaw showed up on the list for potential fences in the area. In fact, he's the most likely person to be able to fence such a high-priced item."

"No way!" She'd caught the receptionist's attention and lowered her voice. "You're sure he's a possible fence?"

He nodded. "His name is all over the dark web. His screen name is AntiquityAssassin."

"Clever."

Hayden looked at her with the burning focus he was known for. "The name might be, but he wasn't clever enough to hide the trail to his real identity."

She shook her head. "How was I so wrong about him? Sure, he came across as defensive of the woman in his shop, but otherwise he seemed reputable. Clearly he isn't. I'm in Seaside Harbor right now and need to pay this guy another visit."

Hayden narrowed his eyes. "Just be careful, okay. I have no idea if someone who deals in stolen antiques is dangerous, but he could be."

The last thing she wanted to do was put herself in a life-threatening situation. "Does it appear as if he has any partners in crime?"

"As far as I can tell, he's a loner."

"Then I'm good to handle him."

"Sheriff Abby Day to the rescue." Hayden saluted her, then laughed. "I'll continue to run my algorithms for him, but let me know if I can do anything else."

She ended the call with a sharp swipe and started to dial Burke, but the attorney stepped into the waiting area. Burke would have to wait.

Now came the boring time prepping for the deposition.

Would she be able to focus? Or would her mind spiral with everything Shaw might say when she talked to him again—every awful, impossible, true thing?

∼

Abby pulled up to the antique shop and used the SUV's infotainment speaker to dial Burke's number. The call went straight to voicemail. Drat. He was likely meeting with Sheriff Ryder. She wouldn't distract him by leaving a message and ended the call. She could catch him up after she talked to Shaw.

Light from several crystal chandeliers shone through the antique shop's front windows, casting a glow on the twilight-darkened sidewalk. Abby killed the engine and climbed out. Before she entered, she paused to peer through the glass door. The store was empty, and Shaw wasn't behind the counter. He was probably working in the back.

She entered and made her way down the main aisle, calling, "Anyone here?"

No reply.

If she owned a shop with such a pricey inventory, she wouldn't leave the counter unattended. She was about to shout louder when a woman's light footsteps approached from the back room.

Abby turned and came face to face with the same woman she'd seen earlier. No question in Abby's mind. She was looking at Estelle. The same large, dark eyes. The same olive complexion. Wavy hair pulled back in a bun. The only changes in her face were wrinkles around the eyes and skin that had lost its elasticity. She'd stayed in shape and looked quite fit for a woman her age.

"Estelle Lemoine." Abby kept her gaze fixed on the woman. "Is this where you've been hiding all these years?"

Her eyes flashed wide, but quickly constricted. "I'm not sure who you're referring to."

"Oh, come on," Abby said. "You're Estelle Lemoine. Victor Lemoine's wife. You disappeared, never to be heard from again."

She lifted her chin. "You're mistaken."

"I don't think so." Abby eased closer to the counter.

Estelle jumped back.

Good. Abby had unsettled her. Abby displayed her deputy's badge and introduced herself. "If you continue to deny it, I'll have no choice but to take you in for fingerprinting and questioning. A DNA test too."

Estelle's expression twisted into something dark, sinister as she whipped a pistol from behind her back. Abby tensed —too late.

The gun in her hand gleamed under the light, an old, weathered pistol. Was it the missing gun from Victor's collection?

A twisted smile spread across her face. She was enjoying this.

Abby hadn't seen it coming. She didn't think this older woman would pull a gun on her and had underestimated her because of her age. And now, she had seconds—maybe less—to figure out her next move.

"You just couldn't leave it alone, could you?" Estelle waved the pistol. "Picking, picking, picking, when all I did was leave my husband."

"It's the manner in which you left him." Abby lifted her chin, trying to hide her fear. "And now you've come back to steal the crown from him."

"The crown?" She laughed, the pitch hysterical. "Oh, that's priceless. It's long gone. I took it before I left him."

"So you replaced it with the forgery," Abby stated.

"You figured it out. You're a better investigator than I thought this backwater place would have."

Abby ignored her insult. "If you already have the authentic crown, why did you come back to steal the forgery?"

"Okay, maybe I was wrong. Maybe you aren't as smart as I thought." Estelle sneered at her. "I wasn't after the forgery. I wanted what's in the case. I took the crown to make it look like my target."

Could this be what Victor meant by the crown wasn't the treasure?

"What's in the case?" Abby asked.

"Microsoft stock certificates Valentino bought at the company's initial public offering. With all the stock splits, and the increase in share prices, his initial investment is now worth about fifteen million dollars."

"A lot of good they'll do you. You can't trade stocks in Valentino's name."

Estelle gave her a sly grin. "I've already had a document made showing Valentino transferred the shares to me. I even added Victor's signature as the witness. It's a world-class forgery. No one would question it."

"That would be some haul," Abby admitted. "If you knew about the stock, why wait until now to take the case?"

"No point back then. It wasn't worth much." She frowned. "Foolish me, I figured I'd be set for life with the money I got from selling the crown. Big mistake. I'm accustomed to a certain lifestyle, so I had to come back."

Just what they'd suspected, except it was for stocks and not the crown. "I suppose it cost a lot more to raise a child than you planned."

"You found my journal." She honestly seemed impressed. "Don't think for one minute I had that child. Even then, I knew without Vincent's fortune and title, I didn't want to raise another child."

Abby didn't want a picture of what she had done to get rid of the baby. "So, what happened to Vincent? Did he get smart and leave you?"

She laughed. "I thought you found Vincent's body at the mansion. How do you think it got there?"

"Vincent?" Abby took a moment to process the comment. "You killed Victor's brother and buried him at the mansion?"

She cocked her head at a superior angle. "I was so tired of my life here, and I knew Victor wouldn't leave. But Vincent offered to take me away from it all. Until the day we were going to leave. Then something came over the fool. He felt a sudden need to tell Victor what was going on."

"So you killed him to stop him?"

"No. No. It was an accident. I couldn't risk Victor finding a way to make me stay, so I argued with Vincent. It got heated. I shoved him. He grabbed my locket and the chain gave way. He lost his balance and stumbled. Hit his head on a rock. Died instantly."

"If it was an accident, why didn't you report it?"

"And stay here?" Her voice skyrocketed. "Maybe end up in jail here? No. No way."

"So you buried him to hide your crime."

"Hah. Look at me." She wiggled her well-manicured fingernails. "Do I look like someone who could dig a grave and drag a large man into it?"

Yeah, Abby thought it was improbable, but people did amazing things when in shock. "Who helped you bury the body? Was it Shaw?"

"Shaw? You've got to be kidding. He sold the crown for me, then broke in to steal the bogus crown. He also tried to impale your boat with one he'd stolen to silence Victor in case he discovered anything over the years. Fool couldn't even do that."

"Of course, you promised him something in return."

"I might have offered to share a portion of my new wealth." A devious grin crossed her face. "But that's it."

Abby planted her hands on her hips. "I find it hard to believe that's your full relationship with him."

"I'm telling the truth, but you don't have to believe me." She tilted her head. "I don't know why I'm bothering to answer this. Not when I won't let you live beyond today."

Abby had no doubt she would follow through on her threat. Not after she so callously killed and buried Vincent. But Abby would do everything to make sure she stayed alive. She needed to buy time until she could figure a way out of this situation.

"So who did bury Vincent?" she asked.

"Juan. The fool was in love with me and would do anything for me. Even cover up Vincent's death."

Another surprise. "And no one missed Vincent or was looking for him?"

Estelle shrugged. "I was gone, so I have no idea, but Victor and our children were his only living relatives. Vincent's obvious advances toward me made Victor write him off. He didn't want to have anything to do with his brother. Probably wouldn't wonder what happened to him." She gave a guttural laugh. "The perfect crime."

"Not so perfect," Abby said. "We unearthed the remains, and we're hot on your trail."

"Not exactly hot. You found a belt buckle. Something I didn't think to remove. Sure, if you showed it to Victor he would know it belonged to Vincent, but what was your step beyond that? Or did you even have one?"

"We're running the forensics found at the gravesite. Fingerprints. DNA. We're sure to find yours on recovered items. We also found the locket buried in the greenhouse. You didn't say how that ended up there."

"Like I said, Vincent broke the chain when he grabbed it. Juan picked it up and asked me what I wanted to do with it. Victor had given it to me when we got married, and I wanted no part of it. Besides, if I was caught wearing it, no matter any disguise I could wear, it would identify me. So I gave it to Juan. Asked him to dispose of it. He said he'd bury it in the greenhouse. When you and the detective started investigating I figured I better retrieve it."

"So it was you we interrupted that night in the greenhouse?"

Estelle nodded.

"And did you light a fire in the office fireplace that night too?"

She lifted her chin, laughter in her eyes. "I burned some papers hoping it would throw you off. Sounds like it did."

Abby was getting tired of Estelle thinking she was above the law and would never have to serve time for her crimes. "Regardless, we'll find enough to prosecute you for Vincent's murder."

"And then what? I'm leaving town tonight. No one could find me before. What makes you think you'll be able to find me now? And even if you did, because of Vincent's advances toward me, it wouldn't be unlikely for my DNA or fingerprints to be found there. I had no motive to kill him, but Victor did. He would be your most likely suspect."

She stopped talking and jiggled her gun. "Enough of this. Remove the gun from your holster—slowly—and put it on the counter."

Abby couldn't bring herself to hand over her weapon. As a law enforcement officer, it'd been ingrained in her not to surrender her firearm unless absolutely necessary. "Everyone on my team knows I'm here. If you harm me, they won't stop at anything to hunt you down."

"I wish them luck." A sinister laugh rose up out of her mouth. "As I said. They'll never find me."

"I wouldn't count on that. Far more technology tracking your every move exists now that didn't when you disappeared before."

She jerked her pistol. "I'm getting tired of this. Gun on the counter now or I'll just shoot you right here and leave Leonard to take the fall."

Now, Abby had no choice. Glaring at Estelle, she took

out her weapon. Laid it on the counter as instructed and would look for ways to overpower the older woman.

"Now step back," Estelle demanded.

Abby complied. Estelle snatched up the gun and shoved it in her waistband. She jerked her pistol toward the front door. "Lock the door, and we'll go out the back."

Abby slowly walked to the door, scanning through the window to find help, but the street was deserted. Feeling like she was sealing her own fate, she twisted the lock. "Where are you taking me?"

"To see my good friend Leonard."

"Where is he?"

She jabbed the gun in Abby's back, her strength very surprising. "The sooner you get moving, the sooner you'll find out."

Abby took her time walking to the back room. She entered, but her steps faltered.

Blood. Was that blood smeared near the exit door handle?

She whipped her head around to look at Estelle. "Is this your blood or Shaw's?"

"The silly man was going to tell you the truth about the crown. I couldn't let that happen." Estelle growled like a wild animal. "Take out your phone and leave it here."

Was Estelle confessing to murdering Shaw? Abby wouldn't put it past her. Gone was the woman everyone had described when they talked about Estelle in their interviews. Or this was the real Estelle, and she'd just been pretending to be the woman they'd all known.

Abby couldn't afford to make her angry, so she set her only lifeline on a worktable.

Estelle shoved hard on Abby's back, pushing her through the exit and directing her toward a blue van with the side door open. At the vehicle, Estelle gave Abby another hard shove. She slammed into the cargo van's metal floor.

Abby continued to be amazed at this woman's strength. Sure, she looked as fit as a younger woman, obviously maintaining her shape and likely working out to maintain her muscle strength too. As much as Abby didn't like that she'd gotten a drop on her, she had to admire the older woman's fitness.

Estelle gave a sharp punch to Abby's leg. "Pull yourself in so I can close the door."

Abby couldn't let the door close. No way or she'd be dead. She frantically scanned the vehicle for a way out. Two bucket seats in the front. An empty void in the back.

Nothing. Absolutely nothing useful for an escape.

"Fine." Estelle dropped her finger to the trigger and aimed at Abby. "The same offer from inside stands. I'll kill you right here. Either way you're dead."

Abby's pulse pounded. No way she wanted an instant death. If she hung on she might somehow escape on the drive to wherever Estelle was taking her.

She drew up her legs and curled into a ball. Her thoughts ricocheted through her brain. She could hardly focus.

Prayer. She needed prayer.

She closed her eyes and lifted up her request.

I don't want to die. Not when I've just found a possible future with a wonderful man like Burke. Please let someone find me before Estelle takes her revenge.

25

Phone to his ear, Burke paced across his department's floor as he waited for his call to Abby to connect. Voicemail. Just like the last five calls he'd made in the past hour.

He'd think she didn't want to talk to him, but their last conversation told him they were beyond that stage. At least he hoped they were. But if so, where was she? Why wasn't she answering?

He wasn't one to panic. At least not normally. But his feelings for her added a strong measure of unease.

What should he do next? He could ask Ryder to have her phone pinged, but he didn't have enough justification for such a request. If the only evidence they presented to a judge was a woman who wouldn't return his calls, they'd be laughed out of his chambers.

So then what?

Call her team.

He stopped pacing. Was that a good idea? If nothing was wrong, he would come across as extremely needy. Not something he wanted to portray when they were just starting to think about a relationship. Normally, he wasn't a needy guy.

Wouldn't even be thinking of calling her team. Would just leave another more urgent voicemail. Or not even that.

"So give it time," he mumbled under his breath and returned to his desk.

He settled into his chair and took the time to read through the original missing person file, hoping something would jump out at him. Something they'd missed. He flipped page after page. Nothing popped out at him.

His phone rang. *Abby*. His heart soared. Fell. Not Abby, but Sam was calling.

He swallowed his disappointment and answered. "You haven't heard from Abby this afternoon, have you?"

"No, why?"

"She hasn't been answering her phone for the last few hours."

"Do you think something has happened to her?"

"I'm probably just being paranoid."

"Because you care for her."

Though she spoke the truth, Burke wasn't going to acknowledge it. At least not until his relationship with Abby became official. "You must have forensic results if you're calling me instead of her."

"Way to sidestep the question." She let the words hang in the air.

No way Burke would say anything, and he waited her out.

"So, yeah," she finally said. "I have additional fingerprint information for you."

"Good." He tried to get enthused about her call instead of worrying about Abby. Failed. "The investigation has kind of stalled, and we need something to go on."

"One set of prints on the crown hiding place belonged to Leonard Shaw."

"Shaw?" Burke could hardly believe what he was hearing. "How did you get his prints for comparison?"

"He wanted his high-end antique customers to know he was above board, so he had a background check done."

"Smart move for a legit operator," Burke said. "Foolish one for a criminal."

"Maybe these days, but not when he had it done," Sam said. "Before 2014, those prints weren't kept in the FBI's database, so investigators couldn't locate them there. But I have a buddy who has access to the older state files. He ran the prints as a favor for me. Not a legit favor. Means if you prosecute the guy, the prints can't be used."

"Point taken. But the print locations could indicate he killed Estelle and stole the crown."

"Exactly. And if it helps, the prints on the crown's hiding place are current. The locket, much older as you would expect."

"So he could be the guy who broke in recently and took the crown."

"Looks like it. Unless he visited Victor."

"I can have Gabe search the ferry key card log to see if Shaw ever visited. If he doesn't show up, though, doesn't mean he wasn't there. He might not have a card or he has access to a private boat. In fact, if I was going to steal the crown, I would do it late at night when ferries stopped running and arrive in my own boat."

"Agreed. That's all I've got for now, but I thought it might help if I got this information to you quickly."

"Absolutely, and thanks, Sam." He ended the call and immediately dialed Abby. Straight to voicemail again.

That niggling concern in his gut grew into a full-blown cramp of worry. He called Gabe.

"Yo, bro," Gabe answered right away. "What can I do for you?"

"I need you to check the ferry boat logs to see if Leonard Shaw ever visited Victor."

"The antique dealer? Okay. Got it. I'll get right on it."

"Before I go, have you heard from Abby in the last few hours?"

"No. Is there a problem?"

"I hope not, but she's not answering my calls."

"Hold on. Let me try her in case she's blowing you off."

Before Burke could argue about being blown off, Gabe put him on hold. He tapped his foot under the desk as he waited for Gabe to come back on the line.

"Yeah, man, you're right. She's not answering. Maybe she's just tied up in a meeting."

"Could be, but I'd rather be safe than sorry. I'll call your team headquarters to see if anyone there has heard from her."

"Sounds like a plan. And I'll get right on your request." Gabe ended the call.

Burke dialed the LLL team headquarters. The phone rang three times, before it was picked up.

"Lost Lake Locators, Hayden Kraus speaking," he said, sounding as if he'd been schooled in positive customer service. "How can I help you?"

"Hayden, it's Burke. Have you heard from Abby lately?"

"Lately? Nah. Last time I talked to her she was in Seaside Harbor waiting to meet with the prosecuting attorney for tomorrow's deposition."

"How long ago was that?"

"Ah," he paused. "Five maybe more hours ago. She's not likely still there though."

"She's not answering her phone or returning my calls, and I'm concerned."

"That's not like her," Hayden said. "Let me give her a call from my cell to see if she'll pick up for me."

Again, Burke didn't bother to argue. Just like Gabe, Hayden seemed to think she could be blowing him off. He'd obviously given her teammates cause to believe such a thing. Or maybe she had. Either way, he didn't think these guys had a positive impression of him.

"No answer," Hayden said. "Went straight to voicemail. If you're really concerned about it, she has an iPhone, and the Find My iPhone feature is active on all of our phones. I made sure of that so we can find each other at a moment's notice. You want me to check it?"

Did he? If nothing was wrong, he didn't want her to think he was spying on her. But something might be wrong —terribly wrong—and at this point he wouldn't take a chance. "Do it."

"Hang on."

He heard Hayden's fingers moving over a keyboard on the other end of the line and sat back to wait for the information. He couldn't sit still. He jumped up and started pacing.

"She's at The Gilded Gallery in Seaside Harbor," Hayden said. "Isn't that the place owned by the expert Nolan mentioned?"

Burke's blood turned cold. "Leonard Shaw isn't just some expert. Sam just confirmed his fingerprints were found on the crown's hiding place."

Hayden's voice dropped. "Shaw's also the guy I warned Abby about right before her meeting. He's on my list of known fences. And he used to be close to Estelle before she vanished."

Burke's stomach twisted. "Then he could've stolen the crown and killed her."

"And Abby said she needed to talk to him. She was planning to go alone, but she said she'd contact you first."

A call Burke never received. A bolt of panic ripped

through him, nearly buckling his knees. "We need to get to that gallery. Now! I'm in Surfside Harbor—it'll take me too long. Can you get over there? Take the team. Just go. Check on her."

Burke heard shuffling. The scrape of a chair. Footsteps.

"Already leaving," Hayden said tightly. "Team's coming with me."

Burke's gut clenched like a fist. "I'm heading out. Call me the second you know anything."

"You got it."

Burke shoved his phone into his pocket and tore out of the office. Thank God his work vehicle had lights. He planned to keep them on—sirens too—until he reached Shaw's place.

If anything happened to Abby, he'd never forgive himself.

∾

The van bumped over uneven roads, and Abby rolled around on the hard metal floor. Estelle had bound Abby's hands behind her back, so she couldn't right herself or brace against the rough road. Miles had passed. Miles where she'd planned to somehow stall Estelle or slow her down. Failed.

Abby had to buy time until she found an opportunity to escape or someone realized she was missing and came to help. Problem was, no one knew where she'd gone. Hayden had the iPhone app set up for all of them and would at least track her to the antique shop. But then what? They'd have no idea where Shaw was, that Estelle was still alive, or that she'd taken Abby captive. All they would find were her phone and blood on the door. That would tell them something bad had happened, but not what. They could assume the blood was hers.

The van came to a sudden stop. They hadn't traveled far. Maybe five or so miles. The sun had set fully now, so she couldn't tell which direction they'd been heading. Especially since Estelle had whipped around several corners. Abby got turned around. She was certain they'd left town and had driven on uneven and bumpy roads. They were out in the country or down by the beach. Either way, not likely places for anyone to come looking for her.

The van door slid open. The sound of the rushing ocean and the salty, fishy smell came whipping into the van from nearby. They had indeed traveled to the beach.

"Get out." Estelle's sharp tone sent Abby's fear soaring.

Abby knew what Estelle would do if she didn't comply. She wiggled her way to the edge of the floor and sat up, then slid out, her gaze quickly traveling around the area.

Only the headlights Estelle had left on threatened the black sky with zero light pollution from the town. They'd most certainly left Seaside Harbor behind. A tall, narrow structure rose up on the beach. A lighthouse, she presumed. It didn't transmit any light so not likely one in service.

Estelle ground the barrel of her gun in Abby's side. "Head for the lighthouse. No one around to hear us, so any stupid move and I'll shoot."

Abby didn't doubt the woman's words, so she took careful steps through the deep sand toward the dark structure. Footprints led the way through the mounded sand. With nothing filling the impressions, she figured someone had recently been there.

Had the blood at the antique shop been Shaw's? Had Estelle brought him out here to kill him too?

She gave Abby another shove. She stumbled, but managed to right herself.

Estelle laughed.

"What's wrong with you?" Abby swiveled to look at the

woman. "How can you be enjoying this? Finding joy in someone else's struggle?"

"Struggle? You don't know what struggle is." She revealed deep anguish in her tone. "Try growing up without a penny to your family's name. Literally without a penny. No food on the table. Going to bed hungry more times than not. Wearing rags to school and being belittled every day."

"I'm sorry that happened to you, Estelle," Abby said sincerely. "But it doesn't mean you need to resort to killing people."

"I'll do anything. *Anything* to live the life I want. Escape from my childhood. But that didn't happen until I married Victor. I worked hard to drag myself up out of the gutter and make myself socially acceptable. I had to before someone like Victor would stoop to marry me. Once I caught his eye, I had to fake my feelings for the imbecile. Bear kids for him. Just so I could have the life I deserve."

Shocked by her statement, Abby stared at her captor. "No one deserves such a life. It has to be earned."

"Really?" Her eyes flashed open, and she panted like a dog. "Did Victor earn it? No. He simply had the good fortune to be born into a rich family. He's never worked a day in his life and never will." Her eyes turned hard as iron. "Now go."

Her look sent shudders over Abby as she turned to follow the footprints. At the lighthouse door, she tried to get a good look inside, but the darkness hid everything. Estelle pushed her ahead and flipped on a light, flooding a circular room with large windows all around.

"Go to the stairwell to your right. We'll be going down to the basement." Estelle shoved her harder, and she continued on across the room. She gasped.

To her left, Shaw lay in a heap, his eyes wide, blood infusing the front of his white shirt.

"So now you can see I mean business," Estelle said. "We aren't here for fun and games like you seem to think."

"Trust me," Abby said, her voice barely getting out of her throat. "I didn't think we were here for that. Is there anything I can do to convince you not to use your gun on me?"

"No." Estelle fired Abby an undeniable look of certainty. "You're going to die tonight."

~

Burke stabbed the call from Hayden on his phone mounted on his dash. "Tell me you found her, and she's okay."

"We didn't find her. The shop's locked. The lights on. The back door open."

"And?"

"And we found her phone on the work table, blood on the inside of the back door."

"Blood?" Burke couldn't control his tone, the high pitch reflecting the inner turmoil threatening to destroy him. "It could be hers—" And he was still thirty minutes away from Seaside Harbor. He couldn't do anything about it.

"It could be." Hayden's tone was level, unemotional.

"How can you be so calm?" Burke snapped.

"Trust me. I'm not calm. Just trying to keep it together. You should probably do the same. Won't do her any good if you get in an accident."

He was right, but Burke couldn't calm down. Not with Abby missing and blood found on the door. "Did Shaw hurt her? Where could he have taken her?"

"Could be another property he owns, but I don't know of any. I'm on my laptop now, checking county property records."

Burke needed to pick up his speed, but he couldn't

concentrate on the phone and go faster. "Call me back the minute you know anything."

He didn't wait for Hayden to agree, but ended the call and punched the gas pedal. If anyone other than Abby were missing, he would still do his best to get to them. But his emotions wouldn't be wrapped up in the need to find this person, and he could drive more rationally.

If anything told him he cared about Abby—maybe loved her—this clarified things for him.

He gripped the wheel, roaring around curves, his tires squealing. He'd taken many defensive driving classes and was confident in handling this road, slowing when he had to but hating every second of it. Hating every minute that passed when he was no closer to knowing where Abby had been taken.

Nearing the lights of Seaside Harbor, his phone rang. "What did you find, Hayden?"

"Nothing."

Burke slammed his fist against the steering wheel. Pain shot up his arm, but it didn't compare to the pressure crushing his chest. "So that's it? We've got nothing?"

"Just a long shot," Hayden replied. "I found a mention in a local paper. The sale's not final, but Shaw's in the process of buying an old lighthouse. Coastal property."

Burke didn't care about final. This location was a lead. Right now, it was all he had. "Send me the coordinates."

"On it. We'll meet you there."

A chime lit up his phone. The GPS loaded instantly.

His pulse spiked.

The lighthouse was on the edge of Seaside Harbor—his side. He was only three minutes out. Three minutes from possibly finding Abby alive.

Or not.

He floored the gas pedal, tires screaming against pavement.

Hold on, Abby. I'm coming.

~

In the basement with big construction work lights burning bright, to the floor. "Don't make a move."

Abby tried not to be afraid. Tried to pretend it didn't matter. Pretend she wasn't concerned with what Estelle was about to do. But inside, her stomach rolled and acid burned up her throat.

Please, please, Lord. Don't let Estelle win. Don't let her kill me. Sure, I want to live, but I'm not asking for myself. I'm asking for Burke, who has finally been able to consider loving someone again. For my team members who don't need to deal with the loss of a teammate. Even for my family, though I don't know how they'd respond.

Estelle had made a call while Abby prayed, and she tuned into it now.

"What do you mean there's some question about my trip back to France?" Estelle nearly screamed into the phone. "What's wrong with my passport?"

Tapping her foot, she listened carefully, her eyes narrowing into spiteful slits. "You better figure it out. I'm leaving tonight or you'll pay the price."

She shoved her phone into her pocket.

Abby was certain the gun would now be trained on her again, only this time the unstable woman would fire. Instead, she started pacing, running her hand over hair no longer rich black like earlier in her photos, but brown and laced with silver.

She suddenly spun and stared at Abby. "You're law enforcement. You can fix it so the authorities aren't questioning my passport."

Abby likely couldn't do any such thing, but she wouldn't tell Estelle. "Sure, but I'll have to go into the office to take care of the paperwork."

"Don't think I'm stupid." Estelle's stare turned into a challenge. "You don't help me, I get that hunky detective you've been hanging out with to do it. Then I'll kill him too."

Abby stifled a gasp. "If I call him to do the paperwork, I'll have to tell him you're alive, and he'd have to insist you stay in the country until the investigation is resolved."

"What about one of your teammates? I read their bios on your website and know they're all former law enforcement officers. One of them must have a contact who can make something happen under the table."

"Sure, yeah, that might work." Once again, Abby was certain they couldn't sidestep federal law, but someone on the team might have a contact who could help. "I'll have to tell them where I am and why I didn't come home after my meeting today."

"Lie," Estelle snapped. "Say you and the detective have a thing for each other, and you're on a date."

Abby's stomach twisted. "What if he calls them?"

Estelle's gaze sharpened. "Is that likely?"

"With everyone working on this investigation, it could happen," she said, though even she didn't sound convincing to herself.

Estelle's eyes narrowed. "I don't believe in chances. I believe in instincts." She cut the ropes on Abby's hands and held out her phone. "Pick the team member most likely to have the right contact. You have five minutes."

Abby froze.

Five minutes. Just five. For a decision that could mean the difference between life and death.

The weight of the clock pressed against her chest.

One call—one person—could save her life. Or end it.

26

Lights glowed from the lighthouse, spilling onto the pristine sand. Burke scanned the area. Mounds of sand. Moonlight glistening on the water rolling in and out on frothy waves. Pure solitude.

And no sign of Abby's team. Unless the cargo van on the side of the road belonged to them.

One way to find out. He slammed on the brakes and skidded into place behind the van, his tires spitting sand.

He fought the urge to make a fast dash from his cruiser to Abby. Shaw had most likely stashed her in the lighthouse with lights burning through the windows. He forced himself to cool down, pick up his radio, and call in the van's plates.

He waited for dispatch to respond to his request, his legs and hands jittery as each second passed. Each of his heartbeats stabbed like a hammer blow, fast, hard, relentless.

He was ready to jump out of his skin. Finally his radio squawked. He listened carefully, then bolted from the vehicle. The plates had come back as a rental. So not the team. Likely belonged to Shaw. Likely the person who'd abducted Abby.

He fixed his focus ahead. Nothing to hide behind, just

an open beach between him and the lighthouse. On the bright side, he could go straight to the building. A slower evasive route wouldn't help in this situation.

He charged down the bank toward the structure.

I'm almost there, sweetheart. Almost. Hang in there.

He slowed as he approached the open doorway. Drawing his sidearm, he glanced inside. One big room. Empty. Not totally. A crumpled body lay on the far side next to a cardboard box.

His legs threatened to give in.

From the doorway, he took a good look at the figure. No. Not Abby. Too big to be her.

Thank You! Thank You! Thank You!

He approached the body. Shaw! It was Shaw with a bullet wound to the chest.

Someone had killed him, but who? More importantly, if he were dead, who had Abby?

Voices drifted up from a stairwell on the other side of the room. He silently made his way over. Listened.

Abby was talking. Asking for help in getting Estelle Lemoine's passport cleared so she could leave for Paris today.

Stunned, he took a step back. Estelle was alive, and Abby was trying to help her.

A creak of the floorboards sounded behind him.

He spun. Lifted his weapon. Aimed. Prepared to shoot.

Gabe stepped into the room.

Burke let out a long breath. Crossing the room, he held a finger to his mouth to warn Gabe to be quiet. "Keep it down. I'm not sure if Abby's in trouble yet, but she's in the basement."

Gabe jerked a thumb at the body. "That Shaw over there?"

Burke nodded. "It was probably his blood on the antique

shop door, not Abby's. She's talking to someone about helping Estelle Lemoine get back to France tonight."

Gabe blinked hard. "Estelle? So she's not dead."

"Apparently not. I'm wondering if she killed Shaw and brought Abby here. Sounds like Estelle is having a problem with her passport and isn't able to leave the country."

"And she's making Abby fix the problem. Probably at gunpoint."

"Probably," Burke whispered. "Which means we need to figure out a way to get down there without alerting Estelle. Or entice her upstairs before she hurts Abby."

Gabe nodded. "I circled the building when I got here. No outside egress from the basement. Only one way in and out. A perfect place to take a hostage."

"Then either we storm the basement or entice Estelle out."

"We could wait for the team. They're on the way. We could storm the place in numbers."

Burke shook his head. "I don't think numbers will help. This is a more delicate operation. Somehow we need to get eyes down there to see exactly what's happening."

"I have a flexible camera in my car. We should be able to snake it down the steps without Estelle noticing it."

"Get it and call the team while you're out there. Tell them what's going on and ask them to hang back until we signal."

Without a word, Gabe took off, silently making his way to the door and outside.

One one thousand. Two one thousand, Burke mentally counted to keep from pacing. *Three one thousand. Four one thousand. Five one thousand...*

Finally, Gabe returned, the camera in his grip.

"I'll take it." Burke held out his hand for the black snake-like device.

Gabe held back. "She's my teammate. I can do it."

"I know you *can* do it," Burke replied, doing his best to keep his voice down. "You're a temporary deputy. If Estelle suddenly needs to be taken out, it would be better for a regular deputy to take the shot."

Gabe sighed in resignation and passed the camera to Burke, then held out his phone to him. "The camera app is on here."

Burke took the phone and plugged the camera into it. The app opened, and Burke moved the lens around, the screen displaying the room.

"Perfect. It works." He looked up at Gabe. "I need you at the stairs for backup."

His sharp nod gave Burke a measure of relief.

They traveled across the room, creeping side-by-side. At the stairwell, Burke dropped to his knees. Flattened out on his belly. He signaled for Gabe to stand by and be ready to head down the stairs if needed.

Burke unrolled the camera coil with practiced precision, hands steady despite the adrenaline surging through his body. Silently, he fed the end into the narrow gap where the stairwell met the ceiling below.

His phone screen flickered, then lit up.

Abby!

She sat on the cold floor, knees drawn tightly up to her chest, clutching a phone to her ear like a lifeline. Her lips moved as she talked on the phone, but her wide, terrified eyes were locked on Estelle.

The older woman stood motionless, a handgun trained on Abby. She didn't speak. Didn't need to. Not when her posture was as lethal as the gun she held. She watched Abby the way a lion watched an injured deer—patient, certain, already tasting the end.

Abby lowered the phone. "My teammate said he can get

your passport cleared. He'll do his best to fix the problem tonight, but he can't promise he'll make it on time."

Estelle planted her feet wide. "You better convince this guy to come through for me or I'll take you both out."

Abby arched an eyebrow, her posture suddenly defensive. "You're going to kill us no matter what we do. You can't let us live. Not when we both know you're alive."

"So what?" Estelle laughed. "You'll still do what you need to do. You have to. You want to stay alive as long as you can. You especially. Foolishly hoping someone rescues you. Face facts. No one knows where you are. No one is coming for you."

Burke fought the urge to call out, "Hold on, sweetheart. I'm here for you." He bit his tongue instead.

Abby remained motionless, Estelle's comment seeming not to bother her.

"Then the only thing to do is wait for your teammate to succeed in his task." Estelle marched to Abby and held out her hand. "Phone."

Abby slapped it on her palm. In a split second, she lurched up and went for Estelle's gun. They clashed. Struggled.

A shot rang.

"No-o-o-o!" Burke cried out and waved Gabe on.

Sidearm in hand, he charged past Burke and down the steps while Burke got to his feet and bolted after his partner.

In the basement, Estelle and Abby were struggling over the gun. Gabe clamped his hands on Estelle's shoulders and ripped her free as if she were a rag doll.

Burke raced to Abby, trying to ignore the blood on the floor. He dropped down in front of her and scanned her body for obvious injury. "Are you okay?"

She nodded. "Estelle took the bullet."

Burke glanced over his shoulder.

Moaning, Estelle was stretched out on the floor, already handcuffed. Gabe leaned over her, applying pressure to a wound on her leg.

"Ouch!" she complained. "Not so rough. I'm not one of those peasant girls you're used to dealing with."

Gabe rolled his eyes. "Her Royal Highness isn't going to die from this, but we should call 911."

Burke turned his attention back to Abby and took out his phone. "You're sure you're all right?"

She nodded. "A bit shaken up, but no injuries thanks to you and Gabe."

Dispatch came on the line. He gave his badge number along with the details. The dispatcher promised an ambulance was on the way.

He stowed his phone. "Ambulance will be here soon."

"Thanks." Gabe looked up from his first aid duties. "I'm certain I can keep her alive until then." He laughed.

Burke chuckled. He'd actually come to appreciate this guy's humor in the face of difficult situations, but right now all he could think about was Abby. He took her hands. They were trembling and icy cold, sending waves of anger rushing through him. Not only anger for her discomfort, but anger for the way she'd been treated. Anger for not being there to stop her abduction before it happened. Anger for failing her.

"What is it?" She leaned closer, looking deep into his eyes. "What's wrong?"

He didn't want to tell her, but if they were going to have a future together, he needed to let her in. "I failed you," he choked out. "If I'd stayed in Seaside Harbor with you, this wouldn't have happened."

"I don't see how you could've stopped it. If you'd been here, it would've happened to both of us. If so, we might not have been rescued."

"Hey, I resemble that." Gabe laughed. "I was the one doing the rescuing."

"Because I told you to move in," Burke fired back, but ended with a grin.

"You doubt I could've done this myself, Mr. Big Shot detective?" Gabe lifted his chin in a playful challenge.

Burke laughed, thankful they could be lighthearted to help ease Abby's tension, but she didn't smile. He sat on the cold concrete beside her and drew her close to him.

She rested her head on his chest, her body shaking. His anger grew, but he swallowed it. The last thing she needed was to see him lose control.

She suddenly sat up. "Call Hayden. Tell him where we are, and that I'm okay."

Burke held up a hand to ease her stress. "Don't worry. He already knows you're here. He's the one who found this location, and he's waiting down the road with the rest of the team."

"Then call him, please." She gave him a wobbly smile. "I don't want him to worry any longer than necessary."

Burke got out his phone and shared the good news with Hayden.

The team wanted to see her for themselves, but they couldn't risk contaminating forensics needed to put Estelle away, so the team waited outside.

Abby scanned the walls as if searching for something that wasn't there—a safe place, a way back, a moment before it all unraveled? She looked impossibly small, like a child lost in a world too cruel to understand.

"Come here," Burke said softly.

She didn't hesitate but collapsed against him again, her surrender telling him more than words could ever convey.

He held her tighter than necessary, as if his arms alone

could protect her. If he had any say in it, nothing like this would ever touch her again.

And for as long as she let him, he'd be there—at her side.

~

Abby enjoyed every moment of being held by Burke. It helped keep thoughts of Estelle and her cruel behavior at bay. It also helped to see the medics carry Estelle toward the stairway. She fired a deadly look at Abby, but Abby didn't flinch. No way she would show that woman how much she'd scared her.

"I'll wait for you two upstairs." Gabe strode to the steps behind the medics.

Remaining comfortably in Burke's arms, Abby relayed everything Estelle had said about the past and the current theft of the crown.

"So it's Vincent's remains we recovered." He shook his head. "If we'd shown Victor the belt buckle, he would've told us that."

"Probably. At least we don't have to do it now." At the thought, she tried to swallow, but her mouth was as dry as burnt toast. "Unfortunately we do have to tell him his brother is dead. Worse yet, Estelle killed him. I hope he's strong enough to handle it all."

"If he's smart, he'll continue his search for faith to help him get through it."

Abby nodded and closed her eyes to pray for Victor. If anything positive existed in this whole situation, it was that Victor might have come to faith.

Burke's phone rang, and Abby opened her eyes.

"It's Kelsey." He sat forward, taking her with him. "Maybe she has Vincent's cause of death."

Abby's heart jumped.

He tapped the phone screen. "I put you on speaker so Abby can hear too."

"I'm glad you're both there." Kelsey's voice held her usual enthusiasm for her work. "I've identified a cause of death. I found depressed fractures in the back of the skull. Indicates he suffered a blunt force trauma."

"That makes sense." Abby described the story Estelle had told her of how she'd pushed Vincent.

"Seems like we have an ID, but we'll have to confirm it with DNA. I'll extract it from the teeth and send it to Emory Jenkins—our DNA expert—to process. If you can't provide anything of Vincent's with his DNA for comparison, we can match it to his brother's."

"We'll meet with Victor or his son tomorrow to ask if they have anything belonging to Vincent." Burke looked at Abby as if asking for confirmation.

She nodded. "Once we have it, we'll get it right over to you."

"Excellent." Kelsey ended the call.

Abby sighed. "I don't look forward to telling Victor about all of this."

"We'll get through it with God by our side." He squeezed her shoulders.

"And at least the cause of death indicates Estelle's telling the truth. A bonus we can't downplay."

Burke rested back against the wall and stroked her hair.

She would love to stay snuggled in his arms. Forget everything bad in the world. Enjoy the warmth and caring radiating from him. But life wasn't always a smooth road. There were bumps and ruts too, and it was time to ditch her makeshift prison.

"Time for us to get out of here." She pushed free and stood on wobbly legs, then headed for the stairs, taking them slowly until she reached the main floor. There she stopped to take in the room she'd moved quickly through before.

Gabe paced in long strides near the exit, and Burke strode past her to join him. They both stopped to look at her as if she were made of fragile crystal.

"You don't want to stay in here," Burke said. "Let's head outside and get some fresh air."

His suggestion sounded good, but her gaze shot in the direction of Shaw's body as if a magnet drew her. A cardboard box sitting next to him captured her attention. "I didn't see that box before."

"It's been there since I arrived," Burke said.

Abby hurried to it.

"Careful." Burke stepped over to her. "Could be a trap."

"Not likely," Abby said. "Killing me wasn't part of Estelle's plan. Honestly, she didn't want anyone knowing she was even alive. When I showed up at the shop and called her out, she looked genuinely shocked that I recognized her."

"Still," Burke said. "Be careful."

She knelt by the box and looked up at him. "Do you have gloves?"

He took out a pair from the pocket of his tailored suit.

"I'm beginning to understand the point of the suit now." Gabe laughed.

"Has anyone mentioned you're not quite as funny as you think?" Burke grinned good-naturedly. "You never said how you got here so fast."

He shrugged. "I talked to Hayden after you said no one had heard from Abby in a while. He said he tried to call her too, but she didn't answer, and I got a bad feeling. So I hit the road in case I was needed, keeping in touch with the team. Then he mentioned the lighthouse. I was closer to this place than they were, so I came straight here."

"Always the hero," Abby said with a grin, flipping open the box. "It's the crown case."

She pulled it out, tipped the box, and set the case on top. Inside, the crown nestled in velvet. "Looks legit, right? But Estelle told me it's the fake one she commissioned. She stole the real one back in the eighties—Shaw sold it for her."

"If she knew it was fake, then why steal it?" Gabe asked.

Abby told them about the Microsoft certificates. "Supposedly they're in this case."

She lifted out the crown and held it up to Burke. "Can you hold this?"

"You're wearing my only gloves so give me a sec." He peeled off his jacket and held it open so she could set the crown inside for protection.

She felt around the inside of the case. "No holes or tears in the velvet. The piece we found in the greenhouse must not be from this box. And I don't feel any paper in the lining."

She turned the case on its side and ran her fingers over the leather. "There's a seam here. Looks like a hidden door."

Using her fingernails, she carefully pried it open, revealing cream colored certificates with a forest green scrolling border. The name Microsoft appeared in bold black letters at the top. In the middle, a grayish green box held Valentino Lemoine's name as the registered holder.

She counted the certificates. "Ten of them valued at one hundred dollars each just like Estelle said."

Burke squatted by her. "I wonder if Victor knew about these. Could be the reason he said the crown isn't the treasure."

"Seems logical to me." Abby put them in the box, then added the crown. She stood and looked at Burke. "You might not like this, but we're in Sheriff Mina Park's jurisdiction, and she'll insist on taking over this scene."

"I'm more than happy to let her take it off my hands," he said, rising to his feet. His eyes lingered on Abby. "I'm far too invested in a certain someone to lead an objective investigation."

A slow warmth bloomed up her neck, flooding her cheeks. She didn't need to ask who he meant—his gaze had already answered that.

The case was closed, but new questions had taken its place. *What happens now? What are we when the danger is gone?*

With Gabe in the room, she couldn't ask. But she silently promised herself.

We'll talk soon. When it's just the two of us.

27

Three weeks later.

Eager to see Abby again, Burke parked in front of the inn and charged for the door. He'd gone home after the lighthouse incident, but she remained in Lost Lake. One day, she drove down and they'd visited Victor at the hospital together. He had very little residual damage from the stroke and would go home the next day. He was all smiles as his son decided to move in with him to take care of him.

Then two weeks had passed since he'd seen her, and talking on the phone wasn't the same. Each day, it was all he could do not to jump in his truck and drive up here. He couldn't. Not and close out all the paperwork and loose ends from the investigation. And she was busy with Sheriff Park's investigation into her abduction, along with a new missing person's investigation the team had taken on.

Their separation highlighted a problem. A big one. They lived hours apart. Something they'd discussed at length on their calls without coming up with a solution. This distance could stop them from ever getting together.

"Detective Ulrich?" A blonde dressed in dark-wash

jeans, dress boots, and a leather jacket strode toward him and shoved out her hand. "Sheriff Mina Park."

He grasped her hand, not surprised at her solid grip.

She released him. "I was hoping I'd find you here."

"Something you need for Abby's kidnapping investigation?"

She shook her head. "I'd heard you and Abby were an item."

Not at all what he expected her to say, and he wasn't sure he wanted to respond to such a private question.

"I didn't mean to sound nosy—sorry about that. I just figured if you two were together, you might be thinking about moving out this way."

"And if I was?" Burke asked, still not sure he was comfortable with this discussion.

"If so, I have a detective position coming available."

"You're losing your detective?" When he was thinking about moving here, he'd asked Abby if the county sheriff's department had any openings. They didn't—just one detective on staff, and she seemed like a lifer.

"No, thank goodness. Detective Lyons isn't going anywhere." Mina firmed her stance. "We just received a grant to work cold cases, and I'm hiring a detective to manage them."

"Impressive," he said. "From what my sheriff tells me, grants are hard to come by these days."

"He's right." Mina frowned. "But unfortunately, my department didn't have a very good closure rate back in the day. We're the worst county in the state for outstanding cold cases." She cringed. "On the bright side, it made us the most eligible department for a five-year grant to clean up the backlog. I already talked to your sheriff, and he gave you a strong recommendation. So if you're interested in the job, it's yours."

"Wait. What?" He shook his head. "No interviews or comparing me to other candidates?"

"I posted the job internally, but no one applied. A good thing when many of the cases went unsolved with these staff members employed. It's time for fresh blood, and I was just about to post it outside."

"Even if your staff didn't apply, won't they be upset with an outsider coming in?"

"Not likely. Not when they didn't want the job." She pulled a business card from her jacket pocket and handed it to him. "Even if it turns out one of them does take offense to an outsider, from what your sheriff tells me, you're not the kind of guy to let that stand in your way. If you're interested, let's sit down on Monday and talk about the details. See if we're a good fit."

"Name the time." He couldn't hide his eagerness.

"Eight work for you?"

"I'll be there."

She smiled. "Now forget I interrupted your party with business talk. Nolan wouldn't be happy if he knew I was accosting detectives in the lot on the way in." She laughed.

He did too, and they walked inside together. The faded midcentury décor took him by surprise. He halted inside the door to gawk at it.

"I take it you haven't been here before," she said.

He turned in a complete circle, the furnishings not improving. "I expected something a little more professional looking."

"The team is working on updating the place, but they have little free time."

"I don't envy them. This looks like a ton of work."

"Move here, and Abby just might rope you into helping." She chuckled. "Let's go back to the ballroom. And before you expect a true ballroom, it's really just a large meeting room, but it's another blast from the past."

He liked Mina and could see himself working for her. Was he crazy to hope it would happen? Their Monday meeting would tell him for sure. Nothing to do now other than to tell Abby the good news and wait. He shook off his thoughts and trailed her down a dark, dingy hallway.

He followed Mina through a doorway on the left and into a room exactly as she'd described—a large meeting room with sixties furnishings. Around twenty to thirty people mingled in small groups near a long refreshment table overflowing with appetizers and home-baked goodies.

Above the table hung a sign declaring *Happy Anniversary, Lost Lake Locators!* The company had formed more than a year ago, but they'd been too busy with investigations to celebrate their success.

He didn't have eyes for the food or a desire to celebrate. He wanted Abby. Found her talking to Reece. The pair were extreme opposites. Abby was petite with short dark hair. Model-slender Reece towered over her with her blond hair falling below her shoulders. Finally Abby turned and locked gazes with him.

His heart somersaulted, and he struggled to breathe. He couldn't wait to tell her about the job offer. Even *if* he didn't know if he would take it. Transitioning from the large county office he worked in to a small sheriff's department was a step back.

But, in the long run, the way his heart just responded, it probably didn't matter what job he went to if it meant he could be close to Abby.

Burke strode toward Abby. She could barely breathe. All she wanted to do was throw herself into his arms, and it seemed like forever for him to reach her. Like a slo-mo scene in a movie, each step measured and unhurried.

Reece grabbed her arm. "Breathe, sweetie. Or you're going to pass out before he gets over here."

"I am, aren't I? I've never felt like this before."

"From the look on his face, I bet he's thinking the same thing." Reece sighed. "It's like I have my own romance movie playing before my eyes. Only this is better because it involves one of my very best friends and her handsome hero."

Abby forced her gaze from Burke to smile at Reece.

"Oh yeah," Reece said. "I'm going to be a maid of honor before you know it."

She couldn't deny it. Burke was looking more and more like a forever kind of guy. No matter when she got married, Reece would be her maid of honor.

She turned back to him as he took his final strides to stop in front of her. "Hi."

"Hi," she said back.

Reece laughed. "The two of you sound like a couple of lovestruck teenagers."

Burke arched an eyebrow in her direction. "Good to finally meet you in person, Reece."

"And I can read in your expression what you're not saying. 'Nice to meet you, but take a hike.'" She grinned. "I'll go check the refreshments and give the two of you some time alone."

She gave Abby a pointed look and took off for the table loaded with fabulous refreshments she'd made for the party.

"Speaking of time alone," Burke said. "I know you

should be at the party, but is there somewhere we can talk in private for a few minutes?"

Taking his hand, she led him across the room, her heart thumping at merely touching his hand. She was tempted to step into the hallway and kiss him, but when she kissed him again, she wanted them to be alone. No place more alone than looking over the cliff at the ocean, so she pulled him to the door and outside.

She continued across the lot to the edge of the cliff, the sky blazing with the midday sun, waves crashing in rhythm below. God's majesty unfolding before them.

He rested his hands on her shoulders and turned her to face him, his eyes only for her. "I couldn't wait to tell you what Mina talked to me about on the way in."

Her butterflies evaporated. "Not something about the kidnapping investigation, I hope."

"No, no. Sorry. I should've started another way. It's about a job. Her department received a five-year grant to investigate cold cases. She wants me to be the detective in charge."

Abby squeezed his hands. "What wonderful news. I mean, the best news, right? You could move here, and we could be together."

He didn't answer right away.

A knot formed in her stomach. "You don't want to move here. You want me to be the one to move. I don't want to leave the team, especially since Victor not only paid us the big fee as promised but gave us a very generous bonus, and the business is doing well. But for you, I will."

"No, that's not it at all. I absolutely would be glad to move here to be with you. I just have to meet with Mina first to determine if I'm up for the job, and if we have the same standards."

The knot loosened. "I can't speak to the job, but I do

know you both have the same standards. She's a stickler for protocol and doing things right. Just like you. The only place I could see snags between you is stubbornly butting heads over things you might not agree on."

He waved a hand, dismissing her worries. "Happens on my current job, but Ryder is reasonable, and we work it out. I know Mina is highly respected by her staff, so she must do the same thing."

Her heart soared at the possibilities.

He frowned. "You should know I could be out of a job when the grant ends in five years. I'm not overly picky about the place I work, but it has to be in law enforcement."

"Who knows what the next five years will bring? We can face that when and if it happens."

He smiled, a sweet, soft smile just for her. "Then after I meet with Mina on Monday, we should know more about our future."

Things were still unsettled between them, but Abby raised her face to the salty breeze and let it carry away the weight of any remaining doubt. Her anxiety lifted, replaced by a quiet peace.

"I'm glad you came so we could talk about this," she said.

"I couldn't stay away."

Completely at peace, she watched the waves crash into the boulders below. *Thank You, God, for Your many blessings.*

Burke stood quietly behind her. His silence continued so long she had to know what he was thinking. She turned to look at him.

He took a small box from one of his cargo pockets. Not velvet like a jewelry box, but a cedar box sanded smooth.

"I made this." Uncertainty replaced his conviction not only in his words, but in his expression. "I spent the last two weeks getting it right."

"I can tell you worked hard on it." She took the box, the cedar smooth under her fingers. Whatever it contained, he'd handcrafted the box for her. She lifted the lid. Inside sat a hand-carved wooden compass, polished with oil, and the needle was set in silver.

She turned it over. Found a single word, etched in careful script— *Return*.

"The compass and box are both beautiful." Emotion choked off her voice.

"It's meant to be more than nice to look at," he said, voice low. "The compass means a return to something real."

To her, that meant a return to who she was. No more trying to be something her family wanted her to be. No more trying to be the unbreakable woman she tried to be when she was sheriff. But now, just Abby. A woman in love with Burke, who reciprocated her feelings.

This man—stubborn, brave, compassionate—wasn't only part of her life now. He was home for her. Not because he rescued her, but because he saw her. Her failings. Her faults. And he stayed.

She stepped closer. "Sometimes the hardest journeys are the ones back to ourselves."

He reached for her hand. "You helped me find something I'd lost. Trust. Faith. Love. I won't get everything right. That's for sure. But I'd like to figure it out—with you."

As a gust of wind swept over them, a quiet prayer rose up within her—a prayer of gratitude and surrender. For love. For the grace that had never really left.

"I wasn't looking for love," she whispered. "For us. I didn't think I deserved it."

"Me neither. In fact, I was thinking I was a lost cause in that department." He stepped closer and circled her in his arms. "But here we are."

She curled her hands around his neck and lifted up on her toes for what she hoped was an inevitable kiss.

To the sound of waves crashing into the rocks, he lowered his lips to hers—a kiss of peace and love. His lips, soft and gentle, didn't demand anything, but simply promised—*I see you. I trust you. I'm not leaving.*

He lifted his head and breathed deeply.

She instantly missed his contact and rose up again to rest her forehead against his. "So... what now?"

"I love you, Abby." He looked deep into her eyes. "Will you walk this path with me?"

"I love you too." She smiled, tears wetting her eyes. "I will, with God's help, every step."

∼

Thank you so much for reading *Lost Cause*. If you've enjoyed the book, I would be grateful if you would post a review on the bookseller's site. Just a few words is all it takes or simply leave a rating.

I'd also like to invite you to learn more about these books as they release and about my other books by signing up for my **NEWSLETTER** at https://www.susansleeman.com/sign-up-2. You'll also receive a FREE e-book copy of *Cold Silence*, the prequel to my Cold Harbor Series, when you do. If you're already a subscriber, you can sign up again and get the free book and it won't put your name on the list twice, but you will receive welcome to my list messages.

And you'll be happy to hear that there are more books in this series! Read on for details.

LOST LAKE - BOOK 4

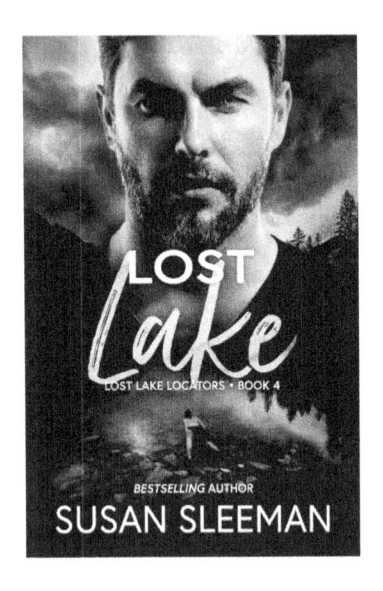

A body in the lake. A child missing.
Detective El (Elaina) Lyons is haunted by her past but relentless in her pursuit of justice. When a woman's body is found in Lost Lake and her child vanishes without a trace, El races against time to solve the crime before it turns into a second tragedy.

A killer and kidnapper still out there.
Enter Gabe Irving—Lost Lake Locator, rogue investigator, and the victim's best friend. He's got a personal stake and zero patience for protocol, putting him at immediate odds

with El. And at odds with their ongoing interest they'd been fighting for years.

But as tensions rise and secrets surface, it's clear the case—and the killer—are far more twisted than either expected. Forced to work together, El and Gabe must navigate a maze of lies and danger. Can they find the missing child before it's too late... or will the killer disappear with the sweet little girl?

PREORDER LOST LAKE NOW!

LOST LAKE LOCATORS SERIES

When people disappear without a trace, those who dare to search for them face a shocking reality: finding the missing may cost them everything—including their own lives.

Book 1 – Lost Hours
Book 2 – Lost Truth
Book 3 – Lost Cause
Book 4 – Lost Lake
Book 5 – Lost Girls
Book 6 – Lost Light

For More Details Visit -
https://www.susansleeman.com/lost-lake-locators/

SHADOW LAKE SURVIVAL SERIES

When survival takes a deadly turn, every step forward draws them deeper into danger—where one wrong move could be their last.

Book 1 – Shadow of Deceit
Book 2 – Shadow of Night
Book 3 – Shadow of Truth
Book 4 – Shadow of Hope
Book 5 – Shadow of Doubt
Book 6 – Shadow of Fear

For More Details Visit -
www.susansleeman.com/books/shadow-lake-survival

STEELE GUARDIAN SERIES
Intrigue. Suspense. Family.
A kidnapped baby. A jewelry heist. Amnesia. Abduction.
Smuggled antiquities. And in every book, God's amazing
power and love.

Book 1 – Tough as Steele
Book 2 – Nerves of Steele
Book 3 – Forged in Steele
Book 4 – Made of Steele
Book 5 – Solid as Steele
Book 6 – Edge of Steele

For More Details Visit -
www.susansleeman.com/books/steele-guardians

NIGHTHAWK SECURITY SERIES
When the innocent are in harm's way, these heroes don't hesitate—they put their lives on the line without a second thought.

Book 1 – Night Fall
Book 2 – Night Vision
Book 3 – Night Hawk
Book 4 – Night Moves
Book 5 – Night Watch
Book 6 – Night Prey

For More Details Visit -
www.susansleeman.com/books/nighthawk-security/

THE TRUTH SEEKERS

A team of six forensic specialists bound by one mission: to bring the truth to light. But when chilling mysteries land on their doorsteps, the hunters become the hunted—and the truth they're sworn to protect may be the very thing that shatters their world.

Book 1 - Dead Ringer
Book 2 - Dead Silence
Book 3 - Dead End
Book 4 - Dead Heat
Book 5 - Dead Center
Book 6 - Dead Even

For More Details Visit -
www.susansleeman.com/books/truth-seekers/

The COLD HARBOR SERIES
The cost of protection is high, but for these heroes, no price is too great—not even their own lives.

Prequel - Cold Silence
Book 1 - Cold Terror
Book 2 - Cold Truth
Book 3 - Cold Fury
Book 4 - Cold Case
Book 5 - Cold Fear
Book 6 - Cold Pursuit
Book 7 - Cold Dawn

For More Details Visit -
www.susansleeman.com/books/cold-harbor/

ABOUT SUSAN

Susan Sleeman writes the kind of romantic suspense that makes you double-check the locks—and maybe fall a little for the hero.

Her clean, high-octane stories are packed with danger, heart, and just enough faith to light the darkest corners.

With 60+ novels, award wins, and over two million books sold, Susan backs up every twist with FBI and police academy know-how.

She calls Oregon home, where she juggles plotting crimes (fictional ones, promise), spoiling grandkids, and running *TheSuspenseZone.com*.

Ready to lose sleep over your next favorite book? Head to SusanSleeman.com.

Made in the USA
Monee, IL
03 November 2025